Books by M K Scott

The Talking Dog Detective Agency
Cozy Mystery

A Bark in the Night
Requiem for a Rescue Dog Queen
Bark Twice for Danger

The Painted Lady Inn Mysteries Series
Culinary Cozy Mystery

Murder Mansion
Drop Dead Handsome
Killer Review
Christmas Calamity
Death Pledges a Sorority
Caribbean Catastrophe
Weddings Can be Murder
The Skeleton Wore Diamonds

The Way Over the Hill Gang Series
Cozy Mystery

Late for Dinner (June 2018)

Bark Twice for Danger

By
M K Scott

Copyright © 2018 MK Scott

Print Edition

To obtain permission to excerpt portions of the text, please contact the author.

All characters in this book are fiction and figments of the author's imagination.

Chapter One

WHAT HAPPENS TO a girl who can't say no? Most people would assume she'd end up pregnant before her fifteenth birthday. The idea made Abby wrinkle her nose at the impossibility of that happening to her. It would involve someone asking her to do something more interesting than pet sitting their parrot or running papers to a client on her way home. Truthfully, she didn't mind too much. She didn't have children to drive to soccer practice or the need to start dinner for her partner when she got home from work. What she did resent was people assuming that since she had no life, she'd automatically do the things they had no time to do.

Delivering papers wasn't in her job description. Technically it wasn't on anyone's in the office. The others were smart enough to make themselves scarce, while Abby merely took the papers and agreed to go out of her way to Carmel to deliver them before the end of the workday. The only perk was she got to leave early to arrive while the client's office was still open.

After she delivered the papers, she exited the art deco building, only to almost bump into *him*. She couldn't say she didn't notice him. He was the type of male who drew all eyes to him by simply existing. He'd erupted into the parking lot riding a wave of sound and testosterone. Instead of a surfboard, his mode of transportation was a Triumph motorcycle. The bike drew her eye first. Back when she was barely thirteen, she longed for a motorcycle. Her fantasies, however, didn't include her hanging onto some guy steering the bike. It was always her bike.

That dream had been squashed by her father, who pointed out that motorcycles were the quickest route to a wheelchair or a painful death. Saying her father was risk avoidant would be an understatement. In his work as a vehicle insurance adjustor, he had to speculate on how much damage a person could do to themselves and their vehicles and how much the company would be willing to cover. He applied the same lessons to raising his daughter. In short, her father's philosophy of child-rearing was everything is dangerous, so don't do it. Okay, maybe only the fun things were dangerous.

Still, there was the man on the bike. He probably felt her gaze on him, because after he parked close to the building, he lifted off his helmet and shook out his shoulder-length hair as if in a shampoo commercial. He did have gorgeous coffee-colored hair. Their eyes connected for the briefest second, but then she looked away, embarrassed at her ogling.

Mr. Gorgeous Hair headed her way with a smile that caused her to look behind her. No one was there. He held up his hand in greeting. "Ciao, Bella."

"Hello." She'd managed to squeeze out the single word.

He had a sexy accent, too, which just about made her combust on the spot. He'd waggled his eyebrows and gave a husky laugh that had her melting inside.

"Oh, that's how it is. You're going to act like you don't know me." He stopped to slant a seductive smile her way. "You were very friendly before."

"Ah, I think you have me confused with someone else."

He held up two fingers to his forehead as if saluting, then winked. "Who knows? We might meet again."

The unknown man strolled toward the building, aware that Abby watched him briefly before forcing herself to look away. *Weird. This stuff never happened to her.* If Michelle still lived around Fishers, she'd swing by and relate the whole story. Her best friend had been offered a position at Indiana University and full professor jobs were hard to come by. She'd call her tonight. Even though it was hard not to get in one last lingering look, she made a beeline to her car and got in to drive away. It took her another thirty minutes to reach Fishers, but she was almost home. Within minutes, she'd be heating up her diet entrée in the microwave, and her current male in residence would be meowing his discontent about the slowness of his dinner service. Since she'd picked him up at the shelter, Bruno could show a little more gratitude.

Abby made a hard right to turn into her apartment complex. The two-story, vinyl siding apartment buildings resembled the type of drawings a first grader might make. Still, a child would have added grass or a flower, something to cheer the place up. The complex was more about intentions that never took root. There were odd patches of grass here and there. The constant stream of feet kept it from forming an uninterrupted carpet of green between the buildings. The place offered no amenities such as a pool or a clubhouse.

She worked her way through the maze of functional buildings that had proved daunting when she first moved in. They had nothing to distinguish one from the other, except a small number designation that was hard to read while traveling in a car.

Eventually, she taught herself to find her way home, not by the buildings themselves, but by the glimpses of the neighborhood between the buildings. First came the trampoline, which sometimes had kids jumping on it, depending on the weather, then a fenced-in yard with the cute corgi dogs that would sometimes race along the fence the best they could with their short legs. Finally, the blooming burst of color yard would appear. She'd named it the happy gardeners' home since she suspected anyone surrounded by so much natural beauty had to be cheerful. No matter what the season, something was always happening in their yard. In the dark of winter, they interlaced their pine branches with twinkle lights.

Every now and then, Abby would peer out her window in the direction of the lights, imagining what such a life would be like. She'd spotted the middle-aged couple that lived there while taking out her garbage to the nearest dumpster. They were hard at work grooming their yard but still appeared companionable in doing so. When they saw her, they smiled and waved, which was unusual. People seldom noticed Abby.

That's the way it had always been. She was a cog in her insurance company, a low paid one. Back in college, she'd been advised to go into numbers, even told she'd make the big bucks.

"Yeah, big bucks, that's why I'm living la dolce vita."

She snorted at the prospect of living the sweet life. She parked her white sedan in her assigned parking place and headed up to her apartment as she mulled over the accidental meeting of a drool-worthy male.

The encounter still puzzled her. Women like her often married their high school sweethearts, and not out of overwhelming love, either. She hadn't. Could have, but she had some wild idea there had to be more to life. So far, she hadn't found it.

Her footsteps rang out on the open stairway. Her next-door neighbor, Barb, stepped out onto the breezeway clutching two strips of wood with sharp nails sticking out of them.

"Hey, Barb." She gestured to the wood strips. "What are those for?"

The woman grimaced and shook the strips, careful not to impale herself. "Those stupid birds. That's what. Every spring, they make nests in that area between the support column and the roof, which results in waking me up every morning with their infernal birdsong."

"Oh, okay." It was hard to know how to respond to that. Personally, she liked listening to the birds.

Barb was only a few years older than her and single, too. It made Abby ponder if she'd ever acted that crotchety. She hoped not. Lost in mentally comparing her actions to Barb's, she only half-listened to her parting comment.

"Whatever you ordered must have been pretty important for you to rush home from work to pick it up. You whipped in here, snatched it up, and were already on the stairs before I got the door open."

What was the woman talking about? She hadn't ordered anything. Perhaps she was confusing her with the divorcee who lived across the way. Instead of making an issue of it and correcting her, she nodded and headed to her own apartment. Bruno greeted her with a hoarse meow that sounded a bit like scolding. She flicked on the lights, booted up her computer, then went to the cabinet to retrieve her pet's dinner.

With Bruno fed, and her dinner heating, she scrolled through her email. A subject heading caught her eye, *Your Package Was Delivered.* A click revealed that a red bikini had been shipped overnight to her address. The provided link showed the minuscule scraps of fabric that came with a hefty price tag, never mind the shipping. This had to be a mistake. She'd call the company up and give them heck.

She might be all soft and agreeable in person, but on the phone, where no one could see her, she released the inner warrior princess who could demand refunds with the best of them. Abby pulled a diet soda out of the fridge to go along with her meal. She popped the top of the soda, grabbed some flatware out of the drawer, and placed them both on the bar that separated the kitchen from the living room. It was only big enough for one person or two very small people.

Her mobile phone chimed, and her friend's face popped up on the screen.

"Hello, Michelle. I was going to call you."

"That's why I called. I had a feeling something was going on."

"Huh?"

"It was a hunch. So, what's up?"

"Besides meeting some movie-worthy hunk in a parking lot? Too bad he mistook me for someone else."

"Ha! He was hitting on you."

"Please." The microwave dinged, alerting her that her correct portion entrée was done. *Yippee.* She rolled her eyes at the idea as she shuttled her hot entrée to the bar. "That's a joke."

"I wish you'd give yourself a chance."

"I know what I am." Her father made it clear to her that she took after his side of the family: simple, salt of the earth folks. He pounded many messages into her with the prime one being that she wasn't like her mother. Her mother had been a circus performer. As a child, she held onto that fact as if it made her somehow shinier or more special than the other children. It hadn't. Her paternal grandmother was quick to point out that circus people didn't make good parents. It was hard to say since she could barely remember her mother. All she knew was her mother had left when she was two.

The most she remembered was her light-hearted laugh and her floral perfume.

"No, you don't." Her friend emphatically disagreed. "You know what you think you are."

She pushed the speaker button and rested it against a stack of library books. "What's the difference?"

"You think you're an ordinary woman with an unexciting job, living alone in a crummy apartment complex."

"Sounds about right." Although, when the words came out of Michelle's mouth, somehow, they sounded infinitely worse.

"No, it's not right. You're extraordinary. You've never allowed yourself to spread your wings. Always playing it safe."

Oh great Scott, here came the *be all you can be* speech. She loved her friend but could do without the inspirational pep talk. "Something else odd happened today."

"What?"

"Someone hacked my online shopping account and ordered an expensive bikini. I think they even had it delivered to my apartment and came by earlier to pick it up."

"Oh, that's not good. Call wherever they ordered it from right away. Close the account. The fact they know where you live isn't good, either. Not only could they be using your card number, the person or persons could be opening new accounts in your name. You need to get on top of this. It's probably some cyber hackers in Russia."

"They'd have a long commute to pick up their swimsuit. It has to be somebody closer."

Her text alert chirped. A notice from her credit card company warned her someone was charging a flight to Bermuda. The text asked, *Is This You*? She typed *No* and closed her eyes for a second.

"It's started. I just got an alert from my credit card company."

"Girl, you need to get on this right now. Someone has stolen your identity."

She knew Michelle was right. All her work to have a safe, stable life was shot to pieces by some unknown culprit with a taste for bright swimwear and tropical beaches. "Whoever it is, they're having a better life than I am."

"You make the calls."

Abby stared at the phone, knowing her friend had hung up. Unlike most people, she had planned for such an event by copying all her credit cards and writing the customer service number down beside the card image That way, if anything happened, all she had to do was pull the file.

Angry that she even had to resort to such a measure, she stomped to the bedroom, flicked on the light, and pulled out the file cabinet drawer so hard she was surprised it didn't come out of the metal frame. Her neat printing labeled the needed file, financial information, that contained everything from her checking account info to her credit card numbers. The file was empty. *It couldn't be.* She slowly opened the file as if it would make the missing paper appear.

Still empty.

Someone had been in her apartment. In the entire six months she'd lived there, she hadn't had one guest. Her father was content to meet at Bob Evans. Michelle was always up for a spa day at Woodhouse Spa, although lately, she wanted to float in those immersion rooms, which did not lend themselves to chatting. She didn't want anyone to see how bland everything was anyway. She'd never got around to hanging a picture or even putting curtains over the utilitarian blinds.

There had to be something she could do. She had a second copy on her computer, but it didn't stop whoever lifted the paper from applying for more credit in her name. She had excellent credit, or she did.

Her dinner congealed as she worked her way through her phone lists. Some were easy. Other businesses were closed for the day, allowing the culprit to charge unimpeded. Her bank, which had a type of phone customer service, agreed to cancel her debit card but insisted she needed to come into the bank during business hours to verify these charges.

That would be inconvenient, but not as inconvenient as having her bank accounts drained. She might be able to stop any future charges, might even be able to get some of the charges reversed. Still, if she couldn't identify the jerk who did it, she was still at risk.

How did whoever-it-was get in her apartment? Despite all her precautions, she felt far from safe. He inner warrior princess was ready to go ballistic on the credit-stealing scum bag, but first, she needed to secure the place. She took a wooden chair from her dinette set and wedged it against the door and her foyer wall. No one was coming in while she was there. Of course, it did nothing to protect her apartment or Bruno while she was gone.

The police would be the natural response to a break in, but they would ask when it happened and what was stolen. They might even hint around that the information had been misplaced or taken by a former boyfriend. She didn't misplace things. A boyfriend would have been something she'd notice hanging around the apartment.

When she got Bruno, there was a chatty employee who had recommended Bruno to her. The other workers called her the *pet matchmaker*. She seemed sweet enough. What was weird, was she insisted on giving her the card of a private investigator. She told her the woman was good and would get to the bottom of any problem.

Being organized, she had filed it under *P* in her card file. She pulled out the card that had an image of a German shepherd using a magnifying glass. Odd, but cute. She entered the numbers into her cell, wondering if she'd get yet another recording telling her it was past business hours.

The phone was on the third ring before it was picked up.

"Nala Bonne. Private Investigator. Discreet is our first, middle and last name."

Chapter Two

THERE ARE UPSWINGS in the private eye business. The winter holidays were one of them. Ironically, Nala experienced another surge in February near or even after Valentine's Day. Instead of potential Romeos and Juliets checking out online dates, verifying everything he or she professed was real, it swung to finding the missing love interest. For reasons too numerous for Nala to count, the holiday celebrated by florists and confectioneries made perfectly appropriate love interests vanish like the morning fog in strong sunlight.

Her lips twisted as she considered the term *appropriate love interest.* If the person was a stand-up kind of girl or guy, they wouldn't disappear due to a sentimental holiday. It wasn't like she was an expert on the matter, but she assumed it wouldn't be the right thing to do. Her phone rang.

Spring break allowed her a solid ten days she could devote entirely to her investigative work. Now all she needed was business. Maybe the call could be just that.

Max, her rescue German shepherd mix, who had been enjoying a snooze in the late afternoon sun, opened his eyes. The phone rang a second time, forcing him to push up into a sitting position. He fixed her with an indignant stare. "Aren't you going to answer that?"

She held up her hand. "On the third ring, I don't want to appear anxious or that we have no business."

He gave a snort as his front legs slid out, allowing him to resume his prone position. His eyes remained open and one ear went up.

"Nala Bonne. Private Investigator. Discreet is our first, middle, and last name."

Her mother thought it was a good idea to have a slogan, but saying it aloud sounded like a used car commercial.

"Oh good." A harried female voice spoke. "I'm not sure this is a case for you, but there was this woman at the rescue center."

"Karly," Nala provided the name, realizing her best friend had been passing out her business cards, which explained the missing chunk of cards. She'd initially thought her mother had helped herself. No way her father would have taken them. Her police captain father considered a police officer passing out cards for his daughter's private investigation business a conflict of interest.

The caller responded. "I think that was her. A real sweetheart who matched me up with my rescue cat. Anyhow, she gave me your card and told me if I ever had an issue to give you a call, but I'm not sure if my situation is up your alley."

It wasn't hard to pick out the hesitation in the woman's voice. She was seconds from talking herself out of why she had called. While Nala's mother, Gwen, hadn't spent a great deal of time teaching her daughter the ins and outs of the design business, she did make a diligent effort to teach Nala how to land a reluctant client.

Inject warmth, and a comradery that didn't exist between the two of them.

It was a tall order and not something she was used to doing in her former, now substitute, job as a preschool teacher.

"Oh, you'd be surprised at the variety of cases I have." Her recent caseload consisted of checking out potential dates and following up on medical insurance scams. "Could I have your name?"

"Abby, Abby Lowenstein. Maybe this was a mistake."

"Abby." She repeated the name, well aware she was one hang-up away from not having this job. "Tell me why you called. Think of it as a free consultation. I'll tell you what I could do for you and how much it would cost. I can tell you I'm the cheapest PI around."

"Well, ah, I don't know."

Great, she'd led with *cheap*. Her mother had warned her about that. People didn't want cheap. They wanted value at an inexpensive price. "I'm able to offer great service at a better price because I'm new in the business. Just trying to get my foot in the door."

That sounded a bit like begging. Max lurched to his feet and strolled over to the desk, placing his head on the surface. "Tell her you have a rescue dog on the team. That will clinch the deal."

Before Nala could say anything, her almost-client asked, "You use a rescue dog?"

Maybe Max was right. "Yeah." She wouldn't make the mistake of saying *use* in reference to Max. Her opinionated canine had a definite bias against being referred to as an animal. With a talking dog, she had no excuses for not knowing what her canine companion had on his mind. "He really helps sniff out crime."

A grimace crossed her face, realizing she'd just used another hackneyed line. Why had no one told her part of the PI business would involve quoting lame lines?

A slight chuckle came from the line. "That's funny."

Her eyebrows shot up. Someone thought it was funny. Either the chick had never heard it before, or she was just being kind. Probably the latter. It would also be part of the reason she was calling. Nice people often found themselves the target of unscrupulous con artists who used their natural niceness and desires to go against them.

"Yeah, Max really likes to take a bite out of crime."

There was silence at the other end. Maybe she had pushed the lame lines a tad too much.

There was an inhale of breath, showing that the woman was at least still on the line. "Um, yeah, that's what I wanted to talk to you about. A crime."

Even though it cut into her business, she had a protocol to follow. "Did you call the police?"

"No. It's not a violent crime. I think someone is using my name and credit accounts to order stuff."

"Identity theft."

"Exactly!" The voice strengthened as the woman explained. "I came home to my neighbor telling me I'd been home earlier to pick up a package. I hadn't, but someone else had. Then I went to look for my file in my cabinet that listed my credit and debit accounts, and it's missing."

"I'm going to assume someone broke into your residence and took this information. You should at least file a breaking and entering complaint. There's the theft accusation, too."

"Ah, there's some issues with that."

Mentally, Nala added *there always is.* "Can you elaborate?"

"There's no sign of a break-in. Since I moved in six months ago, I have never invited anyone over." There was a pause. "I always figured I'd invite people over when I got the place fixed up. My job keeps me pretty busy."

She could understand that. "I want you to file a report anyhow. We need to have the crime of identity theft reported. However, most of the work would be done by you or me if you hire me. Be prepared though, sometimes people report identity theft to entrap a former boyfriend or even a family member."

"I wouldn't do that!"

An indignant response is what she expected from an innocent party. Someone who was trying to run a scam would try to laugh it off or overplay her hand, or she suspected they would.

"This is the reason filing a police report would be beneficial. I'd be glad to assist in the procedure free of charge. Dealing with the police can be overwhelming."

"You'd do that for me?"

"Yes. Give me your address and I'll be right over."

"It's kinda late."

"I usually work nights anyhow."

Nala took down the address and bid the woman goodbye. After thumbing off her phone, she stood.

"Looks like we have a job interview. Let's go, Max, and wow the woman with our charm and expertise."

A loud bark sounded, and Max's lips pulled up into a wide, doggy grin. "My charm and your expertise. Make that *our* expertise."

Please. Her eyes rolled up as she grabbed her purse and checked her gun. Loaded and the safety was on, not that she was expecting trouble, but it always helps to be prepared. In the hallway, she rattled her door knob making sure it was locked. There was more give than she liked in the lock, especially considering not too long ago she discovered her door unlocked and having a wrong feel to the office, as if someone had taken a stroll through. After that, she'd taken all the hard copies of her files home and managed with digital copies stored in the cloud. Her father insisted on a special security door that was beyond her price range. Instead, she settled on a chain lock while she was working, which left a great deal to be desired.

Down on the second level, she bumped into Harry, a personable guy who ran his business out of a second-floor office. To be honest the man wasn't hard on the eyes, either, with his well-trimmed dark beard and hipster glasses. She assumed he had hair to match the beard, but it was only assumption because every time she saw him he had a cap on. Most were superhero caps, but a few just had amusing slogans. Nala put his age at thirty-something. It was harder to gauge how old a man was. He had to have the metabolism of a young male, considering all the fast food she'd witnessed him bring into the building. An older man would have packed on the weight from such a diet.

"How's it going, Harry? What's keeping you here so late? I know you don't have any Halloween costumes to get out."

He stooped down to pat Max on the head and addressed the dog as opposed to Nala. "Listen to her, she thinks the only time people dress up is Halloween."

"Okay. Enlighten me. When else do people need to don superhero costumes? Movie premieres?"

Harry fell into step with her as they made their way down the stairs. "Some do premieres. Not that many. Most of the money is in conventions. Comic Con for one. It's happening here in Indianapolis. Not only do people want their costumes, I'm manning a booth. I need lots of merchandise. I'm pretty much guaranteed to sell out. That's why I was still here. Getting my orders in."

"Makes sense. Think I should check it out?"

Harry stopped on a step and gave her a long look. "Seriously, what do you expect me to say? We're talking my livelihood here. Go. You'll have fun. I can even sell you a costume at cost."

A puff of derision passed her lips. "Oh yeah, just what the city needs, another Wonder Woman prowling the streets."

"I was thinking more like the Black Canary."

Harry fell back in step with her as they strolled to the first-floor landing. "I've given this some thought and felt it was more fitting since the Black Canary was born into a crime-fighting family. I'm thinking of Dinah Lance, the daughter. The mother was the original Canary, but Dinah decided to take up the costume and continue her work."

"Okay." It was hard not to know things like that when Harry spouted stuff from his Geek Universe most of the time. It also made her wonder how often he thought about her, and what type of costume did the Black Canary wear? "Should I ask about the costume?"

He grinned in her direction and waggled his eyebrows. "You sound interested."

She shrugged, not really intending to go to the convention and certainly not putting herself into anything spandex. Her mother would tell her to make the most of her assets while her father freaked when she donned a sports bra for running when she was thirteen. "Curious."

"Most people who play the Black Canary usually don all black. Black boots, pants, and jacket. Those who have money wear leather."

"Sounds hot."

"It is." Harry gave a hearty sigh.

"That's not the way I meant it. Leather is heavy."

"Fake leather, not as much and you can usually get it with a shine."

"I'll keep it in mind." Actually, she wouldn't. She had no intention of going to the convention.

They hit the front doors together. Harry turned and checked the door to make sure it shut. You'd think there wouldn't be an issue with an authorized entry, but Nala still knew there could be. As the three of them rounded the corner and turned toward the line of parked cars, her phone burbled. It rang a second time.

On the outside, she never answered her phone until she was in a safe place. Many a person who was chatting away on their phone or checking out how many likes they had on their social feed either ran into something or became an easy target for a snatch and grab mugging. There was even a video circulating on social media of a man staring at his phone, bumping into a bear.

A quick peek showed her mother's number. Her parents were supposed to be on a cruise. Rumor was there was no cell coverage on the cruises. Any calls would cost mucho dinero. Since Harry and Max were with her as attack deterrents, she decided to take the call. Besides, why would her mother call unless it was an emergency?

"Are you okay? Dad? Did your boat wreck?"

"Nala!" Her mother shouted her name, forcing Nala to hold the phone away from her ear. "We're fine and in a coffee bar in Belize. Trip's fine. Ship's great. We stopped by the bar to use their WiFi. Anyhow, there's some weird stuff popping up on my business credit card. I was only going to check to see if that shipment of jade Buddhas had come in. Everyone wants one for their foyer."

It sounded like her mother, who couldn't let business go even on vacation. "Did the buddhas come in?"

"Yes. There's also some charges for an atrocious red leather living room suite I so wouldn't have approved. I need you to swing by Posh Interiors and see if anyone ordered it. If so, I want to know who. Not only did they use my card but have extremely bad taste. That's not the rep I want for my store."

"Okay, Mom, I'll try." She wasn't looking forward to running interference at her mother's company. Most of the employees she'd known for a long time, and they treated her more like family. There was no way she wanted to accuse any of them of playing fast and loose with her mother's credit. "Go have fun."

"We will," her mother enthused. "Your father just ate iguana, and I plan on trying the zip line that goes out over the bay."

"Sounds great. Wish I was there," she lied. Eating iguana and flying through the air without the benefit of nets did nothing for her.

"Really? We offered to take you with us. There's a fold out bed in our room that would have suited you perfectly. It would have been a free vacation for you. Sweetie, you could use one, too. It would put some color in your cheeks."

No reason to rehash all the reasons she didn't want to be crowded into a pocket-sized cruise room with her parents, especially if her mother switched into matchmaking mode, which she usually did.

"A client just walked in. Bye now."

"Bye, sweetheart. Kiss, kiss."

She cut her eyes to Harry as she lowered her voice and added, "Love ya." No way she'd say kiss, kiss in front of Harry. A woman had to have some dignity.

"Parents?" Harry asked with a smile.

He probably heard the entire conversation since her mother had shouted, convinced she'd compensate for the miles between them.

"You guessed it. They're on vacation. At least my father is. My mother is taking advantage of shore excursions to check on her business. Apparently, she wants me to run errands for her, too."

Yeah, she'd do that tomorrow.

Chapter Three

THE ROBOTIC VOICE of the phone GPS filled Nala's vintage Volkswagen Beetle. *"Turn left at the light onto Elysian Way."*

A place named Elysian Way should have weeping willows bordering the road or at least flowers. Instead, there was gravel and a hardy patch of weeds to mark the way. A discarded fast food bag had Max poking his nose out the window.

"Did you see that? I think there might have been a French fry left in that bag!"

"Not going back. You might not have any pride when it comes to garbage, but I do."

Even though Nala kept her focus on the road, she could still sense the hard stare of her canine. "What?"

"What about the blue chair?"

A sigh escaped her lips. Whoever thought dogs were stupid never had a talking one. Her pooch had picked the debating skills of a first-class lawyer. "That wasn't garbage. The neighbor put it out because she just didn't need that chair anymore."

A barren stretch of land populated with weeds and the occasional wildflower was on the right of the road. An industrial park squatted with endless pole-barn type warehouses, complete with busy semi-trucks and forklifts. The nav app sounded before she could reply to Max's derisive snort.

"Your destination is on your right within a quarter of a mile."

Really? There was nothing there, except for the industrial park, until the boxy form of an apartment complex sprouted out of the flat terrain. No trees, and no water features to pretty the place up. As she drew closer, an oval sign announced Camelot Apartments. In smaller script, it read *Where you're treated royally*.

Never being a fan of the King Arthur tales, she'd never considered where Arthur might live, but she was betting it would not be in the weathered-looking units in desperate need of paint. Nala clicked on her turn signal as Max commented.

"We're not in Kansas anymore."

"Please. It was funny the first time, but not the second, or tenth time. Not sure where you get all your movie quotes, but I suspect Elvin. Look for 311. Not sure what order the buildings are in."

Max pointed up his nose as if insulted. Cats had a reputation of being divas, but they were amateurs compared to her dog.

Nala cut her speed to make sure she didn't zoom past the address. The car behind her honked and whipped around her, belching out oil-rich exhaust that had both Nala and Max coughing.

Even though he wasn't the driver, Max tended to take anyone passing them personally. "Jerk!"

"Maybe he knew where he was going."

They crept past cars with bumper stickers announcing they smoked and voted. Another few stated their gun would have to be pulled out of their cold, dead hands. Duct tape secured one bumper to the vehicle. An inexpensive new car sat next to a primer spotted vehicle It wasn't the worst neighborhood she'd been in, by far, but it was definitely a step down from the well-kept backyards she could spot between the buildings.

Not sure which went up first, but she could bet the homeowners weren't pleased to have a crumbling complex as their backyard view.

Bark! Bark! Bark!

She stomped on the brake without the benefit of the clutch, stalling out the car. "Max!" Whenever he barked as opposed to talking, it startled her. You'd think it would be the opposite. After all, who'd ever heard of a talking dog? Even if his ability to talk was the result of a witch, who, tired of her non-communicative boyfriend, decided to converse with his dog instead. It worked out for a while until she tired of both Max and his owner. Turns out that a man who refused to talk with his girlfriend had absolutely no time for a chattering canine.

A woman stood outside a car smoking a cigarette while talking on her cell. A tiny rat-like dog lifted its rear leg in the direction of a porch support. Obviously, that is what had Max so riled up. A dog. She should have guessed it.

Restarting the car allowed Nala time to discover she had reached building three, which must contain an apartment eleven somewhere.

The smoker shot Nala a glare. "You need to control your animal."

The pint-sized urinator strolled away from the woman toward the Beetle as if to baptize the idling car. Instead of barking, Max uttered in a gravelly voice, "Think again, buster, if you want to keep that leg."

The dog rushed back to its owner as Nala drove up to the next building, determined not to park near Smokey and her pet. Private eyes did their best work when they weren't the center of attention. A glance back in her rear-view mirror showed the woman giving her the finger. Maybe she should drive two apartment units down. The last thing she wanted was a fight. When it came to girl fights, Nala's signature move was to look at her watch as if late, then flee. Sometimes she didn't even look at her watch.

She parked in an area marked *visitors*. The last thing she needed was to tick off someone else before she even found her client. Technically, she hadn't ticked off anyone. Max was the culprit. Explaining her dog made the remark wouldn't save her. There was no Elvin to step in, either.

The second hand on her watch made several swoops, allowing Smokey plenty of time to get back to her apartment. While she waited, Nala counted the number of times she'd been in a fight on one hand. Early on, she'd been a feisty five-year-old and punched a neighborhood boy who accused her of cheating at the basketball game of horse. Her mother wanted her to apologize, but her father insisted that would just make it worse. She'd survive the next ten years unscathed. Possibly due to the fact she never earned the envy of her fellow females since she was neither popular nor shockingly good-looking. At best, she was average.

As a person riding the crest of mediocrity, she was surprised when a bigger, tougher girl targeted her in high school, making Nala slip around the school, doing her best to vanish in plain sight. Her ability to blend in sometimes allowed her to pretend she was a spy or a famous detective like Sherlock Holmes. Finally, the six-foot avenging female left her alone. Nala first put it down to her superior hiding skills, but later found out Elvin had said something to the girl. She was never sure what it was. Even more odd, Nala never asked. High school breathed life into Elvin's social awkwardness, making him into an inferno of nerdy comments and double entendres. It was probably better not knowing what had been said.

Max nudged her with his nose. "Client, remember. Not sure what is so fascinating about your watch."

She pushed his head away. "I know. I was giving the woman you irritated time to move on."

"Ha! Her." Max snapped his teeth together. "I'd bite her and gobble up her tiny dog, too. Not that it looked much like a dog. Weasel, maybe?"

"Really?" She cut a look his way. "Weren't you the dog who bit the culprit and complained about the taste?"

Max coughed and looked out the window, muttering, "She tasted really bad."

No need to belabor the point. Her canine companion had done what she needed him to do at the time. No one wanted a dog who made a habit of biting people. That would result in a quick call to animal control. A thorough glance showed no evidence of Smokey, but a large man who could have easily served as a bouncer or professional wrestler walked down a flight of stairs carrying a small dog.

Her dog leaned out the open window before turning his head back toward her to comment. "Is this tiny dog land?"

"No, but when you live in an apartment, a big dog like yourself isn't practical. Just be glad I have a house. Let's hit it. Put your game face on."

"Does that mean I'm on my game?"

Nala swung her door open and exited the car, pondering the question. Since her rescue dog had a varied life before he ended up with her, he sometimes said peculiar things. Sometimes she tried to mentally trace down who might have said them or if he was watching too much television.

"Yeah, I guess you should bring your A game."

The German shepherd nodded, then jumped over the gear shift and bounded out of the car. She pulled out her purse, settled the strap on her shoulder, and took time to lock the vehicle while Max sniffed out the area. The earlier dog came to mind and she shouted,

"No cars!"

The elegant nose elevated somewhat, telling her what he thought of such a suggestion. While they were in public, he generally didn't speak as per Nala's orders. Still, he occasionally would blurt out something like he did earlier and blame it on the moment.

Her body turned away from the apartments which served as a shield as she talked to her canine. "I wasn't trying to insult you. It's just that people are sensitive about their cars."

The nose went up higher, exposing his entire throat and chest. He was going to be that way.

"All right, you would never do anything like that."

His nose dropped, and his lips went up in a doggy grin. "I have, but not recently. I was trying to remember how to bring my A game. It's something about getting a girl to think you're better than you are. Should we lie about how many cases we've actually solved?"

It didn't take a psychic to know her pooch had been listening to Elvin bragging to one of his guy friends. If that was a man's definition of having an A game, Elvin so didn't have it. Women recognized him as a hopeless geek seconds after meeting him. If they gave him a second thought, it was usually to set up their smart television or fix their laptop, which he could.

"That's not what I meant. Sure, we want to look our best, but there is no reason to lie." The two of them meandered back to building three, stepping over patches of hard packed dirt with a few sprigs of grass in it. Despite its current circumstances, the grass was making a valiant effort to survive, as possibly were some of the residents. The entire place had the feel of a temporary stop. Her mother would point out that was the whole purpose behind apartments. In her world, people who lived in shabby apartments did not need design services.

As they reached the correct apartment building, she'd counted the number of cases she'd solved, which was almost all of them. There was one date profile she'd looked up for a nervous dater, but by the time she'd discovered he had a habit of romancing wealthy women, her client refused to listen. The dossier still sat on her office desk. Her mother suggested mailing it in about three weeks before the woman lost everything.

An identity theft should be easy compared to piecing together the history of the duplicitous Romeo. The wide swath he'd made through wealthy widows was easy enough to follow. The harder part was getting them to say anything bad about him. The dating scene must be even tougher for those over forty if they were willing to pay big bucks for the man's company. No reason to mention that case. It wasn't pertinent.

Her father would remind her to let the client talk and observe. Meeting at her house was a plus, because it would give her much more info. The fact the woman was okay with it meant either she was desperate or way too trusting—possibly both.

None of the numbers on the bottom unit were eleven, which meant she'd have to check the second floor. Even though her house was in a neighborhood filled mainly with retirees and the occasional young family, her father still bemoaned how it would be a snap to break into her ranch style home. A second-floor apartment would be more difficult with only one door, and it would be hard to escape notice trotting a television or a sofa past nosy neighbors.

A few of the second-floor doorways sported wreaths announcing team affiliations. There was a half-dead plant by one door as if the owner shoved it outside for a breath of air or to give it a chance at life. A paper list taped to one door announced the owner didn't want to try out vacuums, buy fundraising items from children, or attend nearby churches. Unfortunately, the paper covered the number. She lifted it up to see what number it was the same time the door opened.

"Can't you read?" A man holding a beer demanded as he squinted at her and held onto the doorframe as he weaved slightly.

A little flustered by the unprovoked attack, Nala opened her mouth to explain. Before she could, Max's baritone voice sounded.

"I can read. Can you, human?"

The man never took his eyes off Nala and slammed the door.

"Stop that! Do you want to get yourself in trouble?"

"He never looked at me. I doubt he could see you too well, either."

The dog had a point. It was the wrong door anyhow. The only one left had no wreaths, hateful notes, or half-dead plants. There was nothing besides a number and a plain doormat that did not say welcome or make a playful statement such as *wipe your paws*. The outside of apartment 311 showed no personality. A man or woman could live there, or it could even be empty and the doormat was a leftover. She knew better and knocked.

The door opened, and a woman holding a cat gave the two of them a curious glance. "I'm going to assume you're Nala Bonne and her detective dog."

"That's us. This is my dog, Max. He won't bother your kitty."

She nudged her canine who appeared to be way too interested in the cat. What was it with cats and dogs?

"I'll go lock Bruno up just the same. Don't want him to get out. Come on in, I'll only be a second." Abby hurried off down the narrow hallway with a struggling Bruno tucked under one arm.

The bare walls, the boxes, and the fact that there were no curtains on the windows made her wonder how long Abby had lived here. From appearances, she'd say yesterday, but on the phone, the woman had mentioned six months. It could be a very temporary stop for her or by not fixing up the apartment, she could pretend it was only for a little bit.

By the time Abby returned sans the feline, Nala had determined that the woman not only did not have a significant other in her life, but she also wasn't looking, either. The lack of any men's accoutrements along with the solid lack of any couple photos solidified that deduction. The TV screen still exhibited the programming schedule Abby had been scanning through, most probably summing up Abby's social life. For a moment, Nala almost pitied her until she realized her life was somewhat similar.

If it wasn't for her family dinner every week, hanging out with Karly, and a late client call, she'd be home scanning her own schedules. The best thing to get her mind off her own lack of a social life was work. To do that she needed to put on a good front.

Max strolled up to Abby and sniffed her hands. He rewarded her head pat with a tail wag, then dropped his head for an inch by inch examination of the apartment. Since her canine was on duty, she should do her part. He padded around the room, then stopped at the closed bedroom door and barked. Something was up. They couldn't converse like they'd normally do. She could get the lowdown in the car.

"He must smell the cat," Abby gestured to the door.

It was probably more than a feline. Max had smelled more than his share. It could be the woman was trying to hide something and would tell her in her own time, if ever. That was the problem with being an investigator. People wanted her help but left out key information in the telling. She could only do what she could do.

"I'll call the police. I know a good many of them since my father is a police captain. If they're under thirty, my father probably trained them. You have nothing to worry about. I'll coach you through everything."

Abby managed a strained smile and handed her the phone.

No reason to call 911 and have sirens blaring as they screamed into the complex. It would be better not to, especially if the thief was nearby, which she imagined she was. Why else would she show up to pick up a package that contained a bikini?

She dialed the central number, identified herself, and heard the familiar voice of Hazel.

"Little Nala Bonne, haven't seen you in forever."

The warm, motherly response had Nala switching the phone to speaker. It would build Abby's confidence to hear how well respected she was in the police community.

"Grown up and not too little anymore. I need some help."

Hazel's voice issued from the mobile. "Your father isn't here. I thought you knew."

"Yes, I know they are enjoying themselves on a tropical cruise. Dad is stuffing himself with iguana while my mom is trying to manage her business long distance."

This wasn't the conversation she wanted Abby to hear. She considered taking it off speaker which would look suspicious. Obviously, she proved the police knew her, which was her intent.

"That sounds like Gwen. The woman can never truly take a day off. I was sorry to hear about, you know…" Hazel trailed off.

The problem was she didn't know. There was genuine regret in Hazel's voice, which meant she should have known. Had Dad's longtime partner died? It didn't seem like the right time to ask.

"Hazel, I have a client who has been the victim of identity theft. Do you have an officer that might take a report?"

There was a long pause that did nothing for Nala's credibility. Then Hazel came back online, sounding breathless and happy. "Good news. I found an officer nearby who can take a statement. You'll have to contact the attorney general, too."

The last part she didn't know about, but she'd make a note of it since identity theft cases could support her along with the insurance fraud work. "Okay. I'm at Camelot apartments on Elysian Fields Drive. Apartment 311."

She hung up the phone. The dispatcher's attitude certainly changed from full sympathy to a mischievous bounciness that made no sense, but something else she couldn't put her finger on bothered her. When her parents came back, she'd make a discreet attempt to pry the recent gossip from them as they waxed nostalgic about their exotic travels.

Nala handed the phone back to Abby who stared at it. "I've heard your phones can be used as a GPS device, but I thought you had to turn something on. Apparently not, since your friend mentioned a police officer being nearby before you told her where you're at."

That's what was bothering her. She closed her eyes, having a good idea why Hazel was so chirpy.

Chapter Four

NALA WIGGLED TO the edge of the seat while she wrote down Abby's response. The woman impressed her with her organizational skills and no-nonsense thinking. "You called all the card services you could?"

Abby sat directly across from her on the matching chair. Her hands went up to her hair and pushed the locks hanging in her face behind her ears, then her restless hands dropped to the chair arms where she drummed her fingertips on the fabric. Couldn't say she drummed her fingernails. She had none to speak of. They, too, were practical, as was the rest of her appearance. This was not a woman who would have opened her door to a smooth-talking player who'd also clean out her bank account.

"I did. Immediately. I try not to use credit, so there weren't that many to call. I also got credit alerts via my phone and computer. That's how I knew a red bikini had been delivered and an attempt to book a tropical vacation. At least I blocked that."

"Good. Do you have any other messages about purchases?"

"I'm not sure." Abby picked up her phone and started to scroll through her messages. "It's been so busy at work today. Normally, I turn the sound off on my phone while I'm at work. My boss gets freaked out if someone's cell rings. It's like he resents people having a life outside of work."

A co-worker might be a possibility. All someone had to do was remove Abby's credit cards, make copies of them, then put them back. No telling how long the person had the information before they decided to do a little shopping. Before she could suggest that possibility, a knock sounded at the door.

An owner should open their own apartment door, but Abby gave her an imploring look. Nala pushed to her feet and sighed. Maybe it was just as well. There was a tiny little foyer that would give her some privacy if who she thought it might be was on the other side of the door.

The strong knock came again. She thumbed off the deadbolt and swung the door open. Snickerdoodles, it *was* him. Her habit of using cookie names to curse, which started when she was much younger, didn't do a great job of expressing her aggravation. Worse, Tyler appeared unusually appealing in his uniform. Surprised that no one had used him for a recruiting poster—at least for the police academy. There was an inner toughness that could be the result of his military service. Defiance showed in his eyes, or maybe it was plain bullheadedness. At times, he reminded her of a coiled predator ready to leap into action, but he could shake it off fast and turn enigmatic. He kept his hair short, shorter than most of the officers. Maybe his shoulders were broader. Whatever, she was glad to see him.

"Aren't you out of your jurisdiction?"

He pointed to the uniform. "Changed counties."

"Oh." That's what was different. "I see. Why'd you change?"

He sighed heavily. "I think you know why."

The sound of dog nails on the wood floor meant Max intended to investigate. It didn't matter how Nala felt about Tyler. Max loved Officer Goodnight. He didn't have to deal with being dumped after their first real date for another dog. Some people might point out she stood him up on their first date. Not really. She'd been busy rescuing a client. Still, she thought they had something click, but then he vanished. No way was she making it easy for him.

"You have a hard time working with my father?"

An audible gulp sounded, and Tyler doffed his hat. "I never knew you to play dirty."

"I guess you don't know me that well. I can be professional as I assume you can. My client had her identity stolen, and we need a report written up. It's an easy-peasy situation."

His expression suggested otherwise. "Let's do it." He added in a lower voice, "It had nothing to do with your father. He's an incredible officer. I, ah," he stopped looking around the apartment as if a reasonable excuse was hidden somewhere within reach, "needed a change."

Max crowded into the small area and jumped on Tyler, placing his paws on his shoulders. His long tongue lolled out and managed a few sloppy kisses before being pushed away.

"I'm happy to see you, too, Max"

Nala considered the words. Did that mean he was happy to see her? If the man wanted to see her, he had her number. After their brief actual date, which she thought went well, he had disappeared. Her mother, unfortunately, was the one who clued her in on the possibility of another woman. Understandable, but did that prevent him from picking up the phone and saying, "Hey, it's not you, it's me?"

Her nose crinkled at the idea. That would have been way worse. Everyone knew that it was always *you*.

Abby joined them in the small area, forcing Nala to stop her pointless analyzing.

"Officer Goodnight, this is Abby, my client."

It might have been unfair referring to Abby as a client when they had done little more than exchange names. It certainly sounded better than here's a random woman Karly gave my card. Part of selling was to get the product in a person's hands. Studies showed people were ninety-percent more likely to buy something they tried on, touched, or drove. It was a little harder with investigative services, but if she could get Abby to think of herself as a client who was fighting back as opposed to a victim, the contract was practically signed.

Tyler put out his hand in Abby's direction. "Officer Tyler Goodnight. Good to meet you."

The two shook hands, causing Abby's cheeks to flare with color. Of course, she'd noticed how handsome he was. It was hard not to. Nala sucked in her lips, resenting the woman's reaction. There were more handsome men out there, but she'd never dated any of them. Oh well, she was here for a job, not some dating competition. The last thing she wanted was for Tyler to sense she had the slightest interest in him. The man could be one step away from proposing to his new woman, or they might already be engaged.

That's the thing with men. No engagement rings and no way to tell if they were in a relationship. Even without the ring, women tended to ramble on about their significant other, even if it was to mention how messy or useless they were. Women still talked. Those who never mentioned a spouse or significant other were hiding their status, on their way out of a relationship, or were ashamed of their partner.

"Let's go into the living room and Officer Goodnight can take a statement."

Nala gestured to the main room as if she were the homeowner. It got everyone moving in the right direction. Tyler took a seat in the club chair while Abby and Nala perched on the sofa. Traitor dog chose to sit by Tyler and stare up at him adoringly.

Geesh! Max acted like a twelve-year-old in the presence of his idol. She never saw Tyler picking up dog poop in the park. He didn't keep the kibble and water dish filled. How fast Max forgot. He could be had for a few thrown sticks and a cheeseburger.

The rattle of the metal clipboard, click of the pen, and a clearing of the throat meant Tyler was ready to write up the report. He asked Abby her full name, address, phone number, and to describe the situation.

If a police officer wanted a woman's number, it would be easy enough to get it. How many times had an attractive woman been pulled over only to end up going out on a date with the officer? The possibility made her wiggle on her cushion. Such behavior would make her appear unprofessional. Grabbing the sofa arm for leverage, she pushed all the way back only to have her feet dangle a few inches above the floor. That might not make her appear a seasoned veteran of the investigative arts. Max lifted one eyebrow confirming her initial thought.

Would it look worse if she wiggled back into place? Not sure why she even cared. She didn't, not really. It didn't matter to her what Officer Goodnight thought of her, as long as it was good. How could she let him know she was doing really well without lying?

Max caught her eye and closed his mouth. Most people might think he was gnashing his teeth, but she knew better. The dog had seen Gwen Bonne mouth words enough to try to do the same. Her mother usually exaggerated a word so much it caused her father to ask once if she was having a stroke. Her dog loved to mimic people, but often he picked things he just wasn't good at. The dog lips didn't express words well.

What could he be saying? *Game.* He was saying game. Had she guessed it, or had she somehow picked up on the canine's thoughts? What did he mean by game? Her forehead furrowed as Abby spoke, then she remembered her words warning Max to be on his best game. It was obvious she wasn't at her best.

By then Abby had moved on to talking about calling Nala.

Tyler had stopped writing and nodded in her direction. "What are you going to do about it?"

Oh, did he just imply that hiring her would be a waste of time? It appeared like Abby had swung into immediate action and had taken preventative action.

"I'm going to catch the identity thief before she rips off someone else."

Tyler leaned back in his chair as his lips twitched, apparently fighting the desire to smile. The left side of his mouth went up, losing the battle. "Keep me informed. I may have a few more cases for you. The area has experienced a surge in identity thefts lately."

A gasp sounded beside her. Abby had already had her identity stolen. It wasn't like it would be stolen again. Her eyes rolled up at her own stupidity. Of course, it could. It would result in freezing her accounts and only being able to pay for items in cash. It might even ruin her credit. Maybe she did have a right to gasp. At this point, she needed to assure her potential customer.

"Don't worry. You've taken the right steps. From here, we can tweak things so you won't be a victim in the future."

"That would be wonderful." The woman's relieved smile illuminated her face, turning her from ordinary to beautiful.

Yeah, it all sounded kinda great. Too bad Nala had no clue how to do it. With any luck, Elvin would give her some suggestions. Tyler stood, handed a duplicate copy of the report to Abby, then closed his clipboard. "That's about it. Remember to contact the attorney general. You'll want to put a freeze on your crediting rating, too."

He strolled toward the door, causing both Abby and Nala to stand in response. Max followed him all the way as if he were leaving with the man. It chafed a little, but her dog acted the same way with her father, Elvin, and even Harry. Sometimes she wondered if Max kept trying to replace his original male owner who decided a talking dog wasn't for him.

Abby shot him a huge smile and waved. "Thank you. Bye now."

Tyler murmured, "No problem. Have a nice day."

Have a nice day when the woman had her identity stolen? She'd pointed out more than once to her father that they should draw the line on using that phrase, especially after giving people traffic tickets. Since the very fact that they received an expensive traffic ticket meant the day wasn't going to be nice.

Tyler hesitated at the door, bending to deliver a head scratch to an appreciative Max while keeping eye contact on Nala.

He expected her to say something, but she had nothing. She indicated Abby with a head waggle. "What she said. Ditto."

His eyebrows went up, but he didn't reply. Instead, he centered his hat on his head, opened the door, and left.

Once the door closed, Abby turned the lock. "Not sure why I'm doing it. Obviously, it's no trouble for anyone to get into my apartment."

On the kitchen counter, her laptop was open and on. An oversized television, along with a DVD player took up one wall. There was one of those electronic units that controlled the various electronic devices with a verbal order. These were all fence-worthy items that hadn't been touched. "Are you sure your apartment was burglarized? Do you have any valuable jewelry?"

A loud gasp sounded, and Abby dashed to the bedroom.

In her mind, Nala often gave her clients names based on a particular idiosyncrasy. Oddly, it made it easy for her to remember them. Most people would think a name would do that. Abby might become The Gasper, but that sounded a little harsh. The woman's organizational skills alerted her to the possibility that the thief had vital information. Nala considered her home and wondered if a would-be robber might trip over an oversized rawhide bone and hurt himself.

Identity thieves didn't need to enter your house to get your credit card numbers. Often, people gave them up willingly, never realizing the person providing a service had intentions to defraud. The daughter of one of her neighbors had recently taken a honeymoon abroad, and while they were gone all sorts of credit mischief had gone on. Fortunately, they only used a particular credit card for travel and were able to trace the charges back to their travel agent. Nala had a feeling this case wouldn't be that simple.

"Nothing is missing." Abby returned, carrying a jewelry box. She waved it under Nala's nose as she talked. "Grandmother's engagement ring is still here."

Many house robbers went for small items that were easily concealed. You had to admit moving a fridge down the stairs would attract attention. Still, many bold criminals had done it simply by placing a bogus moving sign on a rental truck. If people didn't know their neighbors well, they'd just assume they were moving. This might be especially true in apartment communities. If her father was here, she could ask for the statistics. Since he wasn't, she'd have to end up buying Elvin a meal later to pick his brain.

The small age-darkened ring made no impression on Nala. If it boasted a diamond, a magnifying glass might be required. No self-respecting thief would have bothered with it, which could explain why it was still here.

Abby pulled out a long strand of pearls. The length alone made the strand valuable, and the luster hinted at a superior quality as well. "My grandmother gave me these when I graduated from college. They are probably my only real jewelry. Everything else is costume."

A thief would have taken the pearls unless they were hard to find. "Where was your jewelry box?"

"On my dresser."

Even though trailing pink and blue ribbons encircled the white box, it reminded Nala of one she had had as a teen. There was no mistaking that it was a jewelry box. It would be natural for a thief to pop it open for a look see. It was looking more and more like she hadn't been robbed. Tyler never asked if there was anything more than the identity theft, and Abby never volunteered. Could be Nala had her own doubts.

"The pearls are nice, and I could see a thief snatching them. Do you have any reason for thinking you've been robbed, other than a missing paper? It could be misfiled."

She shook her head emphatically, then placed the jewelry box on the end table. "I did check the folders around it when I went in to retrieve the jewelry box. Everything was as it should be."

"Locking file cabinet?"

Abby shrugged. "It could be a locking cabinet, but I never bothered with just me here."

A possibility occurred to Nala, and she held up one finger. "How often did you think about this particular folder?"

"Almost never. I made it, then filed it. I had no reason to keep checking it."

That made sense but left her at zero. So far, she hadn't come up with any brilliant breakthroughs that would make Abby desirous of her services. Max, with his amazing nose, might come up with something she missed.

"It could have been taken a while back and whoever has it waited, hoping to confuse the issue."

"Huh?" Abby shot her a befuddled look. "Confuse what?"

Nala had a rich background of crime and punishment due to living with her father and his various associates who dropped by the house. Not too many children grew up practicing their observation skills or learning how to block an intruder from entering. Unfortunately, what happened to be an unusual childhood resulted in Nala thinking everyone else had similar childhoods. It was no wonder Abby didn't understand. The woman probably never played hostage negotiation with her dolls, either.

"Sometimes, thieves or con artists will lift items for later. With credit cards, it's a gamble because most will cancel the cards as soon as they notice they're missing. Others keep cards for emergencies."

"That's what I did." She tapped one finger against her temple as she spoke. "I paid off my cards a while back. I've worked pretty hard to get out of debt. The sensible thing might have been to cancel them, but I wanted that financial security net just in case."

"I understand." Nala totally empathized since she had more than her share of plastic financial nets. "Who knows about that?"

Abby strolled over to the window and looked out.

Not being able to see a client's face made it hard to judge if they were telling the truth. It made no sense for someone who retained Nala's services to lie to her, but people still did. Sometimes it was a test to see if she could catch them out, which she usually did. Other times, they wanted to keep personal information hidden, which ended up costing them twice as much since more billable hours were needed to uncover info they could have told her upfront.

"My brother, Teddy, knew I had the cards." Her tone grew tight with anger. "He's the baby of the family. My father spoiled him. Work is something other people do, not him. Even though he's my own flesh and blood, he's a user. I'd almost call him a sociopath, but as far as I know, he's never killed anyone."

This might be an easy one after all. "Can you think of anyone else? Significant other? Ex-spouse?"

A derisive snort sounded, then Abby twirled around and placed both hands on her hips. "Do I look like a woman with a significant other? The only male in my life is Bruno. That tells the entire tale. For a short time, before I moved, I did meet this fellow I had hopes for."

Her expression turned wistful, letting Nala know how much this man had meant to her. "Do you remember his name?"

Her index finger went back to her temple and tapped. "It was an odd name. Elf something. I thought he made it up on the spot when he heard I was a Lord of the Rings fan."

Couldn't think of too many people willing to call themselves *elf*. "Elvin?"

Her heart dropped as she made the suggestion. Her nerdy friend, who was often her subcontractor, was brilliant. Movies and television shows often featured evil geniuses, when in reality, most criminal successes were due to luck. Elvin, however, if he chose the dark side, would be very, very good at it. It didn't bear considering.

"That's it!" Abby dropped her hand and interlaced her fingers with the opposite hand. "We only had two dates, and he was never in my house. He thought it wouldn't be appropriate even though I had invited him in."

Could they be talking about the same person? Most men tended to run off at the mouth. Elvin did more than most. Still, it was hard to imagine the man refusing to extend a date unless he truly didn't care for the woman.

So far, Nala discovered the woman was organized and liked Lord of the Rings. She was reasonably attractive and boasted a college degree, which would make her a good fit for her friend. It made her wonder why he might have backed off. She couldn't ask because it might not have been him, and he could also be a suspect.

"It would have to be my brother."

Though obvious there was no love lost between Abby and her brother, Nala asked, "Why is that?"

"It's a jerk move. It's kinda his signature."

"Your neighbor reported some woman came back to pick up the package."

"A deluded girlfriend. Women never see past his great hair or perfect smile."

Could be, especially if he was trying to create a smoke screen. "Do you consider him intelligent?"

"Only in the ways of getting out of work. He could write a book about it. It has to be him." She made an expression of distaste, then shook her head. "It amazes me we had the same father. Anything slightly suspect my father was totally against." She threw out her one hand. "When it came to Teddy, he could do anything. Talk about a double standard."

"Could be because he was a boy."

"Sure. That probably has something to do with it."

"You got a brother? You know how it is?"

The thought had her snorting. "No. I can only imagine what it would be like. Not sure if I could deal with another protective male in the family."

As far as her brother went, it sounded as if Abby had already decided. Nala asked anyway, "Would you like me to run a check on him?"

A sly smile tipped up her lips. "I would like that. It would be good conversational fodder for the next holiday gathering. I've always been the good child. Doing what was right while he has majored in screw-ups. In the beginning, I used to be the first to rush to his defense. That was before I realized he didn't really care. He doesn't care what people think about him, and he doesn't care for people. I think I may be the only person who sees him as he is."

So far, he sounded fairly evil. It made Nala glad she didn't have a sibling. "I assume he has the same last name?"

"He does. I considered changing mine so as to not be associated with him, but it would have upset my parents."

Nala pawed through her purse looking for her pad and pencil. Originally, she had planned to record all conversations but after accidentally erasing one before she could transcribe it sent her back to the paper method.

"His first name?"

"Teddy."

It was hard to think of someone named Teddy as being a sociopath.

"His full name is Theodore Roosevelt Kingsley. My father is a history professor. I'm just glad I was named after Abby Miller who was a trade organizer or something. Fortunately, my mother insisted my middle name not be Miller."

"Okay." It also made her own name, Nala, not so onerous. "Theodore Roosevelt Kingsley. He goes by Teddy."

She could see that as a villain name. Unfortunately, most of her online searches would come up with the former president first. Oh well. She heaved a sigh of relief. At least it was better than looking up Elvin. Although, in the end, she'd have to do that, too.

Chapter Five

The fact the day started with Bruno licking her face when the alarm failed to sound should have told her something. Still, she managed to get to work on time. She'd had the foresight to have laid out her clothes the night before and packed her lunch. There was no leisurely coffee or time to do the whole makeup job. Since Abby kept to foundation, a hint of blush, and a single brush of the mascara wand, people seldom knew she wore makeup anyway. Even her lipstick was only a shade darker than her lips.

No way she'd be out partying with some Italian hottie. Nope, that gorgeous man had to be playing a joke on her. Nothing about the scenario made sense. She tucked her hair behind her ear as she met the gaze of the earnest investigator.

The woman had introduced herself as Nala. With her dark curls and high cheekbones, the investigator could pull off an exotic name. Whereas, with her plain Jane looks, it was no wonder her parents had named her Abby. She knew she was named after a woman who broke barriers and never believed in a glass ceiling. Maybe her mother was like that. It was hard to know since her father refused to talk about her.

Oh. The investigator had asked her something. Even the dog was giving her the fisheye.

"Could you repeat that?"

"Did anything odd happen to you today? Did it look like someone had fiddled with your car? Purse?"

The highlights of the day slowly replayed in her mind as if on a movie screen. Her car was locked when she went downstairs. Melvin, the security guard, greeted her with a cheery hello when she entered the building for work, then it was a straight four hours with only going to the restroom once, and she had taken her purse. The rest of the day was more of the same with her boss coming in and asking for that last favor.

"Nothing. My boss did ask me to drop some papers off over in Carmel." She shrugged. "He does this every now and then. People assume because I'm not married and don't have kids that I don't have a life."

Nala coughed, then added. "Been there. Done that. Anything unusual about the delivery?"

It all seemed so silly in retrospect. Even mentioning it would just make her sound incredibly stupid or vain. She sucked in her lips, uncertain. The dog, whose name she couldn't remember, cocked his head as if he knew.

"Well, ah, I'm not sure it's relevant," she hesitated, wondering if she could back pedal now that she had opened her mouth.

"No information is wasted. You'd be surprised how the tiniest things can close a case, even something the observer had deemed unimportant, from a time stamp to a welding union badge on an electrician's uniform. Tell me what you have."

Abby closed her eyes and took a deep breath, then opened them. "There was this guy in the parking lot when I went to drop off the papers. The man looked like a magazine ad for the Triumph motorcycle he was riding."

The dog made a loud yawn, and Nala nudged him. "Go on. Did you two talk?"

"Yeah, we did. That was the weird thing about it."

Nala chuckled and grinned in her direction. "When some hot guy talks to me, I consider it miraculous, not weird."

"I'd say likewise, but he wanted to know why I was acting like I didn't know him"

"You," Nala pointed at Abby, "and him?" She allowed her raised eyebrows to finish the statement.

"Good heavens, no! Trust me, I would have remembered meeting him."

Nala had clicked her pen and wrote down a few notes. The dog stood and tried to look at the notebook as if he could read. She pushed him away, which caused him to drift around the apartment sniffing things. Bruno wouldn't like it, but Abby assumed the dog helped in the investigations somehow.

"What can you tell me about the man?"

"Besides being the best-looking man, I've ever seen in Hamilton County?"

The crinkles beside Nala's eyes hinted at amusement. "I need a little more than that to go on. I ask a dozen women what the best-looking man in Hamilton County looks like, and I usually get a dozen answers."

"He was tall." Abby stood, trying to imagine where she would have hit Mr. Sexy. "I probably came up to his chin. I was wearing flats like I usually do. I'm five and a half feet tall. That should put him around six feet."

The shepherd pattered back to Nala and nudged her notepad until she bent down and turned her head as if listening to the dog. She straightened up and raised a finger. "Do you remember if he was wearing boots?"

"Yes, he was. How did you know?"

"Those who ride motorcycles often do. Helps keep their feet in place. It would also mean he was probably shorter."

"Never thought about that. It was just a greeting really. He had gorgeous, long hair. It was rich brown with a hint of red in the sunlight. You really don't see that type of hair in men around here. It wasn't too surprising he had an Italian accent."

"Not too many Italians around here, either."

Nala wrinkled her nose. "My real question is did he know you or did he just pretend to have met you to hit on you?"

Hit on her. No way. "It would have to be a first."

Nala smile and half nodded. "Most identity thefts are fairly impersonal. Hackers grab your number from a file, sometimes sell it, use it, but seldom swing by your house to pick up a package. Didn't you say your neighbor thought it was you?"

"Yes, she did." Here she thought things couldn't get any worse. "I don't know how far away she was or how good Barb's eyesight is, though."

"There may be no connection between the two incidents."

"I'll need you to look into this immediately."

"That's the plan."

Her hand pressed against her chest as she realized the full ramifications of her situation. "I had to freeze everything. I have no credit and no way to pay you."

The dog abruptly stood up and went to stand by the door. Nala snapped her fingers, which made the dog return, sigh, and plop down beside her.

"Don't worry about that. Normally, I ask for a retainer, but you have special circumstances. You can pay when I close your case." She waved a warning finger. "Don't go worrying about the cost. I'll give you the special rate."

At last, something good was going her way. "I'm grateful for everything." She stood, waiting for Nala to stand, then held out her hand to shake.

"No problem." Nala grasped the offered hand and gave it a sturdy shake. "I'll call you tomorrow."

The dog gave a final sniff before trailing its owner out of the door.

★

MAX WAITED UNTIL they were safely in the car before speaking. "Either that cat chick is lying or she's clueless."

Chick. That was a new word. She bet she could place that one on Elvin, too. "What do you mean?"

"I know what I smell like."

"Yeah." She inserted her keys into the ignition and started the car. "I assume you're going somewhere with this?" No reason for her to turn to see her canine's icy glare, she could feel it.

"You think?"

He even sounded like Elvin. "I don't have all night. Spit it out."

His nose tipped up and gave a slight sniff. "Not until you tell me I'm a valuable member of the agency and you couldn't survive without me."

Calling her one-woman investigative firm an *agency* was her mother's idea. It made it somehow sound legit. Having a diva of a canine on board wasn't that much of an asset, but there had been some cases where Max's assistance had proved helpful. "Okay. I couldn't do it without you."

"That's not what I said."

Her eyes rolled up briefly before she turned onto the main road. "At this time of night, it's all you get. Keep it up and I might bypass picking up supper."

Max's ears went up. "Don't go nuts on me. I'll talk." He continued speaking in a rushed fashion. "My smell I know. Your smell, got it. Pass cat chick several times and am very familiar with her smell. Cat smell…" He paused to grimace, "…can't get it out of my nostrils."

"How is any of this helpful?"

"There was another human in the apartment."

With the amount of transient population those apartments attracted, numerous folks could have rented the exact same apartment. Most complexes would have at least slapped a new coat of paint on the surface and cleaned the carpets, but this place? Maybe not. "Recently?"

"Less than a week."

"It would be good to know who it was. Could have a bearing on the case. It could have been someone who asked to use her bathroom." Since she hadn't seen any other doors opening off the living room, the bathroom could only be reached by traipsing through the bedroom. Perhaps someone decided to take more than toilet tissue. "Odd. She swore no one came in."

Max nodded his head as if following the conversation. "It was the mail carrier. You can't trust them. Sneaks. Creeping around on people's property."

"They're delivering the mail." This wasn't exactly stellar help. Then again, he probably was as tired as she was. When had she sunk to expecting answers from a dog? Nala couldn't remember turning that corner, but here she was. At least there was no one around to witness it.

"That's what they want you to think."

"Forget your grudge against the mail carrier. I need real possibilities."

"Avon lady?"

She crinkled her nose and slowed for a changing light. "I think they do all that online now. Besides, Abby doesn't look the type to be caking on makeup or perfume. She'd have as much use for toiletries as you would."

"It's hard to use what you don't have."

Really, her dog wanted toiletries now. A familiar phone chime saved her from responding.

"Hey, Karly."

Her friend greeted her with a long drawn out. "Whaaatsssuuuup?"

"Just left a new client courtesy of you spreading my business cards around."

"You're welcome. I wanted to see if you and Max could come by because I have an idea. It's a brilliant one. I think you'll love it."

No, she wouldn't. Karly was her oldest friend and closest one, but she usually didn't love her ideas. They usually centered around meeting men and not particularly wonderful guys, either. The speed dating fiasco garnered her two geriatric stalkers and one determined illegal immigrant who would wed for a green card. Most people would never assume the brunette, who usually wore her hair in a pony tail, would even have time to come up with wacky scenarios to meet men, since she was a hundred percent about the rescue animal placement. Still, Nala knew when something was up. "Tell me over the phone."

"Not doing it. You can be a joy sucker at times. It's something you have to see to appreciate."

"I'm tired and hungry."

"I'll spring for pizza. It might even beat you here."

Max gave a long howl of approval.

Karly responded to the dog's enthusiasm. "At least someone will give me the time of day."

Gingersnaps! Her friend could be every bit as dramatic as her canine. If she didn't go, Karly's feelings would be hurt. Anyway, pizza sounded good. "Make sure there's pepperoni and banana peppers on it."

"Done."

Did she say done? It sounded as if she'd already ordered the pizza with the expectation that Nala wouldn't say no. "I'm not doing that speed dating thing again."

"Oh please. What I have in mind will be fun."

The light turned green allowing Nala to make her choice. Straight would take her home, while a right turn would take her past her friend's apartment. A honk from the car behind her curtailed any lengthy decision-making process. She veered right.

Most of their adventures were along the line of sushi making, that ended up with food poisoning, to swing dancing that did not end well. A violent spinner had whipped Nala around like a top so quickly she had hit a pole in the dance studio and busted her lip. Swing music usually made her run for cover now.

"Just to be clear, I'm coming for the pizza only."

Her friend chuckled. "Yeah, that's what you said last time."

Oh brownies! She had turned into her dog. *Easily had for free food.*

Chapter Six

THE EVENING SHADOWS lengthened as Nala drove. It was way past supper time, and her stomach growled on cue. Usually, her dog would have made mention of going so long without food.

As if able to hear her thoughts, Max nudged her shoulder. "Can you hurry? I'm starving."

Of course, he was. "You never mentioned it until now."

"Hey, I was in work mode. My body is a well-tuned machine that needs fuel for energy."

"I know."

She recognized that well-tuned machine remark from Elvin, her high school friend. Well aware she wasn't part of the popular crowd, Nala had tried to fly under the radar in high school. Elvin drew attention to himself when he should have been silent, making him a natural target. As a skinny kid who set the grading curve, he lacked emotional intelligence and often became the scapegoat for a few of the athletes. His flair for the dramatic resulted in a series of freak accidents bedeviling the muscle-bound bullies. That's when she knew he had skills. He added some height, bulked out over the years, and became very interested in current fashion. His wavy hair was often artistically mussed with the use of styling products. It looked more like the result of a wind tunnel accident, followed by a healthy dose of hairspray.

"When did you start quoting Elvin all the time? You used to

quote just the television or my father."

"I know." Max resumed his place on the passenger seat and tossed his head. "Elvin has way better lines."

That made Nala snort. His lines were so wonderful he had zero women in line waiting to date him. The image made her think of her newest client, Abby. She said she'd dated someone named Elvin? She considered her wise-cracking friend, who considered himself a player, despite the fact no one else did. Would a practical gal such as Abby even give him the time of day?

No way, but Abby didn't appear to have much self-confidence. For some reason, she couldn't imagine some foreign hottie on a prime motorcycle being interested in her. Come to think of it, it would be a stretch for Nala to consider such a guy, either. Those types tend to associate with their own kind in penthouse apartment parties that peons like herself were never invited to.

Maybe Abby did go out with Elvin. The wistfulness in her voice indicated a genuine affection for the vanishing man. The disappearing act did sound like her friend. Oddly, he prided himself on not dating any woman more than a handful of times. He wore it like a badge of honor, but she'd always assumed it was all an act due to the women who dumped him. "I'll ask him."

"Ask who?"

The apartment sign showed on the right, causing her to slow for the entrance. When was she ever going to remember that talking to herself while Max was in the car made him conclude that he was part of the conversation? Her first attempt to explain she was talking to herself only resulted in her dog giving her a *yeah really* look.

"Elvin."

"Ask him what?"

"If he dated Abby." Now she'd done it. Max wasn't great about keeping secrets. Normally, he never talked to Elvin, but a few times he slipped with the result being that Elvin thought he was getting psychic messages from the universe. Somehow, this was more believable than a talking dog.

"You can't do that."

For once, Max was on target. "You're right."

"A male never kisses and tells."

She flipped on her blinker and turned into the complex, slow enough to give her dog a disbelieving look without running into anything. No way had Elvin ever said those words. Maybe he had said them, but he certainly didn't live by them. Her forehead puckered as she tried to recall if Elvin ever mentioned Abby. Nope. Most of the women he mentioned usually had stripper names like Desiree, Pleasure, Treasure, Rhapsody, or Lola. Normally, she assumed he made up the women and the names.

Familiar with her friend's complex, she drove to Karly's unit without squinting at the building numbers and parked right next to the dog mobile, as she often called Karly's car. The station wagon was festooned with doggy bumper stickers. Most would never believe the woman didn't own a dog. Motorists probably peered into the car, curious as to what breed of dog she had.

A man in the familiar red shirt and cap of a local pizzeria came down the stairs with a flat hot bag. Max must have noticed the guy the same time as she did because he gave three short barks, then added,

"Pizza! Let's go."

Normally, Nala didn't feed her canine pizza. It had an unfortunate effect. She'd pull the crust off and gave him that. Maybe Karly had some dog food to supplement the crusts. Other people usually meant an end to Max's non-stop commentary but not with Karly, who spoke to all the dogs, even those who didn't talk back.

The delivery guy glanced at her and grinned. Yeah, he assumed she was the one talking. No one questioned why she had a baritone voice. Probably put it down to being a chain smoker. Nala swung her door open and promptly moved out of the way as Max scrambled across the gear shift and used her seat as a launch platform. He hit the ground running, swerved toward the stairs without even a backward glance to see if she was following. It made her wonder how he thought he'd knock on the door before she got there.

Nala grabbed her purse and locked up the car. Graham Bonne's constant refrain included no place was safe and anyone could be a criminal. It may have made Nala more than a little paranoid. Her father's early efforts to make her into a junior officer had sharpened her observation skills and made her a tad distrustful of the rest of the populace.

Abby's situation could have been something simple enough as ordering something online from work or even a coffee shop with WiFi. Unsecured public areas were easy picking for those with enough tech savvy to pick up numbers or even do a screen capture. Even when you didn't actively use your credit card, those with the right technology could also stroll through your address books, photos, and credit cards stored on your computer. It was never a smart bet using your computer in a public place, especially when money was involved.

She took the steps slowly, making Max dance in frustration at the top of the stairs. Behind him, the door to Karly's apartment opened, and someone attired in a Batman costume filled the opening. Max looked back, then at Nala, his ears pitched forward, announcing his confusion.

It had to be her friend. "Karly?"

"I'm Batman," the woman replied in a husky, but familiar voice.

This was different, and Nala was almost afraid to ask. "I don't care who you are as long as you have pizza."

She reached the landing and gave Max a reassuring pat on the head. They both turned in the direction of Batman/Karly who stepped back and ushered them into the apartment. The spicy aroma of pizza drew Nala in, even though she'd have to hear whatever crazy scheme her friend had cooked up. Her friend spending her days with four-legged creatures obviously didn't discourage her off-the-wall plans.

"Should I ask?" she commented, as she strolled past her friend.

"Comic Con is coming. Do you have your costume?"

Harry had mentioned something about that. In his business, it was a big money-making proposition, but Karly had never shown any interest in it. Until she met Harry, Nala didn't even know Indy had a Comic Con.

"No costume. Don't need one. Not going. What's up with you?"

On one occasion Karly showed up at the local mall where the shelter had the weekend to run an adopt-a-thon for rescue animals in a vacant store area. Traffic wasn't great in that part of the mall where several stores had closed, which meant few people walked in that direction anymore. To clue shoppers in that there were rescue pets waiting for a forever home, Karly donned a large dog head and tried to lead shoppers to them, rather like a canine pied piper. Instead of getting shoppers headed in the right direction, she scared a couple of toddlers whose mother alerted the mall security. By the time the cops hunted her down, she'd already run into the pretzel kiosk and cracked her dog head in the process. After that disaster, Nala figured Karly would have sworn off costumes. Obviously, she was wrong.

Max had edged over to the table where the pizza box was and even had his chin resting on the table. It didn't take a dog whisperer to see what was about to go down. Nala darted to the table and grabbed the box as her friend mumbled something.

"Excuse me. I think the mask must be interfering with your speech."

Karly pulled off the mask and put both hands on her hips. "I know you heard what I said. There will be tons of socially awkward nerds at the Con."

Holding the dinner high out of Max range, she tried to decipher the odd statement. "So, what if socially awkward folks attend Comic Con? I imagine anyone can go. Even you. Why should it matter?"

Karly jostled her, plucked the box out of her hand and headed into the kitchen where she pulled out plates. "Do you want a soda?"

"Sure." Normally, she might have deferred due to the possibility that it would keep her up, but she was already half-past dead. All a soda would do was keep her awake long enough to finish it.

As she imagined, Karly did have a bowl of nutritionally balanced kibble for Max. Unlike at home, the dog ate it with only an occasional side glance at the pizza box. He knew how to play Karly and sneak a slice of pizza. They'd do the exchange when Nala wasn't watching.

The sight of her friend with the giant bat logo on her chest made her chuckle. Using the slice of pizza in her hand, she gestured to the emblem. "Are you seriously going to attend Comic Con?"

"I am. You have some major stars come by. Lots of interesting events, and there are all those nice but dating phobic guys who show up." Her eyebrows waggled excessively to convey the obvious.

"Socially awkward guys." She pressed a hand against her chest. "Be still my heart. I imagine most are living at home with their mothers."

Her last date, which she judged to be fair, was with Tyler Goodnight a couple of months ago. Since there hadn't been a follow-up date, it must not have gone as well as she thought, despite the rumor of his ex-girlfriend on the scene. There was no hard and fast rule that a man had to go back to an ex when said ex made an appearance. Even still, the possibility of dressing up in colorful spandex to meet some guys who couldn't string together a sentence did not appeal. "No, Karly, no. There's so much wrong about this plan."

Her friend waved both hands, interrupting her. "Stop it. You're such a joy sucker. Thousands of people go to the Con. They can't all be socially awkward."

"You said it."

Realizing she'd just been caught, Karly grimaced, but continued speaking. "I was joking. There will be IT guys, engineers, you know, the deep thinkers."

"We all know deep thinkers favor comic books and dressing up in Halloween outfits." She finished up her piece of pizza and contemplated reaching for another. It was pretty late at night, and she was guzzling a sugary soda. If her mother were here she'd be quick to remind Nala that the fast food meal would go straight to her hips. Since hippy women were suddenly hot now, she helped herself to another piece.

"What about Harry? You like him," Karly asked.

Even though the question wasn't directed at Max, he fielded it anyhow. "Harry is cool. He keeps jerky treats in his office for me."

Those treats weren't for dogs, but humans. As Nala remembered it, Max helped himself. Harry had laughed about it, which made him more even-tempered than most. "I agree he is cool, but he makes his living selling the superheroes merchandise to the socially awkward dudes. Also, he's not socially awkward. He talks to me every time he sees me. It's normal stuff. He never asks me if I've seen the latest superhero movie."

Karly put her hands down and no longer appeared to be landing planes, but her squared shoulders indicated the discussion was far from over. "How do you know he doesn't ask his friends if they've seen the latest superhero epic?"

She had a point. The man probably summed her up at the first meeting, probably realizing five minutes into the conversation that she would not be a potential customer for his wares. "That's a possibility. I imagine he has to go see the movies for his business and all."

Karly carefully cut off a strip of pizza, then covered it with her hand. Yeah, so subtle even Max's ears perked up.

"They have some pretty handsome actors in those roles. You might like them." The pizza covered hand moved slowly across the table, then dropped carefully into Karly's lap.

"You do realize you're smearing pizza sauce everywhere, and you're not fooling me."

"Who me?"

"Who else? You're so *not* sneaky. Do not sign up to be a spy."

Instead of being offended, Karly giggled. "I could if I wanted to. You're not fooling anyone, either. I saw you tearing off bits of the crust for Max."

She had been. Her eyes dropped to the small pile of toasted dough. Funny how things had changed once a certain rescue dog had entered her life. As much food as she now shared with her animal, Nala should have dropped some weight, but she hadn't. What had they been talking about before she got sidetracked? Karly's desire to get her to attend Comic Con with her.

Superheroes and people who liked to don their costumes were usually Harry's providence. Her building mate's behavior was friendly, but not anything more.

Her brows came together as she analyzed their various conversations as they tread the office steps together. He always told her what he was doing, or what costume was trending, but she seldom asked more than the bare minimum of questions that showed at best, a polite interest. Nope, he had never invited her to share a superhero movie. It could be because he assumed she had no interest. Then again, it could be the one time he asked her to go to Bru Burger with him for a late-night snack, she begged off.

Couldn't quite remember now why she begged off. It might have been work, but more likely she was afraid that things might get weird. That was her usual excuse to avoid romantic encounters. It hadn't always been like that, but after Jeff, she naturally assumed her judgment regarding men needed a definite overhaul.

"I may save some food for Max, but at least I make him wait until we're done eating."

Karly made a derisive grunt and helped herself to another slice of pizza. No interpretation was needed. The woman practically shouted her disbelief. Maybe she did feed Max under the table when she was eating—sometimes. Make that most of the time. Rather than cede the point to Karly, she chose to change the subject.

"Most of the conversations I have with Harry aren't all that long. Just two folks that happen to share offices in the same building who happen to walk down the stairs at the same time."

"Hmmm, no mention of him being cute and single, which is what you told me when you first met."

Had she said that? Her observant side should have noticed such things. With everyone she met, Nala used her father's training to pick out something memorable or unique about the person. Harry with his trimmed beard and trendy glasses could easily be deemed a hipster, but there was so much more to him than a label. Not too many people would have helped her when a would-be mugger knocked her down, but Harry had. A threat growled by Max sent the assailant running.

"I may have. He's cute in that guy-next-door way."

They both nodded, aware of the context. Max placed his chin on the table. "There is no guy who lives next door to us. There's an old man."

Conversations conducted around Max could be hard. He took everything literally, which was probably a dog's mindset. "It's an expression." Unfortunately, her pooch would ask what it meant. Here she was spending an evening with her best friend, who was dressed in a superhero costume, explaining common expressions to her dog. This was not the cool life of an investigator she had envisioned.

Karly had no issues with explaining things to a dog. "It refers to a perfectly nice guy. He could be a co-worker, schoolmate, even someone who lives in the neighborhood. He usually gets overlooked due to women obsessing on movie-star handsome players, athletes, celebrities, or even cops."

Nala felt the jab. "I'm not obsessing on Tyler Goodnight."

Max' ears slanted forward at the mention of the officer's name, while Karly managed to look smug, which was not as easy as one might think while wearing a Batman costume.

"I didn't mention names. You must be the one with the guilty conscience."

"Hardy, har har! You sound just like my mother." As soon as the word *mother* popped out of her mouth, she remembered there was something she was supposed to do. Her fingers located her cell phone in her front pocket and pulled it out. The glowing time revealed it was almost nine. Probably too late for even the hardest working employee to still be at the shop, especially considering the boss was away.

Better try anyhow. Nala pressed the Posh Interiors number and after two rings her mother's voice greeted her, informing her that her call was important, but the designers were busy whipping up custom creations for treasured customers. Her call would be returned within twenty-four hours.

Obviously, it was a new recording. Her brows came together as she considered the word *treasured*. It implied that those who were paying for services received a better response time. A loud beep reminded her to leave a message. "It's me, Nala Bonne. Mother—Gwen—called." She added the last, realizing some of the employees might not make the automatic connection. "Anyhow, she wanted me to talk to someone about possibly bogus charges on the corporate card. Call me." She added her number and hung up.

Karly held up her index finger and waved it slowly back and forth. "You do realize what you did, right?"

Was this a trick question or what? "My brain's too tired to figure anything out. I waited too late to call? That, I know."

"That, too. You possibly warned anyone who was ripping off your mother you were onto them."

Her hand went up to the back of her neck and rubbed. That wasn't the case here. It seemed like everyone was overly paranoid now. "That's not it. Someone ordered ugly furniture. That wouldn't have happened. We both know Gwen wouldn't have approved the purchase. Basically, she wants me to warn off whoever is making purchases without her approval."

"Hope so." Karly drummed her fingers on the pizza box, which served as an impromptu drum. "You know, with your parents out of the country, it would be easy pickings for a motivated individual."

Posh Interiors had been her mother's baby for almost three decades. One of the employees served as her godmother, while a few others were honorary aunts. There was usually a turnover of new interns every year that hoped to use the store as a springboard into a design career. Her mother seldom ever hired any of the interns in a permanent position. It had been a while since Nala had been inside the store, so it would be hard to know if any new people were working.

"Mother's employees are loyal to her. I can't see anyone ripping her off."

The drumming stopped as Karly regarded her with an open mouth. She snapped her mouth shut and wagged her chin in disbelief. "As an investigator, you should know lots of upstanding citizens do bad things when the opportunity presents itself."

Not exactly what she wanted to hear, especially when she couldn't reach anyone until the next day. "Please. Who would be stupid enough to rip off a woman married to a ranking officer in IPD?"

Max had been cutting his eyes to Nala and Karly as they spoke. Instead of waiting for a rebuttal, he spoke.

"Someone who doesn't know."

Nala hated when her dog came up with an answer before she did. It was an uncomfortable feeling, but not as bad as someone ripping off her mother while she had no phone or internet connection to fight the issue. It sounded more like it was someone who, at least, knew her mother would be unreachable.

Chapter Seven

NALA SWUNG HER door open and stepped inside. For a brief second, it felt empty and silent, then Max rushed in, his nails skittering across the hardwood floors. Without waiting for the dog to ask, she turned on the television to Max's favorite channel. Instead of having a fondness for Animal Planet, he preferred the soap network. It didn't make sense since very few dogs ever appeared in the never-ending sagas of betrayal and heartbreak.

The familiar introductory music meant it must be ten. Her lips twisted as she decided what she should do about her mother's credit issue. She couldn't do anything until morning, or could she? The only person who might be able to provide after-hours advice would be Elvin.

She was halfway through his number before Max looked up from his show. "Who are you calling?"

His tone sounded a trifle accusatory. Who was the dominant species here? "Elvin."

"Elvin's a suspect."

"Not necessarily. I googled Elvin as a name in Indianapolis and came up with over three dozen Elvins. One was even called Elvin Elvin. We don't know which one Abby went out with. Even if it was our Elvin, it doesn't mean he took her credit card information. Besides, knowing our Elvin, he'd have no reason to do something as basic as snatching someone's numbers."

What was supposed to be a reassuring thought didn't have the right effect, while knowing her friend could rip her off at any time. He certainly had enough information to do so, while also having a clue she had nothing of real value to steal.

"Good to…" The show came back on after a commercial break, regaining his attention.

Oh well, she didn't want to waste any more time. Simple etiquette her mother tried so hard to pound into her dictated that you did not call after nine pm. However, Elvin's schedule ran towards stay up half the night and get up late. He might be able to count on one hand how many times he'd seen the sunrise. The phone burbled in her ear once before being picked up.

"What has my favorite private eye stymied?"

The fact he already suspected she had a problem chafed. "It's not me. It's my mother."

Elvin listened without comment as she explained the situation, then offered up his analysis. "It's been stolen."

"How can you say that? So far, the only thing that has shown up is some ugly furniture mother would not approve of. It's her corporate card, not anything she would have taken with her on vacation. All she wanted me to do was check and see if anyone at the company used it. That's all."

He made a disbelieving grumble, probably put out that she hadn't accepted his initial summary. "Believe what you want. I think a smart con artist got your mother's number. They know enough to realize the card is for an interior design salon. They can order as much carpet, drapes, and furniture as they want without triggering an alarm, but once they buy something like a diamond ring or a world cruise, an alarm might post. It depends on what limits your mother has on the card."

"I have no clue." Her own card had very modest limits and blocked her when she attempted to buy a computer online earlier. The credit block supplied enough time for her to rethink her impulsive purchase.

"Do you know if she has been hanging out in dark bars or clubs?" There was an amused tone to Elvin's query.

"You know my mom. What do you think?"

"No. That's where a lot of credit card numbers are stolen. Some of the help are not above writing down the numbers from a card. If a dishonest bartender doesn't get you, the skimmers on the ATM machines will."

"Skimmer?" Half the time, Elvin spoke in code. Unfortunately, it wasn't one she knew.

"It's a device that scammers attach to ATM machines that records your number and password. They are little more than a strip affixed to an ATM machine. What looks like detailing is loaded with technology and is sending info to someone at a remote location. Even before a person pockets the money from the ATM, their number is being used by someone else. By the end of the night, the unlucky sucker will not only have an empty bank account but overdrawn notices for the checks that bounced."

"That's a bad deal. How do you avoid these skimmers?"

"Do your business with a real person inside the bank. The scammers love to put this technology in dark places because it makes them even harder to identify. If you run your fingers over any ATM you can feel if something is out of place. The truly bold will even put them on bank ATMs. They won't last more than twelve hours there since the bank inspects everything."

"Snickerdoodles. You paint a dark scenario."

"Just the facts. As technology advances, so do the criminals.

Nowadays, most can manage a simple virtual mugging by lifting credit card numbers from afar."

"How can I help my mother?"

"Cancel the card."

"I have no clue what the number is."

"Surely it's written down somewhere."

A memory of the last Sunday lunch they shared popped into her mind. Since her parents were leaving the country, her father was a big fan of the worst-case scenario. He escorted her to the den and the file cabinet, pointing out the second drawer, third file labeled, WHAT IF. Her father was a big believer in not making things too easy for criminals such as labeling the file *credit cards* or *will*, which contained both.

"It is. It's in a file cabinet at my parents' home."

Max's head jerked up at the statement. His ears perked as if he caught the scent of something. *Weird.*

"You're going to have to drive over there. There is a twenty-four-hour number for each card you can call. If your mom didn't write it down you can look it up online. Do it now, since whoever has it is charging away. There's no telling how much bad furniture they can buy. Make sure to explain the first suspicious charge. You might have to pretend to be your mother, though."

People often commented that they sounded alike, and the occasional salesperson would ask if they were sisters, especially if Mom was footing the bill. "Can't I just tell them my mother asked me to call?"

The sound of Elvin tsking carried over the phone. It was most likely accompanied by a sad face because she even asked such a thing. Nala continued. "Go ahead and tell me why that won't work?"

"Oh please. I'm shocked that I have to, with you being an investigator, but I will. There are plenty of bitter folks out there. If they could, they'd cancel an ex's credit card just to embarrass them when they tried to use it. If anyone could call with no proof whatsoever, imagine the chaos."

"You got me. Who knew I could have canceled Jeff's credit cards?"

"You can't, but you could have easily lifted them and gave them to some lowlife to max out."

A devious action and one that probably wouldn't have been traced back to her. The fact Elvin had thought of it emphasized the need to have the man on her side. Apparently, he could outthink the average criminal. "All right, I'm supposed to call the credit card agency if I find the number in the file my father pointed out to me. Won't they expect some sort of password or something?"

"Of course. They will ask for an address, birthdate, and usually a grandmother's maiden name. Your mother may have additional questions that you should be able to answer."

Despite having the phone clamped to her ear, she shook it slowly back and forth. Realizing Elvin couldn't see her actions, she spoke into the phone. "You'd think I'd know my parents, but recently they've been doing things that're new to them. They're always taking off on these trips. They never used to travel."

"Kids. Once the kids leave, the parents will play."

She huffed, unwilling to believe she stopped her parents from traveling. If anything, she encouraged it, but before her work had always taken precedence. "I guess I'll head out and hope for the best."

"Good luck. Talk to you later." She hung up the phone and glanced at her dog, who looked superbly comfortable.

Max cut his eyes toward her as if he felt her gaze, then back at the television when dramatic music swelled.

"We need to head over to my parents' house."

"Can't you wait? Tiffany is about to tell Raoul he isn't Raoul Junior's father."

Instead of getting into an argument with her dog, she gathered her keys, phone, and purse. Explanations were overrated, especially when you tried to explain them to argumentative canines. Her hand closed over the remote and powered off the television.

"That was just mean." Max's voice went into a long howl. "Aroo!"

"Let's go Rin Tin Tin. Part of the reason I adopted you was to have some protection when driving around at night." That wasn't the only reason. Karly had told her, as an adult dog who had been unsuccessfully placed in homes, Max was scheduled to be put down. She never mentioned it to him, knowing it would have been deeply disturbing to her boastful dog to learn no one truly wanted him.

His front paws hit the floor as he grumbled, "A dog's work is never done."

WITH THE LIGHT traffic that time of night, the drive to her parents' house went quickly. No need to make a big ordeal out of entering the house. Knowing her father, he'd put the neighbors on high alert if anything unusual happened. Even still, the back entrance would attract the least amount of attention.

As she turned into the driveway, she switched off the car lights. The solar lights her mother had installed along the drive provided a sufficient amount of light. Nala coasted up to the back entrance and cut the engine. Her hand was on the door handle before she thought to warn Max.

"I need you to be quiet. Let's not wake up the neighbors."

Instead of answering, he merely nodded, proving to her he'd gotten the message.

Stillness hung over the neighborhood. A nearby heat pump swirled into operation while a night bird made a mournful call. It felt like the entire world was asleep, except for her. Even Max slid out the car more cat-like than his normal exuberance.

The outside lights were dawn to dusk that snapped on when the sun made its exit. Her father was a firm believer that a well-lit entrance was less likely to be robbed. Criminal types used the dark for their nefarious deeds most of the time. They had rose bushes along the ground floor windows making the option of entering via a window tricky at best.

It had been years since she entered the house when no one was home. She stuck her key in the lock and turned. The lock clicked, which meant they hadn't changed the locks on her. When she pushed the door open, an electronic voice sounded.

"Door ajar. Thirty seconds to disarm."

"Brownies!" Her mother had mentioned an alarm. Even told her the code. It was someone's birth year. She turned on the kitchen light and lunged for the control box. She stabbed in her father's birthdate. She knew her mother's birthdate but didn't know the exact year since her mother tended to fudge the issue.

"Five seconds to disarm."

Not knowing what to do, she put in her own birthdate in desperation.

"Disarmed."

Max gave a relieved sigh. "I was worried I would have to ditch you if the po-po showed up."

Her first instinct was to correct her dog for the use of slang, but she didn't have the energy for it. Instead, she leaned her forehead against the wall. Right now, she should be home, in her jammies, in bed, and halfway through a chapter in the newest thriller she bought. After a couple of minutes, she lifted her head. It would be best to get the job done and leave.

Max followed her upstairs and into the office where Nala closed the blinds before she turned on the lights. The file, holding a sheet of paper for each card, including a copy of the cards, was easy to locate. Her mother had written the phone number to call for help on each sheet. Most of the cards were in either her father's or mother's name. There were two under *Posh Interiors*.

Which one was it? Obviously, her mother hadn't taken her business cards with her. Were they hidden somewhere at work? Maybe not so hidden, since the employees might need access to run the business. If she canceled the wrong card, it might stop business for the duration of her parents' cruise.

She stared at the card numbers and reached for her cell.

Max nudged her elbow. "Use the landline."

"What?" It always surprised her when a dog offered advice. Even more when it made sense.

He angled his head to the pink rotary phone sitting on the desk. She picked up the receiver and held it to her head. There was a dial tone.

"Go on," her dog encouraged.

"Okay. Care to tell me your reasoning?" She started the slow process of dialing with a rotary phone.

"The number needs to match the account."

"Pretty smart for a canine. I would have thought of it if I wasn't so tired."

He lifted a dog brow.

"I really would have!"

Before Max had a chance to answer, the phone rang and was immediately answered.

"Credit Hotline. How can I help?"

In an effort to channel her mother, Nala sat straighter and shook back her hair. "This is Gwen Bonne." She tried for a line between confidence and imperiousness. "I have reason to believe someone is charging fraudulent charges on my card."

"Okay. Let's go through some general information."

The woman asked for an address, anniversary, and children's names. "Nala."

"That's right. Your son's name?"

She had a brother? Did he die at birth? Why had no one told her? She hesitated until her dog bumped her hard with his large head.

"Max!"

"That's it. What charge do you think is fraudulent?"

Her mother said something about some ugly furniture, which could mean anything. "Could you read me back the most recent charges?"

"Red leather living room suite at Furniture Outfitters in Tucson, Arizona."

That was it, but before she could comment that her mother would never shop anywhere with *outlet* in its name, the woman continued to speak.

"Also, a chrome bedroom suite."

She closed her eyes at the mention of chrome. Her mother would have a cow. "Neither were authorized."

"Okay. Tonight, there's been another charge. Wait, it might have been yesterday. Since it takes a while for international charges to go through. Two dozen black velvet landscapes bought in Tijuana."

"Cancel it! Cancel it now. This is horrible!"

Gwen Bonne would be mad about the charges but would be more upset about the damage to her designer reputation. Black velvet paintings! Her mother would rant about them being outlawed or at least they should be. Her own careless comment made when she was ten alerted her to how her mother felt about the kitschy art form.

"Yes, ma'am. Not a problem. We will reverse the charges. You'll still be responsible for fifty dollars of the charges."

She wanted to argue, but fifty seemed like such a small expense to pay. "Just do it."

"We'll send you a new card."

That might not be such a good idea since her mother wouldn't be home to receive it. "Why don't we wait on that until we work out the details of this current fiasco."

"Mrs. Bonne, you've been a loyal customer for the past ten years. We would hate to lose you."

Realizing the woman would push to send the card, she summoned her inner Gwen Bonne. "I said, I would like to wait a while. I did not say I would not use your company, but if you continue to push, I will."

"No, ma'am. Sorry, ma'am. Would you like a confirmation number?"

"Yes." She wrote down the number and managed to end the call civilly. She hung up the rotary phone and picked up the file, ready to put it back in the cabinet, but changed her mind at the last minute. Whoever got her mother's card, might have access to the other ones. She'd take the file with her in case she received any more panicky phone calls.

Max padded over to the window and pushed at the blinds.

"Come on, boy, let's go."

"Heard something. Someone is out there."

Her bed was calling her name, and her day was way past being over. As of this moment, she was off the clock and had no interest in investigating neighborhood sounds.

"Someone could be walking their dog. A teenager is coming home late. There's a thousand ordinary things it could be."

"If you say so."

They walked down the steps in the dim light provided by the hummingbird nightlights Gwen had placed throughout the house. Her mother insisted she did it for Graham, her father, who tended to get up in the middle of the night. It was probably more for her mother who was unwilling to admit she liked the glow of the colorful birds. She probably assumed such an item wasn't in good taste.

The kitchen light was still on. Everything was as she left it. Max stiffened beside her and whispered in a sotto voice, "Trouble."

"Police! Come out with your hands up!"

She should have known her father probably had extra drive-by on the house while they were on vacation. She put her hands up including the one holding the credit card file.

"It's me, Nala Bonne. I'm supposed to be here. This is my childhood home."

Two uniformed officers stood in the kitchen, and one even had his gun pointed at her. The other officer called into his shoulder-mounted radio. "Suspect apprehended. Claims she is Nala Bonne. Some relation to Captain Bonne."

"I'm his daughter!" Neither of the young officers appeared convinced by her claim. "I have identification in my purse."

Max, who had stayed back, padded into the kitchen at that moment. The officer holding the gun lowered it and shouted, "Max! Hey, Brody, look, it's Max."

"It is." He spoke into the radio. "It's a false alarm. Suspect identified as relative."

All it took was a dog to identify her? "How do you know Max?"

The officer holstered his gun. "Sorry about that. Captain Bonne asked us to keep an eye on the house while he was on vacay."

"Understood."

The other officer, whose name tag read Brody, bent to pat Max. "Your father brought Max to work. Mainly to show the K-9 unit how well a dog can work. He's amazing."

How come neither Max nor her father ever mentioned this? She managed a weary smile. "Thanks for your service, but I need to set the alarm and lock up. It's way past my bedtime."

"Hear ya." One of the officers touched the rim of his hat as they backed out.

Once in her car, she had to ask. "Why did you never tell me about going to work with my father?"

"It was need-to-know protocol."

That sounded so like her father. In the end, it all turned out good. "Yeah, I've heard that before. Glad you were my identification tonight."

"You should be, considering you had a file full of credit card numbers."

Chapter Eight

MORNING CAME WITH a wet slobbery kiss and heavy panting. She kept her eyes closed, not to enjoy a hot dream, but to try to fool Max into thinking she was still asleep. The clatter of his paws hitting the floor meant maybe he'd given up, which was so unlike him. A chill hit her body, and she grabbed the blanket to cover up, only to find it missing. Her eyelids snapped open, and she was greeted with a view of her dog with the end of the blanket in his mouth.

"Max!" She sat up in disgust. "This is my only time to sleep late."

His long tail gave a couple of thumps before he spit out the blanket. "My lack of thumbs prevents me from letting myself out. A doggie door would be nice."

"Yeah, yeah, you've mentioned this before." Reluctantly, she pushed herself out of bed and put on her terrycloth robe to minimize the morning chill. The heat stayed at a modest sixty-five to conserve money. Max, with his full coat, never complained, but it could get a little nippy for those without a full layer of hair. "Remember the movie where the burglars crawled in through the dog door?"

"How could I forget? You've only mentioned it a dozen times." He weaved around her and headed for the back door.

Nala followed, anticipating how long it would take to get back to her cozy bed. "Not a dozen times, maybe a few."

"A dozen, two, it's all the same. Hollywood ruins life for dogs everywhere."

She opened the door for Max. He pranced outside as if he were a show horse on display. Still caught up on why a dog door would be a bad idea, she shouted after him. "It's a thing! People are breaking into homes through the pet doors."

A shrill voice carried over the backyard fence. "Dear sweet Lord, no!"

Jeez, another incident where she had been talking to Max and people assumed she was talking to them. She managed a smile at her next-door neighbor who was surrounded by tiny, yappy dogs. "I'm sure no one could get through a dog door for your pets."

"You can never be too careful." The woman fluttered her hand at the neck of her frilly robe. "That's why I let my treasures in and out myself, as opposed to allowing them to run willy-nilly."

Was that a dig at her? Had she let Max run willy-nilly? She had been guilty in good weather of leaving the back door open, especially if she was getting ready.

Her cheeks ached as she held her smile, not knowing how to respond. The woman continued to babble, proving no response was necessary.

"I have to keep an eye on my sweet darlings because someone might try to steal them."

Max had finished his business and strolled leisurely to the door while muttering under his breath, "Fat chance."

Her neighbor's head jerked as if struck. Lemon bars! The woman heard. What could she say that sounded somewhat similar?

The mental scramble for anything that rhymed with fat chance had her brain firing on all cylinders. She'd first came up with tap dance but couldn't make that work. "I said combat stance! You'd take a combat stance if someone tried to steal your pets."

"You better believe I would." Her furrowed brow announced either her feelings about would be dognappers, or her disbelief that the original statement had indeed been combat stance.

Nala gave a wave and waited for Max to enter the house before closing the door. She spun to face her canine, placing both hands on her hips. "We've talked about you talking in front of people."

Max hung his head for a few seconds as if feeling bad. He plopped his rump on the floor, lifted his head, and managed a sly smile. "Come on, I couldn't help myself. No one would steal those hairy rats."

He'd be wrong. There was an unfortunate practice of stealing pets, then waiting for the owners to post a reward. If the people never posted a reward, the joke was on the thief. "You'd be surprised. Smaller dogs are easier to pick up and conceal. Before you came along, one of my mother's neighbors stole the other neighbor's poodle. Kept it for several weeks until the original owner spotted it."

"Why'd she do that?"

Her shoulders went up in a shrug. Back when she was younger, everything had a logical reason, or she thought it did. The crime dramas always featured a believable motivation. None of the mysteries had the detective declaring the culprit was as crazy as a loon and had no decipherable motive or even pattern to his actions. There was a reason behind everything. Even those women who were stupid enough to post online videos of themselves decapitating action figures that their boyfriend or spouse collected had to have a reason. That was her working premise. Most motivations were about greed or revenge.

"She told the officer who was called that she didn't know it was her neighbor's dog. This was despite the dog owner going door to door in search of her dog. Somehow, the collar with the owner's name and phone number had vanished, too. Mom thought it might have been spite because the two used to be friends. In the end, the dog went back home. Since I'm up, I might as well make breakfast."

"I'd like a cheese omelet." Max stood and padded after her. He bumped her hand with his nose. "You could crumble up some burger onto it."

"Remember what the vet said." On their last visit, which included a rabies shot, the vet commented that Max was putting on too much weight. A sign that someone was getting too much people food, and not even good food, but fast food.

"I saw you pay that woman to say those things."

"I paid for the shot."

"Which I didn't need. If I had rabies, I would have told you."

Some things didn't deserve a reply. A visual check assured her the hated kibble she'd put in Max's bowl last night had been consumed. It might not be as yummy as a cheeseburger, but he would eat it. Rather like her and chocolate. Sure, she'd love a chocolate shake for breakfast and could rationalize the calcium was good for her, but the effects would show within minutes after consumption.

After refilling Max's bowl, she had to decide what she should eat. She opened the fridge in search of something healthy. There were numerous condiments, butter, and a mysterious Styrofoam takeout carton. She couldn't remember the last time she ordered takeout, but the imprint was for a nearby Chinese restaurant. Maybe it was still good. She popped open the carton and gritted her teeth at the congealed, noxious mess. Even Max backed up a few steps.

"Smells bad."

Nala had to agree. "It is bad. No breakfast options in the fridge unless I make a fried stick of butter, like at the fairgrounds."

Max's ears perked up. "Sounds like a possibility."

"I was joking." She tossed the container in the trash can, then moved the can to the garage. No reason to smell up the entire house. Maybe the cupboard would yield something munch-worthy. Inside the sparsely supplied pantry, she found a couple of protein bars she'd received as a promo. Couldn't remember exactly when, but with all their preservatives they should last indefinitely. She ripped off the wrapper and bit down into the rock-hard bar. It was the equivalent of chewing gravel. "Must go to the grocery."

"The place I never get to go," Max added.

"Be glad I order your food online. At least you're guaranteed a balanced diet and your food isn't forgotten. As a single person, I have to look after myself."

"How could anyone forget food?"

She took another bite of her bar, refusing to answer her dog who often sounded like one or both of her parents, when he wasn't quoting Elvin. There was still coffee in the freezer so she made some to wash down the chunks of protein bar. She swore the bar maintained its gravel like structure in her stomach.

Her canine was never one to get subtle conversational cues, such as non-replying being the end of a conversation. Instead, he followed her around the kitchen giving suggestions on how a human could remember to buy food. It was easy to understand how the expression *dogging someone's steps* came about.

"Elvin orders his food online," Max told her.

That sounded like him. There were several grocery services in the area that would allow her to swing by and pick up her completed order and even deliver it. The idea had promise for about twenty seconds until she remembered the hassle with her mother's credit card and Abby's identity theft. No, thank you, she'd not be giving out her number to more faceless people.

It might have been a way Abby's number got out there. All it took was one unscrupulous person. What she needed were printouts of what was bought. It might give her a hint if the person was an acquaintance or a total unknown. The first thing she'd do was call Abby, right after brushing her teeth. She knew the woman wouldn't be able to smell her breath over the phone, but it would make Nala feel better and more professional.

ABBY HURRIED INTO Wolfie's restaurant, situated just at the edge of Morse Reservoir. Under different circumstances, she might have enjoyed the reflection of the new spring greenery on the water surface. Instead, she was cutting into her work day to deal with a problem she shouldn't have.

Her brother had joked about her paranoid tendencies when she shredded her ATM slips after recording them and placed the shreds in different wastebaskets over a series of weeks. Felons went through trash looking for financial paperwork that many casually discarded. She'd even found ATM slips by the machine.

The interior of the restaurant was all wood with a hunting lodge feel to it. The televisions were tuned to sports channels. Her eyes surveyed the diners, hoping no one there knew her or why she was there. The fact she even went out for lunch, when it was common knowledge she carried in her lunch every day, raised a few eyebrows. Her boss's secretary teased her about having a gentleman friend. She wished it was that instead of what it really was.

There were a few diners. A couple were staring at the television screen as they munched down on their sandwiches. Another couple stared at their cell phones as opposed to talking to one another. Her eyes drifted over to the lone woman but came back. She was clearly waving at her. That was her investigator.

She returned the wave, pointed out the waving woman, and informed the hostess she'd found her party. Abby weaved around the close tables. Most were empty.

Nala stood as she made her way to the table and held out her hand. "I'm glad you could come."

They shook hands as Abby searched for an appropriate reply. "It wasn't too hard. Most of the employees go out for lunch. I'm one of the few who doesn't."

"It's time you did. First, I'm paying for lunch. I totally understand about your credit situation. So, don't worry about it. I picked this place because at this time it's not too crowded. In a couple of hours, it will be packed. In a couple of months, once the boating crowd hits the lake, it will be hard getting in here."

Abby nodded and took her seat, which resulted in a pony-tailed waitress appearing at their table.

"What can I get you?"

Nala went with a buffalo chicken wrap. Abby followed suit, unfamiliar with the restaurant offerings. Quite frankly, since she discovered someone had been cashing in on her excellent credit and good name, she hadn't felt like eating anything. She had skipped breakfast, and her stomach made a rumbling growl, reminding her of its empty state. Once the waitress moved away, she scooted the chair closer to Nala.

"Did you find out who did it?"

Nala grimaced as if she'd bitten into something rotten. "It doesn't work that fast. There are a few things I need you to do. I think it will help me to find a pattern."

"Okay." She stopped speaking when the waitress showed up with their iced teas. They both murmured their thanks but waited until she moved away to resume the conversation. "I put a stop on my credit cards. I went to the bank and had my bank card canceled and a new one reissued. They even told me about being able to put a lock on your bank card. If I know I'm going to be traveling on business and will just be using my corporate card, I can lock my personal card from my phone."

"Really? This is new."

The thought of her being sent on some corporate trip made her chuckle. It would never happen since she did most of the work around her office. No way would she get the privilege of flying away for a few days. "Not that I could use it, but it's nice to know it's there."

"All right." Nala pulled a slim notebook out of her purse. "Let's go over what I need. I guess I should first ask if you want to use my services."

"I thought I had made that clear last night."

"I thought so, too, but I prefer to put things in writing for both people. Here's a standard contract." She pulled a white envelope from the cover of the notebook and handed it to Abby.

The contract was straightforward without any *therefores* or first party *thereofs*. It must not have been written by a lawyer. She read through the short contract, stating she would not be responsible for payment until her credit was back to functioning. That was taking a major chance with no guarantee of how long that would be. Her finger tapped that segment of the contract. "Do you think this is fair to you?"

"I think it would be unreasonable for you, otherwise." She cocked her head and grinned. "Think of it as an extreme motivator. I need to solve the case so I can get paid. Most people cancel their credit cards, get new ones, or are maybe a little more careful for a few months. They might even start paying for everything they can in cash, but if you don't know how it happened, how can you prevent it from happening again?"

Mercy, she hadn't even thought about it happening again. Abby's hand shot through her hair and tugged at her locks, a habit left over from her childhood that appeared when she was frustrated. What was she, a piggy bank for those who chose not to work a regular job? "Again. I don't even want to think about again, but I would like to track down whoever it is."

"That's why I'm here." Nala placed a pen near the contract. "If you agree to the terms, sign away, and we'll get started."

Her eyebrows lifted in inquiry. "I thought you had already started. I'd hoped you suggested the meeting to tell me who the culprit was."

"I wish. First of all, I cannot proceed without your written consent. Secondly, we're going to have to conference call your credit card people together. We also want to call the credit bureaus to see if new cards are being taken out in your name."

Abby had just taken a sip of tea as Nala explained her strategy. The possibility of new cards being taken out in her name made her choke and tea dribbled down her chin. She put down the glass, took a furtive look around to see if anyone had witnessed her actions. They hadn't. Fortunately, she was not as interesting as a cell phone or television.

"How would they get them if they would come to my address? I have a locking mailbox."

Nala held up one finger. "Those mailboxes can easily be opened with a safety or bobby pin. If the culprit knows it's coming, they could be making regular mailbox checks while you're at work. More likely, they'd list your present address as the old address and put their address as the current address. That's what I am hoping to find. It would make my job easier."

"I'm feeling less safe than I did yesterday." Here, she'd worked hard to create a decent life for herself, and some faceless culprit could undo all her steady bill payments. "Do you think it's because of the neighborhood I live in?"

"No, not at all. Those who are good at hacking are working their way into databases. You're always hearing about breaches. Even the credit agencies aren't immune to them. It could be something like medical insurance where your credit card isn't attached, but there's enough basic information, including your social security number. That info is usually stolen by organized crime and is often sold overseas, but I don't think that is the case here. I think your situation is a snatch and grab."

The server returned with their sandwiches, stopping their conversation once again. The woman offered them a tight smile, probably feeling the awkwardness as she set down the plates. She promised to refill their tea glasses, inadvertently warning them of her return. Both Abby and Nala stayed silent until the tea glasses were topped off and the server moved out of hearing range. The waitress might assume they were spies or possibly criminals. That was a laugh.

"Why do you think that?"

"The parcel pickup, which means it has to be someone close. Max caught the smell of someone else in your apartment. Remembering his barking? I didn't mention what his actions meant then, not wanting to upset you."

"It wasn't Bruno, then who?"

Nala shrugged. "It's hard to say. The best we can do is compare scents. I'd like for Max to take another shot at it. I'd like for him to see if the trail goes to the filing cabinet."

Bruno would not be a fan of the visit, but maybe she could lock him up in his carrier. In the end, it would confirm if someone had been in her apartment and had taken her financial information and remove any lingering doubt that she'd simply misplaced the file. The confirmation would make her feel less safe, if that were possible. How would she stop the culprit from making a return visit after she'd replaced her cards?

In the end, she needed to buck up as opposed to crawling under the table and assuming the fetal position.

Chapter Nine

MAX RODE SHOTGUN in the beetle with his nose sticking out of the cracked passenger window. Nala learned early on that driving around with the windows shut would only result in nose-smudged glass. Suffering a little chill didn't prevent all the nose art, though. Her lips canted down into a frown. She hated dropping the possibility on her newest client that whoever stole her identity could easily come back for round two. Worse, she rattled the woman, who acted as if she had lost her best friend, and then sent her back to work with the promise that she'd look into it.

So far, she didn't have much. Her initial plan had been to work from home, but she decided against it. Even though she was her own boss, technically speaking, she still had a hard time marshaling her thoughts at home where dirty laundry needed washing and the television tempted. Nope, it had to be the office with its four uninviting walls and no entertainment option. The worst that could happen would be she might catch herself in a daydream.

Max may have thought she had picked him up out of consideration, instead of caving to Karly's determined nagging. Not that Nala would ever tell him that. The alleged office break-in that had happened a few months ago made her reluctant to be alone in the office, especially at night. She never mentioned it to anyone, except Harry, since all she had was a feeling and an unlocked office door. Her father would imply she had forgotten to lock it, which would make her sound like she was ten years old again. Even worse would be her mother trying to lend her money to install a better lock. Both potential scenarios stunk and would make her feel less than professional.

What she did instead was rattle the door every time she left, making sure it was locked. Max served as her constant companion. She hoped his occasional barking served to let any would-be burglar know there was a vicious attack dog on the premises. *Vicious* would be an overstatement. All Max did most days was sleep and occasionally watched the pigeons, who preferred the third story window sills for roosting purposes.

The traffic offered little challenge today, allowing her to speculate on the case. Elvin appeared to think snatch and grab, as far as identity theft, was old school. Most thefts came from cracking databases or using skimmers on ATMs. He never mentioned anything about the devices she'd seen used in a crime show that featured a hottie on a cellphone casually bumping into people and recording the signal from their credit cards. Technology invented cards that could be merely waved at a credit machine and two seconds later, the criminal element created a way to capture that information.

Plenty of companies also developed sleeves and metal wallets to prevent that. It was odd how Elvin had overlooked that. It wasn't like him. Her devil's advocate reminded her Elvin could still be a suspect. It would be to his benefit to not be totally forthcoming. She wrinkled her nose as she spoke, "Nah, it couldn't be."

Max's head swiveled in her direction. "If you're asking if we could stop for a cheeseburger, then my answer is yes, it can be."

When was she ever going to get used to the fact that Max would always reply when she talked to herself? "No. Remember, the vet pointed out you were putting on weight."

His hopeful expression vanished as he hung his head. Nala took the ensuing silence as the perfect time to call Elvin. Fortunately, he was on speed dial, which didn't involve too much distracted driving. Her thumb depressed the speaker icon and placed the phone in her lap, which should work unless she made a sharp turn.

The phone burbled twice before a drowsy "Yo?" sounded.

"You still in bed?"

"What if I am? I don't have to answer to you."

She almost asked if he were alone but decided against it. Some things deserved to remain private. "True, you don't. I got a question."

"I figured as much." There was the sound of dishes rattling, then the hum of a microwave. "I'll do my best without my morning coffee. Shoot."

"Make that early afternoon coffee. I called you last night about identity theft, and you never mentioned anything about the radio-frequency identification theft. I saw an episode on Crimes Abound where some chick was using a scanner to pick up people's credit card numbers. She was just bebopping down the street, grabbing numbers right and left."

The microwave pinged loudly, allowing Nala to mentally track what Elvin was doing. She'd give him a couple of seconds to stir in his nasty instant coffee mixture and take a sip. When she once questioned him about his preference for instant coffee, he declared it was an international favorite, which she found hard to believe.

There was an audible gulp before he spoke. "Nala, Nala, there you go, believing everything you see on television."

Her fist tightened on the steering wheel. "Is there a scanner or not out there that can steal people's credit card numbers?"

"There is."

"Aha."

"Still, you have to get very close. Not something you can do with a common stranger. The scanner is expensive and not always a hundred percent accurate. A would-be felon would have to have the unit on him, then go around slapping into people. That's not exactly low profile. People would complain about this. I don't think this is an issue in Noblesville."

This Indianapolis bedroom community wasn't bursting with people, although a recent housing boom had pushed up the population numbers. Still, the scanner existed. "There's all types of wallets and sleeves you can buy for your credit cards to prevent theft. Why is that, if it isn't a problem?"

"Nala."

"Don't start." Somehow Elvin thought repeating her name made him sound like an old black and white movie star. "Answer the question."

"Fear sells."

"That's it?"

Max leaned toward the phone and whimpered.

"What are you doing to that dog?"

"I wouldn't stop at the drive-thru."

"For shame. Anyhow, to answer your question, many things are sold due to fear. Locks, guns, pepper spray, even deodorant."

"Deodorant?" She couldn't see holding off an attacker with a stick of deodorant.

Elvin chuckled, then replied, "Sure, most people worry about smelling. Deodorant promises to keep them socially acceptable. Even if people *don't* need the RFID blocking wallets, if it makes them feel safe. It's a small price to pay."

"You're right." Nala considered her own cute RFID blocking wallet. At least she hadn't paid a lot for it. "Where might someone use an RFID scanner?"

"A huge tourist trap where there are thousands of people. Some bumping into each other. In the end, they're all going somewhere. None of them are staying there. Someplace like Times Square or a huge international airport. Those who had their numbers scanned will be flying far away, none the wiser about what had just happened."

"Okay. I can accept that. Is that why you never mentioned it last night?" Stupid question. No one would admit to concealing information to protect themselves.

"I didn't think that far ahead. You called me in the middle of my movie. I gave you the most likely scenarios. I haven't even heard of an RFID scanner takedown happening. Criminals can buy credit card numbers on the dark web without too much trouble. Hackers who crack open databases are your real issue."

"Yeah, I remember."

"Don't forget your amateurs at your local dark bar, either."

Abby, who apparently only worked and had very little social contact, which Nala gleaned from their two conversations, would not be a candidate for bar hopping. "Appreciate your help."

"Don't you want me to run some searches on your client?"

Normally, she would. Part of her was reluctant to reveal her client. If Elvin turned criminal, he would be smart enough not to leave such an obvious trail. If he had dated Abby, it could get sticky. She didn't expect Elvin to show up on Abby's doorstep, but it could end up being embarrassing. Eventually, she'd probably break anyway. Her old school friend could unearth vital information in minutes whereas it took her much longer. "I'm good. I'll let you know if I need anything."

"All right. Talk to you later."

Elvin ended the call. Did "talk to you later" mean he suspected she'd break and end up calling him before the day was over?

"Stop!" Max shouted. Nala slammed on the brakes not even taking the time to consider what caused such an order and didn't see the mother duck leading her ducklings across the city street until they'd stopped. Her heart pounded loud enough for her to hear each beat.

Fudge! That was close. You'd think city birds would be a little smarter, but they have to depend on the kindness of motorists and observant dogs. "Thank you. I didn't see them."

"I noticed."

She watched the fuzzy little ducklings waddle across, stopping traffic on the other side of the street, too. There was a pond not too far away where they could be heading. In a world where people ripped other folks off every chance they got, it was good to witness something life-affirming, such as the ducklings and other motorists stopping for them.

"I owe you, Max."

"Cheeseburger?"

"How about a run in the park?"

"Not sure how you consider that a favor."

"We both could get in shape."

"Yay." His forced tone gave lie to the word. "Yippee. Just the other day I complained about going to doggie boot camp."

"I know, but every now and then we have to run down suspects. The ability to burst into a fast run might be the only thing between us and a bullet."

Max snorted, then added, "You mean you. I'm much closer to

the ground. People don't aim that low."

"Whatever." No need to add that plenty of canine officers had been shot in the line of duty. Frightening one individual a day should be her limit. There were two empty spaces near her building which meant no parallel parking. Every now and then, she got lucky.

Car parked and locked, they both headed to the building. Even though Indy had a leash law, she figured the short distance to the building wouldn't matter. For her father, Max walked on a leash just fine, but for her, he turned drama queen. He pretended to choke and cough, when she snapped the leash on, usually attracting sympathetic bystanders. Other times, he complained about the color or weight of the leash.

Nala let herself into the building and met Harry on the first-floor landing. The sunlight picked its way through the dusty tall windows, highlighting her building mate. Normally, she'd agree with Karly's assertion that he was nerdy delectable, but today he looked a little green.

Her dog surged ahead and bumped against his leg. He bent and petted Max with his free hand while managing to keep his coffee cup turned upright. Most people tended to move their hands in the direction their other hand went.

"Hey, Harry. What's up?" Even though the greeting was a general one, she bit her lip wondering if it sounded intrusive.

His smile didn't reach his eyes, and he gave a heavy sigh. "Nala, I know in your business you expect to see the worst of humankind."

Well, not exactly. Her goal was to help people, not visit the dregs of society. She'd give the comment a pass. Seems like she was doing a great deal of that today. "Okay, but what has got *you* so down?"

He met her eyes, and the pain shimmered in them. Not enough to break into tears, but enough to broadcast his disappointment.

"Credit card chargebacks."

The whole world must be celebrating credit card obsession day. Every now and then, she got a chargeback when something she ordered wasn't available. "This is upsetting how?"

"Remember me talking about all the orders I had coming in for Comic Con? At least, I assumed it was Comic Con. It could be anything."

Their footsteps echoed in the stairwell as they proceeded to the second floor where Harry's office was.

"Yes," she encouraged, unsure of where he was going with this.

"I got a message from a credit card company that they would not honor a payment since it was fraudulent. I hate it when nerds go bad."

If Harry hadn't appeared so despondent, she would have thought his statement was a comic one-liner. "Me, too. It could just be a mistake. The customer could be over his or her limit."

"No." Harry shook his head. "That's immediate. The charge won't even go through then."

"He could have changed his mind." Suddenly, Nala felt the need to assure her friend that nerd crime was not on the rise.

The three of them idled in front of Harry's office door. A light glowing behind the glass-fronted door revealed it wasn't his first trip of the day up the stairs. After taking a sip from his cup, Harry sighed again. "A person can cancel three different ways. They can call, email, or just click cancel on their invoice. I have a very liberal policy about returns. No, it was fraud. The good news was, I only had one of the Avengers costumes when the order came in and sent it. I was waiting for the giant Hulk hands to come in and ship all of the rest at once to save postage. The hands alone would take up most of the space."

"You just lost the money on one, right?" It wasn't like when she did all the PI work only to have the wife decide she didn't want to know if her husband was cheating and refused to pay her. For the record, he was, and Nala did not get paid, which resulted in her asking for a retainer fee on her future cases.

"Right, that and my faith in nerd kind. My bank will charge me though. It's rather like a bounced check."

Max rubbed against Harry placing his head under his free hand. Most people might not think petting a dog would cheer someone up, but her canine could always sense when she was down. Personally, Nala preferred the quiet dog presence as opposed to Max giving life advice, which he did, too, frequently. Most of it consisted of eat cheeseburgers often, sleep more, and chase cats and the occasional tiny dog.

Harry squatted, put his coffee cup down and hugged Max. It must be bad. Nerds and the people who loved them were his customer base. There had to be some way she could put a spin on the situation. "Maybe…" She thought of the endless crime dramas that featured cons robbing banks with Halloween masks on. A superhero costume would be more of the same. Although they'd have to rip off some clothes to display the entire costume. "Someone or a bunch of someones were going to use the costumes to commit a crime. They probably stole a credit card because they didn't want the purchase to be traced back to them."

Harry looked up from his crouched position beside Max and a hopeful light flickered in his eyes. "That's possible."

Not really. Who wouldn't notice a half dozen people dressed as comic book characters? Unless they were going to Comic Con? "They weren't nerds. They were going to rip off nerds."

"Of course!" Harry jumped to his feet. "I should have known that. It's so obvious. People are always trying to take advantage of nerds."

If that meant selling them lots of comic books and sci-fi merchandise they didn't need, she'd have to agree. Still, that could be true of anyone who had a hobby or an obsession. Harry opened his door without the benefit of a key and waved in their direction.

"Thanks, both of you."

Nala smiled as she made for the third floor. It was nice to have successfully helped someone. Max kept pace with her, bumping into her every second step. It wasn't that he was clumsy. His behavior resulted from his having something to say and trying to wait until he was far enough away to avoid being overheard. When they reached the third-floor landing, she gave him the signal he'd been waiting for. "Go ahead."

"Did you hear him say *both of you*? I helped. Mainly, it was me. Not sure he bought your superhero robber theory. Someone other than us has been on these stairs."

Someone other than them—maybe a potential client. The possibility made her lips tip up as she replied to the initial query. "I heard. As for my costumed robber, it could happen. Although probably just the mask."

Her phone burbled as she was getting ready to unlock her door. The familiar tune meant it was her mother. They must be ashore again. For a cruise, it seemed they did very little cruising. Max put his nose to the floor and made an audible sniff.

"Hello, Mom. I took care of the Posh Interiors card."

"Good. Was it Raylene? She struck me as lacking in taste, but I felt I could teach her."

Why did she hire the woman if she thought she had no taste? At times, her mother could be a true enigma. Her control freak parent wouldn't be pleased that she had had her identity stolen. "Ah, it wasn't Raylene. Someone hacked into your account. They were busy buying chrome bedroom suites and black velvet paintings."

Gasping came over the phone, then her father's voice. "Nala, what did you say that upset your mother so? She's speechless."

"Someone hacked her Posh Interiors card and was buying black velvet paintings from Mexico."

"That would do it. You handled it?"

"I did." Even though she didn't want to mention the police encounter, she thought she should. Otherwise, the neighbors would mention it. "I went to the house to get the card numbers to cancel the accounts and a couple of officers thought I was breaking in."

"You told them you were my daughter, right?"

"I did, but they were newbies and had never met me. They did recognize Max, though."

Her father gave a hearty laugh. "Yeah, all the cadets love Max. Everyone is always asking me why he isn't a police dog. You know he'd make a great one."

"No, he wouldn't."

"Your mother wants to talk to you."

"Nala?" Her mother half-gasped her name. "I need you to do me a favor. If someone hacked my Posh Interior card, what's to stop them from hacking the rest of our cards. Can you get Elvin to run a check for us?"

She could. It might be a test to find out how much he could find. "I will."

Her mother murmured to someone on her side of the phone, then came back online. "Juan, our scuba guide, is here. Gotta go."

When did they learn how to scuba? Nala stared at her phone, then shoved it into her pocket. She inserted her key into the lock, but the door pushed open before she could even twist the key.

"Not again."

Chapter Ten

NALA PUSHED THE door open with one foot and motioned Max to go in first. Her dog backed up, demonstrating his reluctance. To think her father thought he'd make a good police dog. Her top teeth came down on her bottom lip. The deal with being a private eye included you were on your own most of the time, especially a small business concern such as hers. Yeah, it was time to pull on her big girl panties, but there was no reason to be stupid about it.

Her hand rooted through her purse in search of her gun. Her large wallet rested on top of everything, forcing her to pull it out to dig deeper. Her police captain father would have lectured her that a weapon that wasn't easily accessible was more of a hindrance than a help. Finally, her fingers curled around the holstered weapon.

A tissue fragment stuck to the holster of the expensive Glock. Definitely not an image she'd want anyone else to see. Nala took a deep breath, shucked the holster, and switched the safety off. Previously, when she found her door unlocked, she'd made a lot of noise, hoping if there were any culprits inside they'd flee, not that they had that many options. Her office was on the third floor, and there was only one entrance.

Come in low. Her father's instruction replayed as she took a crouched position and entered the office. The blinds were closed, but the sunlight still filtered into the room, leaving stripes across the wood floor and oriental carpet. Her eyes cut to the blinds, knowing she'd left them open to give her light when she entered due to the light switch being five feet away from the door.

Even with the blinds shut, everything was visible. The orange crushed velvet couch remained in its usual place. A pillow had fallen to the floor, but that could have been Max. The dog in question jostled her back. His reluctance to take the lead point made her glad for a change. She didn't want to accidentally shoot her dog.

These after-hours visits were getting old. With any luck, she'd catch the culprit in the act. There were creaky spots on the aging floor that she carefully avoided. Anyone watching her might think she was doing an odd dance with a large step to the left then a careful slide forward, then she'd reverse the order. The minuscule size of the outer office made it easy to see no one was crouching in the corner. The door to her shallow closet stood open demonstrating whoever tossed her office made no effort to be discreet. Her heart kicked into overdrive as she neared the closed entrance to her inner office. Her actual work took place behind the closed door. After the first break-in happened, she no longer left her laptop or any concrete records out in the open.

Her fingers reached out to the door as she held her breath, certain that whoever was on the other side had heard her entrance, especially with Max's loud panting. They would probably expect anyone to be standing upright—that gave her the advantage. There was no resistance, which meant the door had been pulled shut, but not latched. Nala allowed herself a long silent inhale, then punched the door wide.

The metal doorknob slammed against the wall. Nala jumped up and brandished her gun. "Freeze! Police!"

Max entered barking. Unfortunately, all that was in the room was her oversized desk, client chair, her desk chair, and the decorative carpet she used to cover the cut in the floor. The sunlight streamed into the room from the top of the blinds where one of the slats was broken. Instead of buying new blinds she had repaired it with masking tape to match the same shade of off-white. Apparently, the tape had broken.

The frenzied barking echoed in the room. Nala snapped her fingers, hoping that would end the racket. Max must not have heard her over his own barks.

"Desist!"

Nothing. Must not be a word he knew. "Stop it! There's no one here."

The sudden silence was equally disconcerting. There was no one here, which was a good thing in theory. Too bad the adrenalin pumping through her body hadn't gotten the message. It was as if she had the need to sprint or at least pistol-whip a bad guy like in the movies.

The sound of feet running up the stairs penetrated the office. Nala pivoted with the Glock still in her grasp.

A breathless Harry burst into the office. "Are you all—Oh!" Harry took a step back. His pupils had become unusually large at the sight of the firearm. "You have a gun."

"Yeah, I have a gun. Always had. You've just never seen it."

His eyes focused on the weapon. She had to move around him to get to her holster and purse that were still in the hall.

Her would-be rescuer followed her. "What happened?"

"Someone broke in again. No doubts this time. They didn't even try to be subtle."

"Did they take anything?"

Nala stooped to gather her purse and stowed her weapon. Her

fingers closed over her purse strap as she stood. "Don't know. I have so little to steal. After that first incident, I keep nothing of value here."

"You need to call the police. I honestly thought I heard someone yell police."

The walls were thin in the building since its original purpose had been a department store. With the appearance of malls with inside walkways, plenty of free parking, and a children's playground, the appeal of downtown shopping died a fast death. Most of the big stores were only open during the day. The shift to two-income families sounded the final death knell for downtown stores. A savvy owner of their building had thrown up walls for offices and apartments on the top floors. Still, she'd had no clue she could be heard a floor down.

"Ah, that was me." She managed a forced laugh. "I guess some kids grew up pretending to play air guitar, or winning the Indianapolis 500, but I was always jumping through doorways with my thumb and forefinger shaped like a gun, shouting 'police.'" She shrugged her shoulders, realizing the confession made her seem a little off-centered.

"That was normal compared to me." He gestured to her open office doorway.

She entered first to see Max stretched out on the couch with his head on his paws. He looked at her and sighed. Yeah, those few seconds wore her out, too.

Harry followed her in and folded his arms. "I'm staying until you call the police. For whatever reason, someone has a need to be in your office."

"I noticed." Her lips pushed into a grim line. Her intention was to call the police, but she might have talked herself out of it if Harry hadn't insisted. Still, some things should be her choice. One hand found purchase on her hip. "When did you get to be so alpha all of a sudden?"

His face flushed, and he reached up to fiddle with his glasses. "Um, aw, I didn't think I *was* being alpha. I guess it comes from my younger years when I donned my homemade Superman outfit complete with a bath towel cape." He held up his hand with the palm out. "I'm just trying to help, not irritate."

"Point taken." She relaxed her stance, allowing her hand to drop. "Are you still going to stay until I call the police?"

His short nod announced his actions, and her hand found her hip again. Just when you think you knew someone, another facet of their personality would make an appearance, blowing away everything you thought you knew. Harry had a stubborn side. Her mother would insist all men did, and you never saw it until something that mattered to them was threatened.

Her purse landed on the small entry table. She'd have to empty it to find her phone. *Wait.* Hadn't she just talked to her parents? A quick pat down located her phone in her pants' pocket. She held it up to show Harry. "Calling now."

Her father being who he was, preprogrammed the police, EMS, and the fire department into her phone. At the time, she presumed she'd use those numbers very little, but she was wrong. An operator came online. "State the nature of your emergency."

"There's been a break-in. The robber is gone, but I need a report filed." Nala gave the operator her address information.

"An officer is on the way."

"Thanks. I'll have to buzz him into the building."

She ended the call and arched an eyebrow. "Are you satisfied?"

"No. I'll stay until the police get here."

Here she thought her father was bad. Nala placed the phone by her purse, then turned to confront Harry who had suddenly morphed into someone else. "I can take care of this. Remember, I'm a private eye."

He folded his arms and lifted an eyebrow in response. "Yeah, I saw your gun. Humor me. Remember, I helped you tail a target a while back."

"Yes, you did." His services might be needed in the future, too. If all he wanted was to wait with her, then there could be worse things. "How did the robber get in?"

Harry's shoulders went up in a shrug. "This time I didn't let in any suspicious water guys like last time. Are you sure he didn't take anything?"

"I'll look." She snapped her fingers for Max, who stepped so slowly from the couch it was almost like a slow-motion replay. He put his nose to the floor and sniffed around the outer office as Nala strolled the area. "As you can see not a lot of places to store stuff. The most valuable portable item I have is my individual cup coffee maker. It would be easier buying one at the store as opposed to getting past two locked doors."

The coffee maker sat on its own table next to the wall. Inside the closet hung the trench coat she thought was a necessity for being a private eye but decided—in hind sight—it just made her more obvious. Max moved into the inner office and stopped at the folded back edge of the rug.

In her adrenalin high, she'd missed that detail. The outline of the cut on the floor showed. When she first viewed her office, she noticed the imperfect square. The realtor joked about someone making their own private hidey hole, then advised that a rug or furniture would cover it. At the time, she hadn't cared since she was only renting the office, not buying.

Later, she wondered if she should try to pry it up. What if there was some drug stash hidden there, and she was accused? Those who dealt in drugs wouldn't be foolish enough to leave any behind. The possibility of prying up the square and not being able to shove it back discouraged her curiosity. An uneven seam jutted a millimeter higher than the floor. Nala pushed the rug back to examine the entire square. That section had definitely been moved.

The soft tread of Harry's athletic shoes came up behind her. "What is it?"

She pointed to the wood seam, making sure not to touch it. "This has been opened. I noticed it when I first looked at the office. The realtor mentioned it might be a secret compartment or something."

"Could be." Harry crouched down beside her, cocked his head, then stood without speaking. He started backing out of the office, stopping inside the doorway. "The desk has been moved."

Nala scampered to her feet and went to stand beside Harry. Her mother had decided to *help* Nala out by offloading some furniture that was clogging the Posh Interiors warehouse. One morning the furniture arrived, including the behemoth of a desk that had to be carried up three flights of stairs. There used to be a working elevator, but when the department store went out there was no real effort to keep it running.

Her mouth twisted to one side as she regarded the desk. "I can see what you mean. Gwen Bonne would never allow the desk to be off center, considering there is nothing else in the room to balance it out. The square must have been under the desk."

"My thoughts exactly." He ambled to the desk and pushed on it without any movement.

The buzzer sounded, drawing Nala to the wall panel. "Hello?"

"Police."

"Okay. Third floor." She pushed the release button, then rushed to the window and peered out. There was a radio car idling near the front door in the spaces marked loading only. Well, maybe they could get away with it. Nala, never wanting to push her luck, parked elsewhere.

Harry joined her in the outer office, a little flushed from his efforts. "It had to be two guys."

That did nothing to reassure her. With her training, Glock, and Max, she felt she was the equal for any criminal, but two was one too many.

Two of Indy's finest entered the room and were greeted by an exuberant Max. Was there a cop in the city he didn't know? The officer kneeling beside Max didn't look old enough to be out of high school, which would make him an excellent undercover officer for high school or college investigations. The other officer she would have placed closer to forty. Should have made detective by now, but he could have decided on a career change and started as a cop later. He removed his hat, revealing a buzzed haircut, making her suspect former military.

They introduced themselves as Officers Lopez and Ballard. The older one would be Buzz in her mind. They were not all that interested in the fact that the robbers had closed the blinds.

"Ms. Bonne, it would be almost impossible to get fingerprints off those thin cords. What we need to know is if anything was taken."

Nala's eyes connected with Harry's. It would seem foolish to call the police when nothing was missing. They would assume she hadn't locked the door. It would cause her to be labeled a nervous Nelly, one of those silly women who called the police when they heard something fall in the closet. It was not a good rep for herself. "Not exactly."

Harry cleared his throat. "This is the second break-in in Nala's office. I believe something was left in the office that they were trying to get. Tonight, we found a hidden spot in the floor that wasn't visible before and has been pried open. The desk has been moved."

Both policemen straightened up and acted more responsive when Harry spoke. To be fair, Harry's wide stance indicated he meant business whereas she was being way too apologetic about everything. The urge to add *what he said* almost overwhelmed her.

The officers went into the inner office to peer at the floor. Nala joined them and added, "We didn't touch the panel or desk. You should have clear prints there."

"I should have known Captain Bonne's daughter would be familiar with procedure." He rocked back on his heels, then stood. "We'll try to take prints. There may be none if they were smart enough to wear gloves, and we'll check the hole. I heard some stories about this building when I started on the force about seven years ago."

Did she really want to hear this? Was her office the site of a triple homicide or something equally reprehensible? Before she could make up her mind, Harry said he'd like to know about the building, since he'd been a renter for the past couple of years.

Officer Buzz, aka Ballard, put his thumbs in his belt, warming to his subject. "Rumor was a criminal duo had a regular office in the building. Folks who had need of them would come for a visit. Had business cards and a phone and everything. They were hard to catch because the cards never said what they did. Most of their clients were not criminals who attracted attention."

It was hard for her to believe respectable people hired someone to commit a crime. "Who were their clients?"

"As far as we can figure from the folks who were robbed, most were embittered ex-spouses, former business partners, even family members. The victims were quick to name people they suspected, who turned out to have a solid alibi, which in itself was suspicious."

"Why?" Harry asked.

The younger officer replied from his position on the floor. "Most people go home after work. Watch a little television, then go to bed. Those who need alibis make sure they're somewhere where they'll be seen by plenty of eyewitnesses."

Buzz nodded in agreement. "Our first clue came when a happy customer bragged about the service he'd received and how easy it was. We had a clue that business was conducted in this building, but we couldn't finger any one person. The second tip came when an emerald heist went bad due to the owner's dog getting a good bite of one of the burglars."

Max looked more alert, and his lips tipped up.

"What happened then?" A better question would be why did the realtor never mention any of this?

"They arrested the dog bit dude, but his partner got away, supposedly with the emeralds. Might as well pry open the floor. Sounds to me like a double cross." The older officer motioned to the other. "Get the kit." His former attitude shifted some as he smiled in her direction. "And a crowbar."

The younger officer hurried away to get the needed tools. Nala wasn't thrilled at all over the black fingerprint dust she would have to clean up or any possible damage that might be done to her floor. "Make sure you write up that you pried open the floor in the investigation of a crime. I don't want to take any heat from my landlord. Do you know the name of the guy who got caught?"

The officer inexpertly covered a smile with his hand. He cleared his throat before replying. "Don't remember his name, but I'm sure he's still in prison. Armed robbery and all."

His words weren't the least bit reassuring. Emeralds would attract a jewel thief. Lopez returned in a couple of minutes without buzzing for entrance. Maybe the entry door wasn't locking as it should.

Before Lopez kneeled and pried open the space, she knew he'd find nothing. She wasn't surprised when they didn't find any prints, either, not even hers. The desk had been wiped clean. Her only hope was that her robbers got what they came for and would not be back.

Chapter Eleven

THE CLOCK RADIO made a small click before Sonny and Cher started serenading her with their familiar ballad. The early light penetrated the curtains, creating a soft golden glow. Nala blinked twice and stared up at the ceiling. It reminded her of a movie about a man having to repeat the same day until he got it right. In her case, she might not be repeating the same day, but almost the same actions. Her mother called her about a credit problem, and she'd handled it. Abby called her about a credit problem, and she was in the process of handling it. Then there was Harry, who had someone charge a ton of uniforms on a stolen card. Was it her or did everyone she knew get their credit cards hacked simultaneously?

A few more minutes in bed wouldn't hurt as she planned out her day. If there was a breach in some database, it might explain all the sudden issues. If the world was moving toward a cashless society, there had to be some type of mechanism to protect people from hackers. Elvin would know.

A crash somewhere in her house had her jackknifing to a sitting position. *What was that?* Even though she knew it wouldn't do her much good, she glanced around for Max to send him to investigate. No Max, which probably meant he was the source of the crash.

Gingersnaps! She pushed herself out of bed and inserted her feet into her oversized slippers. As she padded down the hallway, she could hear stuff skitter around her floor. The noise gave her pause.

Didn't mice skitter? Although she often heard the expression as quiet as a mouse, too. Besides, Karly, her animal buff, had mentioned that mice leaving the walls in the daytime signaled a crowded population. Surely, she'd know if she had mice. She hoped she didn't. After reassuring herself, she turned the corner to the kitchen to find her black dog covered with flour.

He was using his paw to push the remnants of the flour canister into a pile. "What happened?"

Max started, then swung his gaze to hers. His dark eyes staring out of all the white almost made her laugh, but not quite since cleaning up this huge mess was not on her list of things to do.

"Umm…" He looked down at the mess, then up at her. "I have no clue."

She crossed her arms and tapped one furry slipper that did not make any noise being soft, but Max still made noise despite his padded paws. Probably due to her general irritation, she snapped, "What were you doing in the kitchen?"

"Hungry. I thought you were going to sleep forever."

"It wasn't time to get up."

"Sun was up."

"Daylight savings time. You could have let me sleep until the alarm went off." No reason to tell him the alarm just went off.

"My bad."

That goes without saying, but she chose not to say it. Nala pulled the trash can out from underneath the sink where she hid it, picked up the pieces of the canister, and threw them away. Max crowded her and licked her hands, which only made them damp, causing flour to stick to them. "You aren't helping."

"Sorry." He backed up, but instead of sitting, Max left the room.

Probably just as well, considering how she felt about the mess. It showed intelligence, leaving the scene of the accident. It did, however, only made her wonder what her dog was up to.

The ceramic canisters lined up on the counter were more for show than anything else. Since her mother bought them for her, she had displayed them and filled them. Flour and sugar were easy, but she had no clue what to put into the others. Since she enjoyed an occasional treat, one held cookies and the last one she used for dog treats. That explained it.

The broom failed to get all the flour up, and Nala had to resort to mopping the floor and wiping down the counter before breakfast. People babyproofed their houses. Maybe she should dog proof hers. The first thing to go would be the canisters. It wasn't like she was going to whip up a cake anytime soon. Any cakes eaten in her house would come from the freezer section of the grocery store.

Electric kettle plugged in, she went off in search of Max. All she had to do was follow the flour footprints. He'd returned to the bedroom and had smeared flour all over her dark floral comforter. Even though he was curled into his sleeping position, she could tell he wasn't asleep. Similar to some people she knew, Max would pretend to be asleep to avoid unpleasantness.

"Max!"

He opened his eyes and gave a sleepy blink as if he'd fallen into a deep sleep in the time it took her to clean up. Nala pursed her lips as she debated what to do first. "You're a mess. I don't have time to clean you up. Maybe I can get you into Bill's Dirty Dog Spaw. I hear they open early."

Max lunged into a seated position. "Not that! I've heard about those places. They spray you with perfume and put whimsical bandanas around your neck."

Personally, she thought those were good things but was surprised her dog knew about them. "At least it will get the flour out of your coat. They may not have an appointment open. I'll call anyway."

She ignored the whimpering as she reached for her phone. Max stood on four legs on top of the comforter and shook for all he was worth, sending a shower of flour all over the room and liberally dousing Nala. His coat, instead of being bleached flour white, was more of foggy gray.

His lips tilted up. "See, I fixed it."

"Not really. I'm not even sure how you got so caked."

Max leapt off the bed and butted up against Nala. "Not the dog spa. Maybe you could brush me?"

"I could, but now I have to shower, sweep the bedroom, and take my comforter to the laundromat where they have the oversized washing machines. Any way you look at it, I'm behind schedule because of you."

Her dog dropped to his belly and put his head on his paws, giving her his most soulful look. Normally, it would have worked, but this was a really big mess. "Max, I need help. Quite frankly, you're no expert on identity theft."

He made a small whimper.

"Not dissing you. Just saying how it is."

He lifted his head up to reply. "I'm good at smell. I could smell there was someone in your office."

"True. It doesn't do much good unless we run across that person again, and I can't guarantee we will. Who would be foolish enough to come back to the scene of the crime?"

"Criminals."

Her eyes rolled upward at his answer. "I know television crime dramas promote the theory that criminals return to the scene of the crime, but that's just to tie up the show in under an hour. Most criminals get as far away from a crime scene as possible and usually as quick as possible, too. The police often look for people leaving the crime scene area in a hurry."

"Then they shouldn't leave."

"I can see your point, but distance often makes it hard to track a criminal. Local law enforcement has to call in the aid from those wherever they think the criminal has fled. The new folks get a late start on the chase and often can't pick up the trail, which is why it's usually beneficial for the criminal to run."

"Why did the guy return to your office?"

The turn of topic was to keep her from calling the groomers, but it did make her think about her unwelcome visitors. "Obviously, they thought there was something in the office they wanted. There was only one of them the first time, and he didn't take anything." Her eyes rolled up as she remembered the scenario from a few months ago. "Harry let in a man dressed in a water delivery shirt who had no truck and no water. If he were the B and E person, he may have entered the office and discovered he couldn't budge the desk on his own. He must have made plans to return with help."

"Will he come back?"

Nala wished she knew. Her shoulders went up in a shrug. "Depends on if he got what he wanted. It irritates me that everything is so easy for him. The doors don't seem to stop him."

"Could be a pro."

"It might help if I could find out a little more about who rented my office before me. The realtor won't help. That's for sure. They never want to tell you anything bad about a property. Who would know?"

"How about lightbulb guy?"

At first, she thought Max meant someone dressed as a lightbulb, but her dog tended to describe people by their smell or activity if he didn't know them. Who could lightbulb guy be? Recently, she had complained about lights out in the stairwell and the super came to fix them. He also made a point of knocking on her office door and showing her the old bulbs to prove he changed them.

He might know. Although it would involve her being called *babe* and *sweetheart*. The super must have fancied himself quite the lady killer in his younger days. His comb-over and thick gold chain indicated he still did. "I'll see if I can talk to him. Most of the time, my calls just go to voicemail."

"Invite him for a meal. That's bound to get a response."

"Not the one I want. An invitation to dine can be interpreted the wrong way. Now, we need to get you cleaned up."

"Aww!"

"Quit complaining and help me find your brush."

After cleaning up Max, cleaning up the bedroom, and finally a shower and breakfast, enough time had elapsed to call Elvin, or so she thought. If you didn't work third shift, then you should be up at nine-thirty on a weekday.

Her parents' credit file was open on her kitchen table. Copies of the front and back of each card were on file along with customer service numbers to cancel the cards. Her father, in an effort to be cryptic and thorough, included identity questions that could be asked at login. Instead of writing down the answer, which would have been super stupid if the wrong people got their hands on it, he wrote down hints that no one outside of the family would know, such as the name of Nala's favorite childhood dog. She didn't have one. Her parents had insisted their jobs were much too demanding for a dog, so she guessed the answer would be none.

Having Max as a beginner pet made her wonder what the normal experience was like. No one would call Max normal. Her eyes dropped back to the file. Her father used an old cipher he taught her as a child for the pin names. This probably irritated her mother, who would have insisted she had no time for puzzles.

Most people would not give over their credit information to just anyone, but her father wanted Elvin to do a credit search to make sure their other cards weren't being used for a shopping spree. Nala penciled on a sticky note which cards they had with them. It would help to keep the Gwen sprees separate from some scam artist running up the bill. Then again, just because her parents had the physical version of the cards didn't mean someone else couldn't be using the numbers. You'd think a credit card agency would notice a charge for a zip line in Belize happened at the same time as a visit to a coffee bar in San Francisco. Some did and even sent alerts. Others did nothing, especially if more than one card was issued to family members. They assumed another family member had made the charge. People foolishly allowed friends to use their card, as well, much to their regret.

Her father's ability to sum up a person in a glance and a short conversation served him well as a cop. He had no issue turning over his credit information to Elvin. It made her wonder why she even worried about Abby. Despite his posturing and jokes, Elvin could perform miracles when it came to computers. His large network of legitimate friends, as well as those on the fringe of legality, got the job done, too.

The television blared from the living room as Max enjoyed one of his soaps. A spate of excited Spanish meant it was a Telemundo novella. It must be all the action and color that attracted him or maybe her dog could be bi-lingual.

Here goes nothing. Nala dialed Elvin's number and waited. One ring, then two, finally three, which had her debating if she should hang up or not. A person should be able to pick up by three rings.

"Again? You call me at the butt crack of dawn again?"

Well, obviously he was up—now. "Dawn does not have a butt crack, and it has been up for hours. Before you leap into how you get your best information from the dark web after midnight, I need a favor."

An aggravated sigh carried over the line.

"It's for my parents."

"That's different," he added in a more pleasant tone.

Things certainly change when it's about my parents. "Why the change? What if the favor was for me?"

"Please." He stretched out the word. "You and me are buds. You know the drill. There's always some banter in our exchanges. Your parents are an entirely different matter. What's up?"

Banter? Is that what he thought listening to his fabricated tales and suggestive remarks was? To her, it was more like marching through sludge to get to the treasure she knew existed somewhere behind Elvin's glasses. "I told you yesterday that someone was using my mother's charge card. Since they're on a cruise, they can't check into things on their own, but they'd like it if you'd run their cards or even a credit bureau check to make sure no one is charging away. Before you ask, I did cancel that one card."

"Good. That chatter on the police scanner about a B and E at your folks' house. I assume was you?"

Lemon bars! *Were there no secrets?* "Yeah, that was me, but I had a key. The officers recognized Max, or I would have had to pull out my driver's license and a family photo."

"Doesn't mean that would have worked. Most people don't want their family members in their home. Saying you're related to someone doesn't necessarily mean you get a free pass to run through their house at will."

"I know. That's not why I called. Do you want me to give you their card numbers?"

"Sweet Jesus no! You might as well get a bullhorn and announce it to the world."

While it was normal for Elvin to be dramatic, sometimes she wondered if he was channeling a Southern grandmother or a drag queen. It was hard to keep track of all of his personas. Usually, he played the smooth charmer, the middle school version, with forays into movie characters. Every now and then, all the quips and quirkiness would fall away, and he'd be almost normal, or as normal as he could be. However, that only happened with long conversations, since it was hard to stay in character. That's the Elvin she liked best.

"I *am* at home."

"Sweetheart, any use of your cell is easy to listen to. Remember the parabolic microphone you bought to hear from far away?"

That pricey expenditure, resembling a ray gun from the old sci-fi movies, she'd like to forget. She hadn't once used the device. "Yeah, don't remind me. I should assume there's someone outside my house listening with one of those."

"Always. Laugh if you want, but it only takes once. I imagine the elderly population in your neighborhood would provide some good pickings. Not all, but some of the geezer crowd distrust the Internet. They call in their orders and shout their credit card numbers into the phone."

It was easy to imagine her neighbors doing that. If you had an unscrupulous operator, they could be memorizing or writing the number down as they took the call. At least online, most businesses had an encrypted ordering system. "Yeah. I can see that, but what about you? How do you get around that?"

"Jammers."

"What?" Elvin had a wealth of jargon and assumed everyone knew what he was talking about. Sometimes it made her feel stupid to ask what something meant, especially since the word was said with the same aplomb that she might have equated with *rain* or *sunshine*.

"Cell phone jammers. They confuse the signals. They prevent people from hearing clearly or tracing the call."

"Is this legal?" As soon as the words were out of her mouth, she wondered if her colleague would regard them as an insult. If he did, it would take ten minutes of soothing his ego, which she didn't have time for. She crossed her fingers on her free hand and hoped for the best.

"You're asking me if something in my repertoire of tools is legal?"

Before she could answer, Elvin continued, showing no signs of being upset. "I got mine at the local box store, which means they must be legal. I would assume the police wouldn't want you to use them in a kidnapping, but businesses that deal with cell phones use them to block out nosy parkers. Drop the info by the house and I should be able to run it in a couple of hours."

That she could do on the way to the office. Once at the office, she'd call the super and a locksmith. Mentally, she planned out her day as she replied. "Sounds great. We should be there in twenty minutes." Since Elvin was being cordial about running her parents' credit, maybe she could work in Abby's, too. His reaction would tell her if he was Abby's Elvin.

"Since you're going to be digging into the credit websites and all, I was hoping you could do a scan on a client who's dealing with identity theft."

"Sure, I was wondering when you were going to ask me."

Ah, he had noticed her reluctance to do so. She swallowed and reminded herself that suspecting Elvin was a shade short of paranoia. "Abby, Abby Lowenstein." There was silence on the other end of the phone. "Do you need her address? Birthdate to start?"

"No, I know them."

His tone had gone flat, which left her unable to gauge his emotional response, but she did know one thing. Elvin *was* Abby's Elvin.

Chapter Twelve

TOBY'S FROWN DEEPENED as he stared at the building and the very noticeable locksmith truck parked in the loading dock area. This wasn't good. He swore under his breath, knowing there was nothing he could do to prevent the eventuality of the locks being changed on the third-story office he and Gabe once shared. He sunk his hands deep into his pockets and rattled his change and keys.

It surprised him that it took this long for the girl detective to resort to a lock change. It could be someone else, but he doubted it since he only broke into his former office. Mr. Punctual, who sold superhero costumes and always showed up on time could need the services of a locksmith, but his gut told him otherwise. It really shouldn't matter that much. Toby had tossed the office good with the aid of a felon-in-training.

He had picked up the muscle in a bar that ex-cons were known to frequent. At least that way, he didn't have to worry about the guy turning squeamish and taking off like his previous helper. Once they'd pushed the ginormous desk out of the way, which was no easy feat, he pried open the hidey hole. Nothing.

Gabe would never do anything so obvious. The fake IDs and passports they usually kept there were missing, which was just mean. Rumor around town was that Gabe died in a car wreck. An unannounced visit to his sister confirmed it, but no word of the emeralds. The sister inadvertently revealed that she'd been shocked that Gabe had died in a car wreck, considering her mistaken belief that her brother was in auto insurance. She assumed her brother would have been a safe driver, knowing the accident rates.

No help there. Whatever Gabe was selling, the sister bought it. No reason for her to think otherwise of her brother. Still, that left him with the emeralds missing. Sure, Gabe hid them. Some place that would probably make sense only to Gabe. His former partner was a big fan of the old black and white mystery movies. He'd wanted to get a falcon for their office, but all he managed to find was a basset hound statue that was probably a children's bank. When Toby remarked on the statue's woeful expression, Gabe explained that it gave the place atmosphere. Not sure how, unless he was trying to make it look like a flea market.

The smartest thing to do would be to leave the area, but he needed money to do that. His alarm installation job only paid the bills. Despite living on ramen noodles and cereal, he still hadn't saved enough to buy a beater car. He could boost one, but then he'd have the law on his tail, something he was trying to avoid.

A delivery truck pulled up to the building. The driver jumped out and opened his back doors. He loaded several boxes onto a dolly, then carefully pulled them up the stairs. The idling truck gave him an idea. Stealing the truck, though tempting, would have him back in prison in a heartbeat. There was merchandise in the truck, which made the truck more valuable than say a regular truck or a mini-van, and it would be hard to keep a low profile with such a distinctive vehicle. It wasn't the truck that held his interest, but the boxes. Someone was getting regular deliveries. All he needed to find out was who the deliveries were for and then show up with a few boxes. There were holes in his plans such as the person who buzzed him in expecting an actual delivery.

The basement had to hold the secret to the emeralds. Toby had checked out his partner's old apartment, which was now rented to a young couple with a pit bull. Dogs were the bane of his existence. Who knew why most people liked them, but dogs never liked him. They had this sixth sense that people never seemed to notice when they came to him. It was almost like they knew what he was thinking.

The building door opened, and a man attired in coveralls and carrying a workbox climbed into his vehicle. The delivery guy popped out with his empty dolly right after him and left. The old place was hopping today. He could blend in when there was a lot of activity. If he had been on the other side of the street he could have trotted in with the delivery guy or locksmith. Probably not the locksmith. Their sort tended to be distrustful, which probably came with the job.

The sunlight bounced off the glass door as it swung open again revealing the girl detective and that stupid dog. Instead of moving down the stairs, they waited on the second step until Mr. Punctual joined them. Looked like they were friends. Not good, since friends usually told each other stuff like their office had been trashed, which would make the other renters less likely to buzz anyone up.

Toby's eyebrows came together, scowling in the direction of the descending couple. The dog carefully picked his way down, and when he reached the sidewalk, he stared in Toby's direction. Recalling how rabbits often stopped in mid-chase to fool pursuing dogs that often missed the motionless bunny, he stilled his fidgeting, but he knew the dog saw him. Then it barked, which meant it was time to vamoose.

★

THE SUNSHINE HELPED lift Nala's mood, and the fact that the check she wrote out for a new lock and deadbolt wasn't as much as she thought it would be helped, too. A determined thief could punch his way through the frosted glass portion of her door, but her father had mentioned it was reinforced glass, the type used for huge aquariums. Something that could hold in water should provide some deterrent.

Her trip outside had been meant solely as a relief trip for Max, but Harry joined them on the stairs making it more of a stroll with poop bags. She grinned at Harry. "I appreciate the name of the locksmith. He was much cheaper than I expected."

Harry chuckled and pushed up his slipping glasses. "Friend-of-the-family rate. Leo is some type of cousin. My mother could tell you how we're related." His shoulders went up in a shrug. "All I know is we call Leo whenever a lock needs replacing or you lock yourself out of your home or car. I have another cousin who specializes in replacement windows. Are you in the market for windows?"

Not sure if he was serious or not, Nala just shook her head. Max barked and tried to pull her across the street. What was wrong with the dog? She knew he hated the leash, but she only used it when other people were around. A bicyclist pedaled past attired in bright spandex. He probably startled Max, but bicyclists usually had no effect on him. There was light traffic on the street, so that could be it.

Harry addressed Max, "What is it, boy? Is Timmy stuck in the well?"

Lame. Nala rolled her eyes and grimaced knowing Max would object to the tired question as soon as they were behind closed doors. Instead, she forced a laugh. "I think it's more like Timmy is riding a bicycle."

Max gave her a backward glance and a short growl.

His behavior got weirder and weirder. Once she got him alone, she'd demand explanations. Harry pivoted to look in the direction of the departing bicyclist. "Yeah, I see him. He's moving fast, too. I guess we could count ourselves lucky he didn't clip us. You did a good job warning us."

Her teeth suck into her bottom lip, figuring Max would find the remark patronizing. Her pet—animal companion—arched his neck and lifted his head with pride. He almost acted as if he were posing for a photo op.

What had they been discussing before Max so rudely interrupted their conversation? Oh yeah, the locksmith cousin and family rate. "I appreciate the referral and would like to pay you back somehow." There was a bar not too far from the building. It was a bit of a dive, but not totally. She was about to suggest a drink when Harry turned to her and waggled his eyebrows.

"I was hoping you would say that."

Fudge. What had she said? "Umm, something about paying you back?"

"Yes. I need a favor."

Favor talk was usually never good. Usually, it involved going out with someone no thinking human would. "If it involves dating one of your cousins, the answer is no."

"Nothing like that. It could be a big business boost to you, too."

She used her free hand to cup her ear. "I'm listening."

"Good." Harry rubbed his hands together. "I gave it some thought and realized a lot of folks at Comic Con are introverts."

"Really?"

"Yes, really." He laughed and shook his head, probably just realizing her question had been rhetorical since she already knew the answer. "Anyhow, it's hard for introverts to meet people and when they do, they can't always be sure the person they met is good people. That's where your date investigate service comes in."

"I see it, but not sure how I can get into Comic Con. The booths are probably already sold out."

Harry brandished an index finger. "This is where I come in as a white knight."

"Okay." She wasn't sure if she wanted him to be a white knight. "No cousin dates."

"No cousin dates."

"Or friends." There was a limit to what she would do for free publicity. If Karly were here, she'd elbow her and tell her not to blow off someone until she met him.

"No dates. I have a booth. It cost me plenty, but I will need some help running it. It's not a one-person job. I had a friend, who'd agreed to help." He shrugged his shoulders. "Turns out he needed to fly back home due to his sister being in an accident."

"Is she okay?"

"I think so." Harry grimaced. "I didn't get all the details. Something about him needing to help with her kids since she's a single mother."

She nodded, agreeing that was a good reason. Didn't mean it was the real reason. When people chose to beg off from agreed upon activity, she noticed they used either illness or family. Big excuses involved both. At least his favor wasn't going to be something outrageous. "I would be happy to help, especially since you've helped me plenty."

"Glad to hear it." He stopped walking and put out his hand. "Let's shake on it."

Nala grasped Harry's hand and gave it a firm shake before letting go. "Tell me more about the booth and what I have to do."

"First," Harry resumed walking and spoke as he did so. "You'll need to get a placard made of your Date Investigate services and plenty of business cards. You may even want to have your booking calendar because some people may make appointments on the spot."

"Sounds good, but how can I help you?"

"I'll be selling costumes and sometimes the customers come all at once. You can find them costumes in their size, show them the size breakdown sign, run the occasional credit card through, and wear a costume."

Harry's voice faded as he listed the final duty. Nala looked at him. "Did you say 'wear a costume?'"

He nodded. "I'll be wearing one, too. Can't really sell what people can't see."

Her lips twisted as she considered the possibility of donning some bright, short latex skirt and a simulated leather bustier. "I'm not wearing any of those minuscule costumes."

"Never. I'll pick out something tasteful. Maybe you can spot whoever defrauded me with a bogus card."

Ah, she saw what he did there. He glossed over the costume by mentioning catching a possible felon. *Well played.* "I'll help, but I get the final say on my costume."

"Absolutely."

Max pulled on the leash and gave her a backward look that was easy to read. "Could Max come?"

"Only if he was a service dog."

Harry probably thought that settled the matter, but she knew good and well Elvin had a service harness made up for the canine while he watched him when she and Karly had taken off for a girls' weekend. Max had spilled the beans about Elvin pretending to be blind and using him as a guide dog. Elvin brushed the incident off as an experiment without clarifying what exactly was his working hypothesis. She imagined it had something to do with women and if they were more drawn to a blind man as some type of wounded hero character. In the end, Elvin got kicked out of the bar for chatting up the wrong chick. Apparently, her boyfriend had no respect for the blind or most likely saw through the disguise.

They took their leave of Harry and climbed into her vehicle. Nala started it and waited until Harry drove away before she questioned Max. "What was that growl all about?"

"Oh please." He gave an all over shudder. "Timmy's in the well. Go get help. How many times do you think I've heard that?"

"Point taken. I guess that means you'll be glad not to be at the conference. You'd probably hear the same comment a few thousand times."

Max snorted. "People think dogs are predictable. We pale in comparison to your kind who endlessly parrot the same words over and over."

Too bad her dog did have a point. The best way to handle it was to say nothing at all.

Chapter Thirteen

WHAT A WASTE *of a day*. Nala couldn't help thinking that as she steered her beloved vintage beetle toward Elvin's home. She'd wasted plenty of time cleaning up the flour mess, then Max. The only real work she'd accomplished was tracking down Abby's brother to a resort in Mexico. He'd flown out with a female companion over a week ago. Teddy's desire to brag and post photos on social media made it easy enough to track him down. Even his arrival time showed up on his time line. The plush resort photos of infinity pools and smiling service staff demonstrated great hair and a good smile, not to mention a few other things, could buy a lot.

Oh well, it meant Teddy couldn't have lifted the card file. Other than that, not much got done at work, besides replacing the lock and getting an invite to Comic Con, which could be fun and profitable. Karly would call it a date, she thought with a chuckle. Her bestie had the tendency to say everything was a date or a *near date*, rather like Mom would say.

At least her mother had calmed down on that front after the implosion with Tyler Goodnight. The only romance that came out of that non-relationship was the bromance that developed between her father and Tyler, but even that must have fizzled if he transferred to another county. She hoped it wasn't because of her, but suspected it was, considering the fact her father could be an intimidating guy if you weren't related to him. She often joked the screenwriter must have modeled the angry father-turned-action hero to rescue his kidnapped daughter after Dad. Her father was a man with contingency plans. He could drive any type of vehicle from a semi-trailer to a small plane, just in case. Whenever he came across a cadet who couldn't drive a stick, he usually ended up teaching him. You never knew when it might come in handy. It also explained why she never got an automatic.

A stoplight forced her to stop. A nearby car had a dog standing in the back seat, which resulted in Max barking for a solid two minutes. She nudged her dog. "Stop it."

"Okay." He hung his head as she eased through the green light.

"Stop pouting. Your bark can be ear-splitting, especially in a small car. Why do you do that anyhow? You've seen dogs before. For the most part, you have very little to do with other dogs. When we get in the car, you're usually Mr. Chatty."

"I don't hang with other dogs because I sometimes find their way of life so different from my own. It doesn't mean I don't enjoy a game of chase now and then or a round of butt sniffing."

"Please." Nala wrinkled her nose.

"You asked. Anyhow, in the car I'm just another dog. The barking is a game. The dog who barks first wins."

"Oh yay." It meant Max would not stop barking at other dogs in the near future or ever. It didn't take a mind reader to know her dog could be competitive about some things, usually those that didn't involve danger or possible harm to his canine self.

A grocery store on her left meant take the next left turn to reach Elvin's house. Her father would be horrified to realize after all his hard work teaching her to drive, she had picked up her mother's habit of driving by landmarks. Sure, she did use street names, especially when she programmed them into her phone, but landmarks such as the IKEA store stood out and could be seen from very far away. General directions such as going a thousand feet north, then turning west might as well be a foreign language. Usually, it only took her two runs to memorize directions to a place.

With any luck, Elvin might have found something on Abby's account that she could report back, which would make it seem like progress, but it wouldn't be the name of whoever accessed her numbers. The house with all the bird feeders signaled the entrance to Elvin's street. A smile tugged at her lips as she surveyed the neighborhood. It was a picturesque one with well-maintained cottages and yards. A few homes even sported a white picket fence. Others had bridges with no streams and wishing wells without water. One neighbor even had a non-working hydrant placed in the middle of his yard for his dog. Elvin called it the land of kitschy art. It was not the place his player persona would live. She imagined Elvin acted differently here.

His brick ranch actually stood out because there was no bird bath, no gazing ball, or any type of flowers. His curtains were usually closed, too. Not so much that he had anything to hide, but probably because he was trying to sleep while his neighbors headed off to work or when they started their lawnmowers. An older couple pedaled by on a tandem bike and waved at her.

She parked her car in the driveway, exited the car, and waited for Max to jump out before closing the door. An elderly woman popped out of the house next door attired in a gingham apron over her clothes. Two oven mitts adorned her hands, demonstrating she just came from the kitchen. Why had the woman decided to suddenly come outside?

The yards were small, which meant the two of them were very close. It wasn't like they could overlook each other. She waved in the woman's direction. "Hello."

"Oh, hi." The woman bustled in her direction and removed her oven mitts in the process. "I'm Louise."

It was going to be one of those types of meetings. "I'm Nala. This is my dog, Max."

"Good to meet you in person." She bobbed her head. "I saw you come by earlier. It's nice that Elvin has guests. He's lived by me for the last six years, and he never has any girlfriends come by. Not any boyfriends, either. He's a great fellow. Just this spring when my tree roots invaded my plumbing, he snaked out all my toilet and got it working again. A woman would be lucky to have such a handy—"

Elvin opened the door and dashed outside. He waved at the woman, grabbed Nala's arm, and towed her inside. Max followed, but not fast enough and got stuck on the wrong side of the door. He barked three times to get the door to open.

Elvin hissed, "Get in here, Max."

"What's wrong with you? You were rude to Louise."

His hands covered his face, and he moaned. "She introduced herself. That means you're marked."

"You're talking crazy." She should be used to some of his more bizarre theories. What was worse was when they turned out to be true. She hated when that happened. "The sweetheart popped out of her house—"

"Like a deranged cuckoo clock."

"I told her my name."

"Nooooo!"

He shot his hands through his carefully styled hair leaving parts upright, making his do resemble a baby chick's fluffy feathers. Nala decided not to tell him. "What's the big deal?"

"You remember my aunt you met and her flock of red hat

friends?"

On one of the previous cases Elvin had assisted her on, she ended up meeting his aunt who was more than happy to share a few enlightening tidbits about Elvin. "She was a sweetheart, too."

"That's like calling a shark *precious*. Louise next door is my aunt's best friend and competitor in the gossip Olympics. Currently, Louise is the favorite for the gold, which explains her appearance in the yard when you arrived. Even now she's calling her friends to inform them we are a couple." His eyes dropped to Max as he added, "Your dog will be woven into the story somehow. He could have been a canine matchmaker or we adopted him together."

"That's terrible. You spend so little time with our child, I think he's only been to your house a handful of times and only once for an overnight visit."

The horrified look on Elvin's face made her laugh so hard she had to lean against the wall to wipe away the tears.

"Laugh if you want, but the gossip network reaches far and wide. Wouldn't be surprised if your parents don't get a call when they reach Miami."

"Very funny. What do you have for me besides stories about your neighbors?"

"Come into my office." He gestured to the hallway. Max moved ahead knowing his way around the place.

The house was built back in the early sixties before people felt they needed everything huge with vaulted ceilings. It was large enough for a starter home or a bachelor. Elvin had knocked out an interior wall to combine the two bedrooms into an oversized room to hold all his electronics. A metal shelving unit contained a selection of technical books along with a number of electronic gadgets Nala didn't recognize. She assumed they were electronic since most appeared to have cords hanging down, reminding her of tails.

An air conditioner hummed in the corner even though it wasn't warm enough to turn one on due to the weather. A monster computer located against the far wall table heated up the room. There were four monitors scattered around it. Two were on shelves that put them a little higher than eye level while the other two rested on the table. Three of them had records displayed while the fourth had gone into screen saver mode, displaying frolicking puppies, which was not what she expected. Elvin moved the mouse vanquishing the puppies and a website article replaced it.

A small work table met the computer table at an angle. The file she gave Elvin that morning rested on the table, covered with sticky notes full of writing. She moved closer to see what he had written, but Elvin put his hand over it.

"Not so fast, I need to talk to you about the big picture, as opposed to your parents. We'll get there eventually, and Abby, too."

Even though it would take longer, she knew there was no way to get around it. In the end, it would make sense. "Go ahead."

He gestured to the monitor that used to hold images of puppies, but now had some article about Russian hackers. "You've probably heard about various companies having security breaches?"

"Yeah." She wanted to add *This ties in how?* but knew even if she didn't say it the question would eventually be answered. Her eyebrows lifted, urging him to go on.

"One of the targets was the credit bureau which had millions of credit card numbers stolen. They said they notified their customers, which may or may not be true. People cancel their cards and get new ones. Unfortunately, most want their old numbers. The expiration date and security number are different, which they think makes them safe."

"It's not?"

"Consider all the work these hackers used to get through firewalls and unscramble the encryption. They aren't going to give up just because someone canceled a card. They still have vital information including social security number, birthdate, name, and address. Some immediately started applying for new cards under the person's name as opposed to using the old cards. Others will use computer software to figure out the new security code if the card is reissued with the same number, which it often is. No sooner does a person get a new card than it's put into use elsewhere."

"Whoa. I hope mom's credit card company doesn't send her the same number. How can these hackers get away with getting new cards sent to them?"

"I thought we discussed this." He gave her a suspicious look as if she were testing him but spoke anyhow. "Credit card companies will not send cards to PO boxes for obvious reasons. There are these mail and shipping stores that provide a real address that appears to be a residence with an actual house number and street."

That sounded too easy. Something even a twelve-year-old headed in the wrong direction might come up with. "Don't the credit card companies realize this?"

"Only if they get a complaint about the address."

"Wouldn't the people at the mailbox company say something, especially if they see a variety of names going to the same mailbox?"

Elvin patted her cheek. "You poor naïve darling. Many of the people who use mailboxes often have nefarious reasons. Maybe they're getting money they don't want to share with a spouse. Perhaps they've engaged in a relationship on the side, and the private mailbox is the only thing that's secure. Could be a woman is getting ready to leave her husband and directs all her correspondence there. Someone might be trying to stay off the grid. Then, you have your criminals. Basically, when it comes to a private mailbox, mum's the word."

This didn't sound right. There could be a crime network being conducted through mailbox services. "Can't the police do anything about it?"

"Technically, they can at the United States Post Offices, if they have reason to believe the contents of a mailbox could be harmful, smoking, leaking, making sounds, etc. They have to have a warrant to open the box for any other reason. Mailbox stores are probably about the same, harder to catch since they pop up and close down so fast."

"I've been in one of those. They charged me sixty dollars to mail a guitar. That's robbery."

Elvin held up his index finger. "That's making a profit. No one held a gun to your head. You could have gone to the post office."

"Yeah." She moved closer to be able to read the other screens. "Have you been to the post office lately? You have all these people running stores from their home and have a gazillion packages to mail. Plus, you have these people who wander in to get a passport, and they haven't even filled out the paperwork. The mailing stores are more convenient."

"Exactly. There has been another breach. It hasn't been announced yet. Someone in the United States is selling encryption software to the Russians. It's hard to be secretive about anything when your nemesis has the code. Still, I don't think that's what happened to your parents. Except, there's a suspicious charge on your father's card." Elvin picked off a sticky note from the file. "Lola's Luxurious Day Spa for $350. It came through the day they left on their cruise. Doesn't sound like some place your father would be caught dead at."

"My mother wanted to go there. It's a birthday gift. He talked to me about it before he purchased it. Wanted to know what type of package she wanted."

"Okay. That's a dead end. I ran your parents' credit report. Nothing except for that card you canceled. Do you think she had any disgruntled employees she fired recently?"

That seemed like an obvious angle since the card was a company card. "She doesn't really hire many people. Most of the employees have been with her for over a decade. They're a loyal bunch. When the first charge came through, my mother expected someone named Raylene. Thought the woman didn't have the right amount of taste and might have made such a heinous purchase."

"You spoke to her?"

He made it sound like the reasonable thing to do. "It's been less than twenty-four hours." She shot a hand through her hair, possibly making her look as frazzled as Elvin. "I canceled the card last night. I thought that was the end of it."

Elvin wrapped an arm around her shoulders and used his pseudo fatherly voice. "I thought I raised you better. You're not going to allow Abby to get by with just canceling her cards, are you?"

"No, I'm sure someone took the information from her apartment. Max smelled a different person had walked through her apartment recently. She canceled her cards after the first charge was made. The fact that the swimsuit was delivered to her address—makes it local."

"I'm sure you asked her if she invited anyone over?"

"Are you telling me how to do my job?" A thought suddenly occurred to her. She tapped her temple with her index finger. "Are you asking for the case or for yourself?"

"The case."

His cheeks flushed, which was one of his tells she'd never mentioned to him. It amused her to have something on him. "I guess she wasn't talking about you then."

"What did she say? Was it good? Horrible?" His eyebrows shot up, then came down into a V once he realized he'd been played. "Okay. You got me."

"Yeah. I've said too much already. Abby is a decent person who works too much. She has no time for a social life. She informed me no one had been in her new apartment."

"Do you think she's lying?"

"No, it's a sketchy neighborhood. I wouldn't be surprised if someone decided to do a little shopping, but she has a very alert neighbor. Someone ordered a swimsuit, and it was delivered to Abby's apartment. The neighbor saw a woman she thought was Abby pick up the package. She even mentioned Abby swung by during work."

"That's ballsy. I'd talk to the woman. She'd be your best bet if anyone came in or out of the apartment."

"I considered that, too."

Max gave her a quizzical glance, as if to ask why they hadn't discussed this. She didn't discuss every thought that passed through her mind with her dog.

"Good deal. I know you are just getting started on this. I'd like to help any way I can. Abby is a very special person. I won't even charge you."

She blinked and knocked the heel of her hand against her ear. "Did I hear you right? You said no charge?"

"Just for Abby." A sad smile crossed his face, then disappeared.

"Everyone else costs, including your parents."

"That's the Elvin I know."

"Anyhow, this got me looking into identity thefts in the area. They're up. Way up. This is only the people that have reported it. Some people exist in a fog until they can't get any money from their ATM, then they discover they've been hacked. I'm pretty sure your mother's case is personal since they're busy buying things your mother would hate."

"Whoever it is could just have no taste." Which sounded more and more like Raylene. She'd have to hit Posh Interiors before she could call it a day.

"Possibly. I'm thinking local breech, like the hospital. Thousands of locals pass through the hospital doors surrendering their sosh and insurance numbers, along with credit cards. It's a possibility. Worried me enough that I ran my own credit."

"And?"

"Nothing. I have alerts on every card, and I also falsified all my identity questions."

"Excuse me?"

"It might ask what your favorite childhood pet was. I put Rex the Rattlesnake."

"You never had a rattlesnake."

"Exactly, so even those who think they know me couldn't answer the questions."

"Clever. Dad did something similar."

"Since you're here, do you want me to check your credit? It won't cost you anything."

She waved away the possibility, but on second thought, what could it hurt? If nothing else she'd find out if her credit score was high enough to consider a newer car, one that wasn't as eye-catching as the beetle. "Go on. Will it take long?"

"I had it cued up and ready to go."

"How did you get the information?"

He shook his head. "Pay attention, Grasshopper, and learn."

She hated when he made television references. At least she knew Grasshopper was from the old show, Kung Fu. "Go ahead. Did you flatter your contact at the BMV?"

"No need. I had most of the information I needed already from your address, name, and birthdate. Just needed your social security number. Now, if I had an investigator's license like you, I could get the sosh number, if I had a legitimate reason to have it, of course."

"Really?" This was news to her even though she had taken an online course to get her license. Usually, she expected whoever hired her to provide it. "What is considered permissible reasons?"

"Looking for a missing person. Trying to track down a deadbeat parent who isn't paying child support. Trying to discover if an active duty service person is deployed. You can't randomly pull a number to get even with an old boyfriend."

It would have made her Date Investigate service much easier, but it didn't qualify. "Good to know. Should I register with someone?"

"Probably. You look into it. Type in your digits and I'll close my eyes."

Her fingers flew over the number pad. Why was she even bothering with the credit search anyhow? She only had two cards and limited credit. If a person wanted to scam someone, a fatter fish would be preferable. She pressed enter and waited. An hourglass icon appeared as she tried to decide what she had charged recently.

"I used my debit card for gas. I took Karly to Matteo's for her birthday. Charged it since I had no clue how much the bill would be.

Normally, they're reasonable, but we went for the full works, from soup to dessert. I can't really think of anything else. Haven't bought any expensive investigator equipment."

The icon quit moving and a print out of charges shimmered into existence, a long print out. Elvin moved behind her to read over her shoulder. "Online video games. Looks like you bought a round at B-Dubs and some paintball equipment. What's this?" His finger landed on one charge.

Nala read it aloud, "1-900-Hot-Stuff," and shuddered. "Not my charges. Looks like someone has been charging away while I have been running down everyone else's credit issues."

"Don't you have alerts?"

"I did, but I had them sent to my email." She hit her forehead with the heal of her hand. "I changed my email address when I started the business. Wanted it to sound more professional than *celestial princess*."

"You still have that email?"

"You're no longer *lunar knight*?"

"That's my secret email. Very few know it." He held a finger to his lips. "I expect you to keep it quiet."

"I will, but I may need your help on this credit issue, which seems to be spiraling out of control. It looks like a fifteen-year-old boy nicked my credit cards."

"It's a pretty hefty tab at B-Dubs. Cancel the card. Then, let's swing by the place. Someone who spent all that money at once should be memorable."

The phone was already in Nala's hand, along with her credit cards. She went to the trouble to buy an attractive metal wallet, and she still got ripped off. She typed in the customer service number a little harder than she should. The plan was to help people, not be the victim of crime. She reported the issue in terse sentences. The customer service rep read back the current charges to her.

"None of those are mine. Haven't used the card since the seventh at Matteos restaurant in Noblesville."

The rep offered to send her out a new card. "Don't. I'm not feeling very pro-credit right now."

The woman started babbling about their better systems and how she wouldn't be charged. Nothing would change what had already happened to her. She'd been robbed. Even worse, she should have been aware of it happening, but she wasn't. She hung up after receiving a confirmation number.

"Let's go. I'm ready to nail this jerk!"

Elvin leaned over the keyboard and hit a few keys, which caused booming music to fill the room. "I thought we needed the appropriate soundtrack as we strode out of the room. Ready to deliver some rough justice."

Max barked in response. For a brief moment, she could imagine how silly the three of them might look striding into B-Dubs. Make that two of them, but she didn't care. Whatever punks or punkettes who thought it would be fun to rip off local folks just crossed the line and made it personal.

Chapter Fourteen

Elvin, Max, and Nala crowded into her beetle for their trip to the eatery where someone was living high on her credit. Just the thought of it made her growl, and she twisted her key in the ignition. "Incredible! I did all this work to have decent credit and some jerkwad is blowing it."

Max leaned between the console and whispered the word, "Jerk wad?"

Elvin, who had been looking away, swung his head around. "Wow! You're so mad your voice changed. Don't sweat it. You stopped the cards, and we'll nail the culprits."

"You're right." She pushed Max back into his seat before reversing. "Yeah, that sometimes happens when I'm really mad."

"Weird. Guess I've never seen you really mad then."

"Be glad." Nala inhaled deeply as she shifted into first gear. Life could be challenging with a talking dog. There were hundreds of words she said every day he never took time to repeat. Eventually, her friend would catch on, then he'd want to borrow her pooch to impress women. "I don't need to waste my time dealing with my own credit issues."

"It could be whoever lifted your numbers could have lifted your friends' or your mother's."

"That would be handy, but so far nothing about the PI business has been easy. I'm probably dealing with three distinct cases. Doesn't mean that some racket is being run, especially with all the chatter about ID theft."

"I've been thinking about that, too. The most helpful route would be to follow the money. It would be nice if I could find out who else had their numbers stolen."

Nala cut her eyes to her friend. Usually, he would make some reference to calling Batman or another superhero for help. It wasn't like him to talk sense.

"No chance of that happening," he continued. "Most folks believe identity theft is due to something they did or didn't do."

She scoffed, even though she knew he was right. "Agreed. We're heading to the B-Dubs in Fishers to see if anyone can identify my big spender. Later, I'll head over to Posh to see if anyone knows anything."

"Don't forget the police report."

"Nag, nag." She knew enough to file a report, but wasn't looking forward to doing it, since Tyler Goodnight had transferred to Hamilton County. She knew it was unlikely Tyler would take the call, but there was still a chance, and not one she wanted to take. It wasn't like she stood on a corner handing out her personal information, but the guilt still rode her shoulder like a capuchin monkey.

"Just reminding you."

Flashing lights and slow traffic announced a wreck ahead. Elvin motioned to the side. "You can bypass this by using the shoulder."

"Sure. I'm going to drive on the shoulder, right past the cops. That should go over well. We'll wait our turn like everyone else."

Max groaned in the back seat, making Elvin laugh. "See, even your dog wants you to do it."

"Please." It amazed her that her friend would even suggest it. "I know a way around without using 37." Nala switched lanes until she was in the far right and turned onto a side street that would circle around the blockage.

An assortment of vehicles and trucks were in the parking lot the restaurant shared with several other businesses. They could be busy, but it was hard to tell. Some of the cars could belong to employees. Occasionally, folks met, decided to ride together, and left their vehicle in a public place. That might account for a few cars.

"They could be busy. Will anyone want to talk to us?"

Elvin held up his hands and rubbed his fingers together.

"Bribery."

"Not exactly. Instead of talking to us, a server could be making money. Her time is valuable."

She moved into an open parking space and switched off the ignition. "Hope you have some actual money since my credit is no good."

"Oh brother." He flopped back against the seat. "Your credit problems are costing me."

"I'm good for it."

"Okay, Robin, let's go."

Her fingers pressed down the door handle before she fully absorbed his reference. "Why do I have to be Robin?"

"You'd look better in the outfit than I would. You got a private investigator badge?"

His question had all the earmarks of one of his plans. She exited and paused by the open door, which allowed Max an opportunity to jump out. *Great.* Once out, her dog would not reenter the car, especially when no one else was inside the vehicle.

She tried to give her dog the stink eye, which had no effect since the canine stared in the direction of the restaurant, salivating at the smell of roasted meat. Not too much she could do, except inform him he wasn't going in. He'd keep watch outside and would probably bum some food off patrons or try to.

She slammed the door, aware that at times—make that most of the time—her dog didn't always listen to her. Then, there was Elvin. "PIs don't have badges. It's to keep them from impersonating police officers. All I have is a paper card to prove I'm licensed."

Elvin rested his hand on top of the car. "It'll work."

"How?" She blew out a breath knowing Elvin would have an angle. The man enjoyed assuming different personas, plotting scenarios, and playing games.

"People assume a great deal. Walk in like you mean business. Head up, shoulders back, flash your license, state your name, and what you need."

She held up her open hand. "Quacks like a duck, sounds like a duck. You're telling me to act like the police. As a pretend officer of the law, I won't be handing your money over."

"I thought of that."

A laugh escaped her. Of course, he thought of that. "Why not be ourselves? I'm a PI who is looking for a punk using my card, and how could he use my card if I have it still in my possession?"

"That's what we are going to find out. We'll do it your way. Would that make you happy?"

"I'd be happy if I didn't have to track down my credit card, but here we are. Let's go, Starsky." She used the name of an old-time television cop knowing his desire to role play. Nala continued, "You going to Comic Con?"

"Thought about it."

"Figured as much."

He gave her an incredulous look as they strolled across the pavement. "Why in the world would you think I'd go?"

She shrugged her shoulders as they reached the sidewalk. "Don't know. It's just a big thing in Indy, and I know you're always into whatever's happening."

"I hear ya. I think I'll try to make it."

"I'll be there, too."

Elvin put his hand on the column outside the restaurant as if shocked. "You? You got to be kidding."

"Helping Harry with his booth." No way would she mention the costume, which she hoped had a mask.

He gestured to the door. "Let's do this."

Nala entered first and scanned the room. Not as many people as she would have thought, but dinner time and late night were probably their busy times. Most of the diners were finishing up their meals. A couple of servers stood off to the side, keeping an eye on the customers as they chatted. Nala made a beeline for them. One smiled in her direction and went to the wait stand to grab menus. The other picked up a pitcher of water and headed toward the diners.

"Two?" The server inquired reminding her that Elvin was two steps behind her.

"No." She flipped open her wallet quickly, showing her PI license for a brief second. "My partner and I are tracking down an identity theft ring. One of the stolen cards was used today at your restaurant. A bill for over three hundred dollars."

The woman put down the menus and heaved a sigh.

Not exactly the help she was looking for. A folded bill was pressed into Nala's hand. Ah yes, the bribe she could not afford. A nametag identified the woman as Delight. It couldn't be. Maybe it was pronounced differently. Accent on *del* instead *de*.

"Del-ite, I was hoping you could help us. I'd be very grateful."

She brandished the bill which she thought would be a twenty but turned out to be a five.

"The name's Delight. I didn't have an order like that. Sounds more like a pickup order, maybe party platters. Jack does the pickup orders. You'll need to talk to him." She plucked the bill from Nala's fingers and walked away with a sniff.

"Pickup," she informed Elvin.

"I heard. It's to your right."

They found Jack sitting and texting at the pickup station. Couldn't really blame him since there were no customers. Nala was ready to try her pretend policeman banter again. Elvin cleared his throat causing Jack to look up.

"Delight texted me that you were coming."

"Good." She pitched her voice lower, trying to make more gravely. "You know what we want?"

"The big order that the kid picked up."

"That's it. Credit card fraud. Can you tell me anything about it?"

A smug smile tugged Jack's lips upward. "I was right. I told Jose something wasn't right with the kid. A skinny kid with thick glasses. The name on the online order was a woman's. Anyhow, I said something to him, and he told me it was his mother's card. I didn't believe him."

"You didn't believe him, but you still gave him the order?"

Jack made a scoffing sound. "What can I say? The customer is always right. If I argue with one, I get canned."

Elvin put both hands on the counter. "The order was sent in via the computer?"

"Yeah, that's what I said." Jack arched one eyebrow at this questioner.

Nala expected him to add, *did I stutter?* As far as descriptions go, *skinny kid with glasses* wasn't that helpful. Who knows? Maybe Elvin had a plan.

Elvin asked, "Would the order form have a phone number to call if something went wrong?"

"It should. We have an order template with a place for a phone number on it, for just that reason."

"Can you print me out the order?"

Jack went back to his computer, typed a little, then there was the sound of a printer in the distance. He came back with the printout and handed it to Elvin.

Figures he'd assume the male was in charge. If there was a number, they had him. She called out happily to the employee. "Thanks, Jack."

They exited the building and picked up Max who had way too much interest in a trash receptacle near the store. There was a little more bounce in her step than usual, realizing she was close to nailing one punk. Technically, she couldn't do it herself and would have to call the police, but she could pretty much hand them the culprit gift wrapped.

"I can't believe someone would be stupid enough to put their number on an order when they were using a lifted card."

She opened the door and let Max scramble in. Elvin climbed in the passenger side and waited until she was in the car. He handed the paper back to her.

"Look at the number closely. Does it look familiar?"

Why would it look familiar? She held it up, recognizing the 317- area code and the seven digits that followed it. It was *her* phone number. "Lemon bars!"

"Pretty smart, if you ask me. They might cross reference the card, and it should align with your phone number, which it did."

"So, it's useless."

"Not necessarily."

"How will getting the order information be helpful?"

"We can rule out any vegans by the pounds of chicken wings ordered."

Frustrated, she ended up flooding the car engine, which made her feel foolish. Elvin had the decency to say nothing until she got the car running again.

"I may be able to find out who called the restaurant at this time. A little reverse engineering."

"How can you do that?" She held up her hand before he could reply. Some things she was better off not knowing. "Never mind. How long will it take?"

"Hard to say. Not more than a day. I'll call you with the URL. You do realize we could be dealing with professionals."

"Professionals? They used some skinny kid to pick up the wings."

"Could be a smoke screen. A decoy. You might be stirring up a hornet's nest. Please just deal with Posh Interiors and Abby's situation and leave this to me."

Some people might think Elvin was being chivalric but that's not what she heard. "I can do this. I can handle three cases. Keep in mind, I solved every case I've ever had. I'll solve these, too."

EVEN THOUGH NALA was headed toward Posh Interiors, she wasn't following Elvin's instructions, but finishing her mother's request to check on Raylene and her suspicious taste instead. Max sat tall in the passenger seat.

"You think there will be any treats for me?"

Her mother usually kept a box of treats in her desk, which might be what he was referring to. "Could be. It depends on your not jumping on the furniture. Keep in mind, they need to sell that stuff. It's pricey, too."

"I can behave." He gave a disdainful sniff and stuck his nose in the air.

"Can't prove it by me."

"Whoa. I could tell some tales on you, too."

"I'm not pulling garbage out of the can and spreading it all over the floor."

"What about—"

She shot a meaningful look at her canine friend, which dried up whatever he was intending to say. Nala heaved a sigh, realizing she had been arguing with her dog. Normally, she'd have stopped talking before now. All this identity theft had her running in a circle. Maybe all three items were tied together.

Out of habit, Nala parked at the far end of the Posh Interiors lot away from the expensive clients' cars. Even the senior designers had impressive rides. The good news was there were folks still there—possibly Raylene.

Nala opened the car door and waited for Max to exit. The two of them walked up to the front doors, but before entering, she looked down to her companion. "Good behavior."

Since someone was exiting the door, Max settled for a slight nod.

The departing woman stopped to pet Max and exclaimed, "I had no clue they allowed dogs in the store. I would have brought Satan."

Any pet named Satan was not one her mother would want inside the store. "Excuse me, ma'am. This is my medical safety dog. He barks when I'm going into a seizure to get help and to remind me to take appropriate precautions."

"Oh." The unnamed customer tried for a smile but failed, having been given too much unsolicited information. She hurried off to her car, allowing Nala and Max to enter unimpeded.

The soft lighting made the rooms of furniture inviting. Her mother favored classic furniture with an occasional modern piece and a splash of color. There was an open book with a pair of spectacles on top of it. A half-full old-fashioned glass sat on an ornate coaster. Nala picked it up to examine it. Her mother would be no fan of glasses being left in the design rooms.

The ice cubes and liquid stayed in place as she handled it.

"It's fake." Mona, her mother's assistant, commented as she approached. "I thought it might be a fun touch. Your mother likes for people to feel like the rooms could be a part of a home."

"I know." She smiled at the confident red-headed woman, who had been in her mother's employ for at least a dozen years. "I got a strange call from my mother."

Max bumped into her leg, almost sending her into the wing chair. She pushed him away, aware he was trying to remind her someone in the store could be guilty. Not Mona, though. The woman had known her mother for years. Still, she decided to say nothing about the credit card usage.

"Really. She should be soaking in the sun and drinking those meter-long margaritas."

Drinking some plastic meter of alcohol was not her mother's style. It was odd Mona would say that, considering how well the woman knew her mother. "Could be. She wanted me to ask Raylene something."

"What would that be?" Mona crossed her arms and clenched her jaw, then loosened it.

Wow. Something was bothering her. The woman was wound up

about something. "It's nothing. Just a follow-up on an order."

"You can tell me. You'll have to. I fired Raylene the other day."

Her mother would never allow any other employee the responsibility of hiring and firing. That didn't mean Raylene knew that. Odd that Raylene would get canned the same time her mother's corporate account card went into overdrive.

Her shoulders went up into a shrug. "Guess it's not important." She held up a hand. "See ya." She weaved around Mona and headed for the back hallway.

"Where are you going?"

"Restroom. Long drive. Too much coffee." Max padded after her. Mona dogged her steps, too, which would make it hard to get into her mother's office unseen. No way did she want to explain to her mother's longtime assistant that something didn't feel right.

The front door buzzed, and a customer entered, talking. "I'm not happy with my delivery. The delivery guys are jerks!"

Other customers stopped in their perusal and the few designers present looked up, too. Mona shot a glance at Nala, then another back to the upset client. She heaved a sigh and moved toward the customer. Depending on how angry the woman was, Nala's window of opportunity was small.

Her mother had a keypad lock instead of a keylock. Her mother was a big fan of keypads. The number was probably her birthdate. A quick glance assured her Mona was still busy. A few button presses unlocked the door. Inside the office, her mother's trademark perfume still lingered as if her mother had just stepped out.

The filing cabinet would have to serve. She had no time to boot up her mother's computer. Good chance the computer's password was not her birthday to make it easy. She turned on the light and shut the door after Max entered.

"How about a treat?"

"Not now." She tugged at the cabinet door and found it locked. When did her mother become so paranoid? Her mother always kept a metal nail file in her pen jar to keep her nails flawless. That should spring the lock. She dumped out the pens in search of the file. In her haste, she knocked over the treat container.

Nala didn't spend any time warning Max not to make a pig of himself. She needed to get the file and leave. It would appear odd if they didn't leave via the front door and bid the employees goodbye. Anything less would look suspect, or maybe that was her paranoia speaking. The nail file worked, but she wasn't sure if she ruined the lock. Nala grabbed the folder labeled employees and pulled out the typewritten papers with names, addresses, phone numbers, and social security numbers. She folded the papers twice and stuck them in her back pocket.

"Let's go," she hissed to Max, who gobbled up the last remaining treat. She turned off the light and cracked the door, but a nearby conversation had her closing it again. She waited until the chatters turned off into the restroom.

Nala opened the door, slid into the hall, and motioned to Max to follow. She made her way back through the showroom, nodding at the designers and gave Mona a wave, who was still engaged in conversation with the angry customer. As they passed the two, Max jostled Angry Client causing her to pause in mid-tirade.

Nala tightened her muscles to prevent her from laughing, a trick she learned from her father. They exited without any more fanfare.

Inside the beetle, she pulled the papers out of her pocket and dialed Raylene's number.

"She's not answering."

"Geesh. Someone not answering a strange number." His pithy

remark was ruined by a burp.

"You're right. I should at least leave a message." She called again and waited for the beep. "Hi. This is Nala, Gwen's daughter. Mona shouldn't have fired you. I need to talk to you." She added her number, then hung up.

Max was leaning sideways as if he didn't feel good. She should have stopped him from eating so many treats but couldn't break into the file cabinet and manage her dog at the same time. "Are you all right?"

He belched. "Those treats made me a little gassy."

"Lemon bars! The investigator's life is one glamorous moment after another." She started the car and reversed it out of the parking space. Her attention was on the lit window, highlighting Mona and Angry Client. Her mother would never hire a subpar delivery service. Something besides a few bogus charges was happening.

Chapter Fifteen

THE IMITATION LEATHER costume stuck to Nala's skin. She tugged at the black fabric squeezing her thighs, doing its best to become her first layer of skin. The memory of Harry's pleased smile as he handed her the costume, explaining that it included her specification of no bustier, no short skirt, or even latex, irritated. Unfortunately, she had forgotten to mention outfits that were tighter than a snakeskin on her list of things to avoid. Worse, she hadn't taken the time to try on the outfit before Comic Con. Instead, she had to wrestle into a costume that had to be two sizes too small in a tiny convention center bathroom stall.

Her elbow struck the metal wall. "Ouch!"

Getting dressed might kill her. The platform black boots rested on the floor, but there was no way she could put them on in the stall. Harry insisted she only had to wear the boots for a few promotional shots for the booth. Nala was not sure why the booth needed any promotion. Anyone who bought a ticket was already a hardcore comic book fan. They arrived with enough plastic to buy collectibles, autographs, and snacks. Even if they forgot or ran out of money, ATMs liberally dotted the convention hall. Still, a favor was a favor.

She swung open the stall door and kicked the gym bag that contained her regular clothes ahead of her as she carried the boots. A woman attired in a Supergirl outfit leaned near the mirror, applying her makeup. She nodded to her reflection but spoke to Nala.

"Are you supposed to be the Black Canary or the Black Widow?"

"I think the Black Widow. Originally, maybe the Black Canary, but the costume appeared to be missing a bottom. I told Harry if I was helping him I wanted as much of me covered as possible."

Her image in the mirror didn't look too bad. The color made her look mysterious and well—sexy. A wide V of skin dipped lower than any of her tops, and her fingers went to the zipper to tug it up. No luck.

The other woman paused in her application of mascara to smirk. "Sweetie, there will be so many more males and females exposing much more skin than you. A few start with a swimsuit and cut huge chunks out of it. You'll look like a nun compared to some of them. Still, the outfit works for you. Can you let me do your makeup? I'm a pro. I've been doing Cosplay for years. You gotta come to the contest. Might even want to be in it."

Yeah, right. The possibility of her prancing across the stage made her chuckle. "Appreciate the makeup help."

Even though she had applied her makeup before coming to the center, a little extra might help to disguise her since her costume didn't require a mask. The only person she might possibly see who knew her was Karly, but even her bestie would avoid attending the Con solo.

Ten minutes later, she swayed out of the restroom in the unfamiliar boots. They would not be all day footwear. She'd give them ten minutes at the most. Ancient Chinese women used to bind their feet because it made their gait graceful and preventing them from running away. If they had these boots back then, it would have saved them from binding their feet and served the same purpose, although she wasn't so sure she'd achieve the graceful part.

As long as she didn't go outside and scuff the soles, the boots could easily be sold as new with about the same use as shoes tried on in the store. It would be hard to imagine anyone would wear them more than once or twice in a lifetime. Maybe there was money in renting instead of selling costumes and boots, especially at a conference.

Nala strolled past the other vendor booths stocked with everything from action hero T-shirts, mugs, and jewelry, to tiny costumes for pets and babies. Blue-shirted volunteers bustled about with clipboards in their hands. Electronic pings and gurgles came from a collection of vintage arcade games placed next to a colorful semi-truck cab that was the homage to a popular truck turned robot.

So many vendors made it hard to remember where Harry's booth was. It sat near a door at a corner, but the oversized convention halls had two walls of doors. The only place it couldn't be was next to the concrete walls. Vendors scurried about unpacking merchandise and tweaking signage. Too bad, so many had action figures, autographed photos, and T-shirts. There didn't seemed to be an identifying feature—not that she had looked as she went in search of a bathroom. Unfortunately, she assumed it would be easy. So far, it looked like Harry was the only one with full costumes. Several vendors offered hats or masks, but not the whole deal.

A bunch of Star Wars costumed folks jostled each other and made suggestive comments as she neared. Fudge! She'd have to walk past them, too. They must be vendors, because the Con wasn't open for business yet. Normally, she'd skirt the area, but if she did, she might not find her way back to Harry's booth.

Wait a minute. She was a private investigator who had taken down criminals. Better yet, she was the *Black Widow*. Inhaling deeply, she pushed her shoulders back and strolled past, refusing to make eye contact.

Harry had his back to her as he adjusted a banner. "Not right." He glanced over his shoulder, saw her, and asked, "Can you read it, okay?"

"Yes." No reason to add that she was only six feet away. "Have you ever thought of renting costumes?"

He turned around slowly, his eyebrows lifted in inquiry. "Nala?"

He acted as if he wasn't sure who she was. Put on something different, a little extra makeup and suddenly she transformed into another person. Some men took second looks at her and possibly had impure thoughts—definitely impure. It was hard to know how she felt about it. "Of course. How many women in Black Widow outfits have passed you today?"

"Just you, um, you look different. Good different." He shook his head as if still baffled by the change.

"Don't get used to it." She pointed to her boots. "These are foot cripplers. Remember the clock is ticking on the boots. I'll be outside the booth at the exhibit hall opening, then once we change places, the boots come off."

"I appreciate your help—"

A low *boom* shot through the hall from the exterior corridor. A shower of laughter accompanied a few outraged complaints.

"Why not!"

"It was okay last year."

A nearby vendor with pink hair grimaced. "You'd think with the security they have in this place that someone would have stopped the idiot before he got this far."

"What do you mean?"

The middle-aged vendor shot a hand through her hair making it stand up even more. "Weapons. We all know most superheroes have one. It can be a sword, a gun, a saber, or even a bat wrapped in barbed wire. What it can't be is too realistic with the possibility of hurting someone."

It had never occurred to her that someone would walk around with an actual weapon. It wasn't the safest or smartest thing to do. "They can bring in weapons?"

"They can bring in pretend weapons. Stuff you buy at the Halloween store. Some make their own out of cardboard and such and make it oversized. Guards inspect and tag them if they past approval. You still got these Hill Jacks trying to bring in an actual hatchet with red paint dribbles on the edge."

An air horn blast sent strolling vendors scurrying for their various booths. Harry dashed inside his booth, grabbed a handful of flyers, and shoved them at Nala. She took the flyers and glanced in the direction of the low hum throbbing through the open doors.

Harry leaned across the tables that composed his booth. "Remember to smile. Wait, maybe not. Black Widow wouldn't smile. Feel free to snarl as you hand out flyers."

That she could do. All she had to do was concentrate on her left boot, which pinched more than the right. Could be her foot was bigger. She'd read most people did have one foot that was slightly bigger.

The voices in the hall grew louder. Some uniformed officers came through the doors first and a couple took up positions by each of the doors. Two headed their way, one of them turned around slowly as they passed and stopped to give Nala a second look. *Really?*

Before she could channel her inner Black Widow and say something cutting, she realized the officer in question was Tyler Goodnight. Could the man be any more obvious about his ogling? Another officer called out to him. His hand went up in reply, but he kept his gaze on her as he asked, "Nala? Nala Bonne?"

The man recognized her, which made his behavior a little bit more acceptable. She held up one black-gloved hand and waved.

He stepped closer. "Surprised to see you here."

"You, too."

"Providing security. There was a call for volunteers."

The other officer shouted, "Goodnight, assume your station and quit trying to score a date!"

Tyler shot an irritated look over his shoulder. "Got to go. Maybe we could talk later."

What was she supposed to say to that? Her lips tipped up as she handed him a flyer. He took it with a wink, then jogged away.

From her vantage point, she could see elaborately costumed participants having to stop and have their backpacks and purses searched. Most coming down the corridor only sported a superhero T-shirt or ball cap. A few participants veered off, but most came straight toward the hall.

A couple yelled, "Look! It's the Black Widow."

The shout made Nala look behind her. The shouters, two males of indeterminate age with scruffy beards, raced up to her and placed their arms around her for a selfie. One had the nerve to ask, "Could you plant a kiss on my cheek?"

The other friend held his camera phone up, obviously expecting Nala—Black Widow—to comply. No favor involved this. Her platform boot came down on the man's instep the same time Harry vaulted over the booth table.

"Hey! Keep your slimy lips off my girlfriend." A determined scowl made him look a bit like a hipster superhero as he charged. The guys scattered before he reached them, which was probably good.

His unexpected action shocked Nala so much she dropped the

flyers. The two of them bent down to pick them up. They bumped heads as they came up. Nala laughed, then wrinkled her nose. "I guess I cost you some customers."

"Nope. Not worried. Their kind never buys a costume. I think they only come to pick up women." He waved to the rest of the crowd. "Hand out the flyers only. You don't have to do the selfies, either."

No need to mention Karly's plan to come to the conference to find men. At least two of the single men she knew were already in the exhibit hall, proving her bestie's idea wasn't totally lame. "I think that was just a one-time thing. Besides, I stomped the jerk's instep."

"Way to go," he praised her and slapped her on the back.

She stumbled a little, but caught herself, then handed out a flyer to a trio of visitors. "I'm good. Go back to your booth. Remember, I have the instep killer boots on." No need to add they would probably kill her insteps, too.

The next hour consisted of handing out the flyers that promised a discount when the online code was used. A few folks wandered over to the booth and bought some accessories for their costumes. The longest line belonged to the company selling photo opps with the stars. A fan could pose with their favorite attending star for a mere forty to hundred dollars, depending on the celebrity popularity.

A group dressed as the Avengers strolled past, catching her attention. Could they be the people who tried to buy costumes from Harry with the stolen card? Of course, there would be more than a few Avengers attending today. It would be pretty ballsy for whoever used the stolen credit card numbers to attend. If her father was here, he would wave his index finger and explain, with a curl of his lip, that criminals were seldom as smart as television made them out to be. Most were impulsive creatures who took advantage of felonious opportunities. In other words, the perp would be dumb or arrogant enough, possibly both, to attend.

Whoever stole her identity could be casually weaving through the colorful pack of people crowded the aisles. They couldn't use her credit cards since she canceled them, but most of the vendors only had tablets or phone credit card scanners, which only ran the number. Did anyone even bother asking for ID? Right now, other folks' stolen cards could be running up thousands in merchandise.

Many merchants displayed a cash only sign, which surprised her. They probably didn't want to mess with weak cell signals to run plastic or fraudulent charges. A person could also arrive home with a collector figurine that cost a couple hundred and end up calling it in as a lost card, especially after the significant other exploded after seeing the price sticker. It also explained all the ATMs, too.

When Nala wasn't eyeing the visitors with suspicion, she speculated on what Tyler mean by *they could talk*. Then, there was Harry. His charge to assist her was sweet. Maybe Karly was right about him. True, she was helping the man out, but he offered to let her advertise her date research service. Unfortunately, she'd left the signage in the car, which was parked back at the office. So much for good ideas.

She smiled inattentively at visitors as she handed out the flyers. When she reached the end of her stack, Harry handed her another one.

Yay! She pivoted in time to see Karly with Elvin. She blinked. *Surely not*. Karly saw her, waved wildly, and steered Elvin toward the booth.

Her friend whipped out her cell phone and shoved it at Elvin. "Take our picture."

"Okay, but I'll need a selfie of the three of us." The two of them smiled as Elvin clicked away. Nala decided to ask about the obvious. "You got Elvin to come to the Con? I thought you were here to meet men."

"He asked me to come since he didn't want to come alone. Something about some online chatter possibly from your identity thieves who bragged online about going to Comic Con. He told me going solo would make him look peculiar."

A woman dressed as a green Orion slave girl strolled by on the arm of a stormtrooper.

"I think he'd fit in. Besides, if he knew the name of the people, he could call the police. Why didn't he call me?"

"Tried. Apparently, you aren't answering your phone."

Her hands patted down her costume. "No room here for phones. Too loud to hear it, even if someone did call me."

"Elvin," Karly asked as he joined them, "what did you hear that made you think at least some of the thieves would be here?"

"Your chicken-wing boy bragged about it." He handed the phone back to Karly and crossed his arms. He started to lean back against the booth partition to affect his cool persona.

Harry warned him off. "Don't do that. It's barely standing as it is."

Elvin straightened, settled for crossing his arms, and looked slightly awkward. "I surfed social media and found someone who went into detail about picking up the wings. Do read his version. You'd think he was picking up an arms shipment."

"Did you get his name?"

Elvin wrinkled his nose and buffed his name on his shirt. "The name on his account was Rod Steele. He had friends with names like Boy Toy and Soda Pop. I'm assuming they may be aliases.

"Fig bars!" It didn't take a PI to know that wasn't enough information to track down a person.

Elvin gave a heavy sigh and shook his head. "Nala, Nala."

"Stop that. You do *not* sound like Cary Grant when you do it. What's your incredible information that should help me to nail down my personal ID thief?"

He held up one finger. "He mentioned going as Captain America. His friends would be wearing superhero costumes, too."

Chapter Sixteen

HARRY RESPONDED TO the provocative information first. "It's my thief. The one who tried to charge eight Avenger uniforms on a stolen card." He pounded his fist into his hand. "Let's go get him."

Nala had never seen her mellow friend show so much aggression. She arched her eyebrows, said nothing, but tried to catch Karly's attention. Unfortunately, her friend was busy checking out a well-proportioned Batman. The muscles were probably all padding.

Elvin moved closer to the booth, blocking the exit. "Which Avenger costumes were ordered?"

"Ah," the agitated Harry took a breath and held up one hand. "Captain America, Panther, Wonder Woman, Wasp, Hawkeye, Antman, Scarlet Witch, and I was waiting on Hulk's hands when the card failed."

"No Thor? No Ironman?" Elvin teased, not taking into account Harry's agitation.

Harry shook his head, his eyes darting to the area over Elvin's shoulder, then shouted, "There he is!"

When Nala and Elvin turned to look for a skinny Captain America, Harry shot through the opening. Harry, dressed in a Green Lantern costume, blended into the crowd. He wasn't, unfortunately, the only person dressed as the Green Lantern. Several fans had donned their costumes for the opening day.

"What is *he* doing?" Nala verbalized her thoughts. "If anyone should chase the guy down, it should be me."

A couple dressed in street clothes strolled up to the booth, interrupting their discussion. The woman gestured to Nala's outfit. "I don't want the full effect. Yours looks good, though. Can we get some hats or something to get into the mood?"

What in the world did Harry expect to do? He wasn't a cop. Even as an investigator, she couldn't confront anyone. Once she had the goods on someone, she called in the proper authorities. Karly pushed past her as Nala stood, pondering the situation.

Her friend switched into sales mode, holding up some hair fascinators that gave a nod to various characters. She even picked up a pair of sunglasses that were made to look like a mask. "You get the attitude with none of the discomfort of a rubber band stretched around your head."

Nala located the price list stapled to the posts on the booth. A few minutes later, the couple purchased a couple of T-shirts, a hat with bat ears, and a black lace fascinator that draped across the front of the face. Fortunately, the credit card reader was similar to the one Karly used at the shelter, enabling her to charge the purchases.

The couple left, leaving Karly rearranging the merchandise. Her friend showed a natural inclination for sales. A twenty-dollar T-shirt was an easier decision than a pet that would need constant care, despite the fact it would also provide continual companionship. Nala sucked in her lips as she considered Harry's action.

"Why did he take off like that?" She squinted in the direction of his sprint, hoping to see a telltale beard paired with a green costume. Beards, natural and fake, graced a number of faces, and occasionally a female face. Cosplayer often dressed up as the opposite gender, which was no help. The long white beards could be discounted, though, especially when accompanied with a long gray robe.

Elvin gave a derisive snort and arched an eyebrow in her direction.

"What's that supposed to mean?"

He had the temerity to snort again, before speaking. "Broads. What can you do about them?"

The last thing she needed was Elvin quoting some old 1940s movie most living people had never seen or could relate to. She held up her hand to stop him. "I'm not a broad and no movie speak. No one knows half the movies you quote, anyhow."

"Yeah, and it's a shame, too." He sighed and shook his head. "The man was trying to be a hero."

"What?" She used her upraised hand to gesture to the costumed participants crowding the aisles. "Everyone here wants to be a hero."

Karly gave her a nudge with her elbow and waded into the conversation. "Except when they want to be a villain. Take Cat Woman, for example."

It always puzzled her as to why some comic characters should be labeled villains when they weren't too bad. They didn't kill anyone and just caused general mischief, while helping themselves to stuff that didn't belong to them. "Hard to say if she's a villain or not. I liked her some. Classic bad girl. Somehow that vibe even brings in superheroes."

A variety of expressions chased over Elvin's face until he held his hands out, palms up. "Listen to you two. I'm not talking about dressing up like a comic book character. I mean Harry wants to be *your* hero."

Karly punched her shoulder, adding, "Told you."

Elvin grimaced but continued talking. "Yours, Nala. Did you tell him about someone hacking your cards?"

Did she? Her shoulders went up in a shrug. "I don't know. I did tell him about my mother's card and that I had a client with a stolen identity. He told me there were a lot of people who had their identities stolen. I may have told him on the way to the convention center."

Her fingers went to her temples. Too bad she couldn't summon any superpowers. "I need to go find him before he does something crazy."

"Such as?" Elvin fingered a hat and put it on his head. He cocked his head in Karly's direction. "Do you think it makes me look dashing?"

Nala placed a hand over her mouth, not trusting herself not to laugh. Obviously, her friends were not taking this very seriously. Her lips firmed as she tried to figure out what Harry's next potential action might be. "I have no clue." She exhaled, thinking of all the guards placed around the area. "Security is tight. I think there was an incident at another Comic Con. All Harry would have to do is put his hand on someone, and he could be charged with assault."

Mental images of what could happen to Harry crowded her mind, including one of him in handcuffs being led to a squad car.

Elvin held up a hand mirror to evaluate how the long, striped scarf draped around his neck looked. A trio of customers were pawing through the accessories while Karly offered suggestions.

"I think you can hold down the booth while I locate Harry." She strode off in the general direction Harry had gone. The platform boots kept her from jogging, but the extra inches they provided allowed her to see more than she could normally. A few men tried to get her attention, but she ignored them as she worked her way through the crowd. One was unusually persistent, dogging her steps, whispering campy lines that were probably from a comic book.

Tyler's familiar voice cut through the icky stranger's monologue.

"Hey, Nala! Is this man bothering you?"

The security was there to keep things civil, as well as to keep anyone from sneaking in unauthorized props. Enterprising fans had created weapons that resembled the real thing. Some not so creative individuals tried to use real guns. "Yes."

As Tyler moved closer, her unwanted admirer slipped farther away, making Nala heave a sigh of relief. It was hard enough working her way through the crowds in the uncomfortable boots. She didn't need a stalker, too.

He tucked his thumbs into his equipment belt. "Looks like your problem vanished."

Truthfully, Nala never looked her follower in the face. She felt if she did, it would be viewed as encouragement. Besides, she didn't have time to be bothered with some creepy dude. Weird, how putting on a tight costume caused people to treat her totally different.

"Yeah, for now." She pivoted slowly, realizing there was a small cleared area around the two of them. She could see the glass entrance doors. Outside, a man dressed in a Green Lantern costume stood, gesturing wildly. It could be Harry. "Thanks. I think I see who I'm looking for."

Nala had taken a couple of steps toward the door when Tyler asked, "Need any more help?"

"No." A space opened up in the crowd, and she darted into it, allowing the momentum of the crowd to carry her toward the door.

Her hands hit the door bar, and she stumbled outside. The cool fresh air and traffic sounds were a welcome change from the dull roar of the Con crowds and the overheated interior. Inhaling deeply, she started toward the figure she felt certain was Harry. A sharp canine bark stopped her as she neared the man.

Max? What was Max doing here? In a move born of desperation and inspiration, she had asked Abby, her client, to take care of Max. It was totally unorthodox, but there was no one else. The convention folks were not willing to let Max be part of the booth. The insurance the vendors had to purchase did not cover the possibility of animal attack.

Her parents were her usual go-to dog sitters, but they were on vacation. Her fallbacks were Karly and Elvin who obviously decided to pair up and visit the conference. Even though her friends wouldn't admit to it, they were both on reconnaissance missions. Elvin might be searching for her identity thief. Single men were more likely Karly's target, although showing up with Elvin felt counter-productive. Maybe they'd agreed to split up once they arrived.

Whatever their motives, she'd ended up calling Abby to report what she'd found on her case, which wasn't all that much, and mentioned her dog sitting problem. Surprisingly, Abby offered her services, which worked. It wasn't like it would be an all-day thing since Harry agreed to let her go by three.

Across the street, Abby stood with Max seated beside her. Her hands curved around her mouth to magnify her voice as she yelled, "Nala Bonne!"

A male voice shouted, "What! Where!"

Nala spun in the direction of the voice and saw a pair of costumed males heading across the street. Unlike most of the convention attendees, she couldn't identify the costumes, but one had a blue tight-fitting shirt, leggings, and toted a shield. It might have been Captain America, but she wasn't sure.

The two men darted through traffic. One shot a worried look behind him. The pale, white face wasn't one she knew, but she had a gut feeling he might be her culprit. A cacophony of horns alerted her to Harry charging after them.

Brownies! The man was going to get himself killed. She had to do something, especially if Elvin was right about the man's motivation. "Wait! Harry!"

She stepped off the curb into the slow-moving traffic. Most were probably hopeful of finding a miraculous parking spot near the busy convention center entrance. The awkward platform boots made it feel like she was walking in slow motion. Harry had no issue with moving fast and reached the two before she could.

Even though the men were fleeing, not exactly the sign of bravery, two against one would never work out well. Harry tackled the first one, bringing the man to his knees. The one with the shield darted away, surprising even Nala, who expected some resistance.

A few onlookers shouted, "Fight! Fight!" The sound of barking came closer. The last thing she needed was Abby caught in the fray. Indecision gripped her as she cleared the curb. She needed to tell Abby to stay back, but Harry needed her help, too.

The two men rolled on the ground, trading punches. The man in the blue returned, clutching the shield against his chest. "Let my friend go!"

At least he returned, which was more than Nala expected when she saw him fleeing the scene. The man dropped the shield, revealing a gun.

"No!" Nala lunged in the direction of the man, but she was too far away. Harry, hearing her voice, looked up the same time the man aimed, and an airborne canine body arced through the air, hitting the gunman full force.

"Max!"

A whoop of a siren sounded as Max clamped down on the gunman's right arm. Security swarmed around them with some confusion about who did what. There was the possibility they would all be taken in for questioning, and then one of the arresting officers exclaimed, "It's Max!"

Chapter Seventeen

NALA THOUGHT FOR sure that having the arresting officer recognize Max would preclude her from making the trip downtown. It hadn't. At least she was allowed to come of her own volition, whereas they took Harry. Elvin volunteered to drive, and Max came along. He wasn't allowed to stay behind with Karly and Abby, after her client surprised her by volunteering to assist at the booth. The two women promised to stay until Harry returned.

Phones ringing competed with the shouts of a belligerent drunk. Looking around the station, Nala took in the busy officers and detectives. Max stuck his nose in her hand and sniffed, probably trying to determine if she had any tasty treats for him. She didn't. A uniformed officer brought in a pair of women dressed in minuscule skirts and plunging tops. The two women gave her a once over and a decisive sniff.

Really? Were they giving her the fish eye?

When their names were called, Elvin pulled some folded papers from his pocket. "I printed this out before I left. As you know, there has been a series of identity theft cases going on in Noblesville. I tried to find out what they all had in common and came up with nothing until I did discover there had been a breach in the medical community. Not too surprisingly, news of it wasn't publicized. Did you go to the hospital for anything?"

Going to the hospital was a big deal and not something she'd easily overlook. "No. Trust me, I'd remember that. I avoid the emergency room at all costs. I go to the immediate care center instead." Her lips pursed as she tried to remember any recent visits. "A month or two ago, I had a tetanus shot due to stepping on a nail. They prescribed some antibiotics, too."

Harry shrugged. "It makes me glad I don't go to the med check."

Thousands of people did. In doing so, they give up their vital information, as well as billing information. "Makes me wonder how many residents have been affected."

They walked into the small office, took the proffered chairs, and Max laid down beside Nala. The middle-aged detective, who was turning silver at the temples, gave their costumes a glance, then asked, "You're local, right?"

"Yes." Nala answered in unison with Elvin and Harry. Normally, she never used her father's name or reputation to ease her path. Frankly, she didn't need it usually. "I'm Nala Bonne, Captain Bonne's daughter."

The detective gave a chuckle and shook his head. "I should have known. That must be your crime fighter outfit. I heard the famous Max was involved in the takedown."

As if on cue, Max sat up and gave a single bark.

"He was, and he's up to date on all his shots." She gestured to her outfit. "As for this, all I can say is it was a favor."

Her remark made the man grin. "Oh, I expected as much. I should have introduced myself when you came in. Detective Ramirez. I'm sure you three might be able to clear things up for me. The officers on the scene claimed assault and threatening with a weapon from the two in the interrogation box. I never got a clear reason for why you would attack them. They spent time blaming each other. Claiming the other got greedy, then they griped about you."

"Me!" Nala pressed her palm against her chest. Why in the world would the thugs gripe about her?

"Practically admitted their guilt. They weren't talking to me, but we left them in a room by themselves to see what they might say. They didn't understand why you were tracking them down. Why you couldn't just change your credit cards like everyone else did?"

Her bottom jaw dropped. Lemon bars! They ripped off as many people as they could and were upset that someone might not take kindly to it. They had to be stupid or total sociopaths. Nala wiggled on the padded, vinyl cushioned chair. It made an embarrassing sound she hastened to explain. "It was the chair."

The men's exchanged smiles seemed to deny her statement. Nala held up her hand to protest their assumption. "It was the chair. My costume stuck to it. Anyhow, as for the case, as an investigator, I would want to know who stole my identity. I have a client who also had her identity stolen. If I can't figure out who and how her identity was taken, how can I prevent it from happening in the future? These particular creeps stole my identity and several other folks, too. Even Harry felt the bite of their credit card scam."

Ramirez held both hands up. "Okay, okay, I understand. Yeah, you're definitely Graham Bonne's daughter. What I need from the three of you is to swear out complaints, if you want to. It will be helpful especially since the culprits want to press charges against the guy in the green."

"What?" Harry jumped up from his chair. "For what?"

"Assault."

"I was only trying to stop them."

"Attacking people isn't the way."

The memory of Harry flying through the air stuck in her mind.

Had he tackled the fleeing perp or had he tripped? "He may have tripped and fallen into the culprit. The sidewalk is buckled in that area. The city should really do something about it." She debated against mentioning she almost fell, too. In her boots, the fact she didn't fall would make her friend's trip sound suspicious.

"Harry is not a violent person. He called out several times, but the men never stopped. They broke into a run."

"That's what happened." Harry agreed, shooting her a relieved smile.

Ramirez raised an eyebrow but didn't comment.

The crinkle of paper sounded as Elvin slid the papers he brought across the detective's desk. "Take a look at these. These may have been small-time perps, but they have some major hacking skills. They broke into a medical billing system via a backdoor, probably a third-party biller. They probably would have gotten away with it if they hadn't felt the need to brag on social media."

"Hmm." The detective perused the papers, then gave Elvin a curious stare. "Looks to me like you're pretty good at hacking into things yourself."

Instead of making Elvin cringe in fear, he puffed up a little and gloated. "I'm very good at what I do." He reached into his pocket and pulled out a business card. "I've helped agencies and law enforcement across the states. Nala asked for my assistance in her case."

"He's my subcontractor," she felt the need to point out.

"All right." The detective looked at his computer. "Printing out your reports now. You can sign them. Later, you may be asked to testify. You can sign and then go back to your costume party."

Harry cleared his throat. "It's Indianapolis Comic Con, which brings major money to the city."

"Got it."

The three of them signed papers and left. As they were leaving, Nala noticed nothing had been said about Max. In dog bite cases, the dog is often incarcerated in quarantine to prove that it isn't vicious or have rabies. "Looks like Max has the benefit of my father's reputation."

Elvin laughed. "I think it may have served you well, too."

"I didn't do anything wrong."

"True, but it may have taken longer to work it out."

By then, Harry had removed his mask and looked a little frazzled. He shot a hand through his hair. "I just hope my booth is okay. Not sure how well it will do without anyone there modeling the merchandise."

"Your merchandise is killing me." She tried to wiggle her toes inside the boots without any real luck. "If Frankenstein had to wear boots like this, it would explain his grumpy nature."

"No worries." Elvin slapped Harry on the back. "You have two attractive babes in the booth. The merchandise should sell itself."

The words may have been meant to reassure Harry, but when they arrived at the center, they discovered a crowd around the booth. The attendees were in a couple of straggly lines, commenting how fortunate they were to happen onto a sale at the beginning of the Con as opposed to the end of it, when most of the merchandise had been sold.

The word *sale* made Harry groan. Nala could have told her friend a sale didn't necessarily mean the prices on his goods were cut. Many stores raised prices, then cut them again. All you had to do was plaster that four-letter word on something, and it attracted customers.

They battled their way into the booth with a few grumbling

loudly, thinking they were line jumpers. Harry jumped into action in the booth while Nala took advantage of the empty folding chair and slowly removed her boots. By this time, they had practically adhered to her feet. It might take a butter knife to separate the boots from her skin.

Max had to stay outside the building with security, but Nala promised she'd only be inside a second to retrieve her purse and shoes. Elvin promised to take her to her car that was parked by her office. Boots off, she moaned in relief and closed her eyes.

"Glad you're back."

Nala opened her eyes to see who was happy to see her. Abby stared at her with an expectant look. *Great.* She had solved her own case, but two more had opened up. It would be nice if her hackers were somehow responsible for Abby's troubles, but she thought not.

"What can I do for you?"

"Well, I was wondering if you found out anything more about my identity thief considering how you hightailed it out of here."

A person might legitimately think that. "I don't know. We did catch some hackers who managed to work their way into medical billing records. Do you recall going to an urgent care facility in the last couple of months?"

"Why the last couple of months?" Abby's brows drew together as she asked. "No. I never go to the doctor, med check, or anything like that. I have the curse of being stalwart stock, which means I get double the work when anyone else is sick at work, which they often are."

Snickerdoodles. That killed that lead, although her gut had already told her it wasn't these guys. Mainly because they wouldn't be ordering a bikini or hanging out to get it. "Well then, it's up to Max to pick up any new scent leads."

Personally, nothing she said filled Nala with confidence, but at this time, it was all she had. Before she could say as much to Abby, Elvin squeezed himself into the small booth interior. "Hello, ladies. I was wondering if I could interest you in some lunch?"

Abby answered before Nala could. "No. We're on a case. No time to waste."

Max would be sad to hear that. Still, the frost lacing Abby's voice made it clear that the casual invite did not charm. If Elvin had hoped to strike up a renewed acquaintance with Abby, he could have at least used her name.

Maybe her attempt to fill in awkward silence would smooth things out. "We'll head out as soon as I put my shoes on."

Elvin held out his hands, looking a little dazed at how swiftly Abby had shot him down. As a reasonably attractive guy, he probably got a decent return on his practiced banter, though never anything long term, obviously. Finally, he managed to sputter, "I was going to drive you to your car."

He did say that. She'd forgotten.

Abby chimed in. "I can do that. I already have the back seat set up for Max, too."

Not knowing what to do, Nala shrugged in Elvin's direction, then nodded at Abby. "As soon as I get normal shoes on, we can head out. I'll get my bag and change at your place if you don't mind. Not sure if I could manage to peel out of this costume in the tiny public restroom stalls."

"No problem. It will be fun to see what Barb does when she sees you in that costume. No telling what she might come up with."

The joking remark reminded her that at this point Barb's eyes and Max's nose were the biggest leads she had on the case. Most people would say you couldn't nail an identity thief, but she'd already caught hers. Hopefully the same will be said for Abby's. "Yeah, about your neighbor—" Nala pulled on her black flats and left the toe pinching boots on the floor. She kicked them under the table just to keep them from tripping anyone. "I need to talk to her."

Abby nodded. "I suggest you do it in the outfit. It will make her so curious she won't have time to embroider the truth."

The two of them headed out after grabbing the needed stuff and giving their goodbyes all around. Personally, Nala would like to call it a day, but an investigator's work was never done. Technically, Abby was the only person paying her, too.

Chapter Eighteen

ABBY STRODE OUT of the conference center with a jaunty bounce in her step. She'd shut Elvin down. *Good.* He deserved it for not only *not* calling her after their second date but also pretending he didn't know her. He never even used her name when he suggested taking her and Nala out to lunch. It would have been worse if he'd forgotten her name, which could have been a possibility, but he then acted all jolly, like he was doing them a favor. She wasn't sure how Nala and Elvin were involved. He could be a relative or something. Or worse, a boyfriend.

Outside the center, Max gave a welcoming woof. Nala knelt beside her dog and gave him a welcoming hug. Up to now, Abby always thought of herself as a cat person but was beginning to see the benefits of dogs, too, not that Bruno, her cat, would approve of another pet. The rescue feline could be demanding and rather territorial. Sometimes, she jokingly called him her *bad boyfriend*, who wanted everything his way but never cared about what she wanted. A dog tended to be more social, or so she thought. A dog, especially one like Max, would keep unwanted visitors away.

The three of them strolled the four blocks to her car, talking about the convention as if they'd been friends forever. Abby decided to take the plunge and ask, "Are you and Elvin seeing each other?"

"What?" Nala stumbled to a stop and reached out to a nearby building for support. "Did I hear you right?"

From the woman's response, she would say it was an unequivocal *no*. "I asked if you and Elvin were an item?"

"Are you asking if I'm in an annoying, sibling type of relationship?"

"No." She had to laugh since the two of them bore no resemblance to one another outside of the basics of having two arms, two legs, etc. "Romantic."

"Sugar cookies! I mean…" She inhaled once, then explained, "I've known Elvin since school. He's a good subcontractor for me and gets the job done. As for dating?" She shook her head. "I know him too well."

"What's that supposed to mean?" She assumed it meant that the man was the love'em and leave'em type, as she originally thought. It made her glad she froze him out as Karly had instructed her to do.

"Ah," Nala wrinkled her nose, then went for a wobbly smile. "I know you'll read in advice columns that it's good for couples to start out as friends, but I'm not sure I believe that. With friends, you know about all their idiosyncrasies and love them in spite of them. Trust me—Elvin has plenty."

Instead of responding verbally, Abby gave a short nod. As for the issues, she'd noticed a few and suspected a couple more.

Nala continued speaking, taking the nod for affirmation. "When you start dating someone, for the most part, you really don't know anything about them. Often, when you get to know them better, you stop dating them. The revealing of traits and habits that might be deal breakers are gradual. Although," she held up one finger, "I've heard with everything being on social media now that some people just stroll through their feed to get to know the person better. I hear it's the equivalent of six dates. Saves money and heartache."

"Wow! That's depressing. Is that what you do?" There hadn't

been anyone currently in her life she cared to tiptoe through their pages to see their various likes and comments. Then, there was the other issue. She hadn't been involved in social media too much, either. Her father considered it a danger, a way for kids to cyber bully one another. When he refused to allow her to have an account as a teen, at first, she was upset, but gradually forgot about it. Those who were all about friending each other faded away without any explanation. If they had any friends left, it was probably on social media.

"No." Nala had dropped her hand and grimaced. "You'd think that. Most of the time I spend on social media is for work. I do some insurance work, too. Companies pay out disability to employees that are in too much pain to come to work, but on their social media feed, they're jumping on trampolines, skydiving, and dancing on the stage with a male stripper."

The images made her laugh, then shake her head in disbelief. "You're kidding me. Who would be stupid enough to do that?"

"Lots of folks. We tracked down my identity thief because he couldn't resist bragging to friends."

A tiny bubble of expectation grew in her stomach and worked its way upward through her esophagus making her voice squeak on her question. "Does that mean you got my thief, too?"

"Not yet. I don't think, at least."

Abby gestured to her car, and the three of them turned in that direction. Three dogs crowded the window in a nearby vehicle and erupted into a barking frenzy as they approached. She glanced at the car, then back at Nala who raised her eyebrows in silent inquiry.

"Yeah, I considered opening the door and rolling down the window some more, but it could be the person ran into one of the nearby shops for a second."

A low *ah* sounded, making Abby do a doubletake. Nala explained. "Allergies have that effect on my voice" She cleared her throat. "I hope to gain something from Barb, since she obviously watches everything that goes on in your apartment quad."

Sometimes, Abby felt sorry for the eagle-eyed woman since she didn't provide any fodder for the curious neighbor. The most interesting thing lately was coming home to get a package in the middle of the day—that wasn't even hers and not there. "That she does."

"Makes sense the woman might see who came into your apartment."

They'd already discussed this the night Nala and Max first came over. "I told you, no one."

"No one you *knew*."

She held up one hand as if to protest. "I'd know if I gave my key out to someone. Never did. I didn't really trust anyone to hold my key for me. One of them is on my keychain. The other is in my desk at work. I thought it would be foolish to keep an extra key at the apartment, then get locked out."

"Makes sense." Nala took a deep breath as if readying herself for a big announcement.

A quick punch on Abby's fob unlocked the car.

Max, familiar with the drill, scrambled into the back seat. Nala slid into the passenger seat and waited until both doors closed before completing her thought. "My goal is to find your identity thief. Sometimes, it's not always possible. It doesn't mean I'm going to stop trying. Just felt the need to be honest."

The words came as no surprise as she started the car. Getting into the flow of traffic and into the right lane absorbed her attention. "Tell me which way to turn to get to your office."

"You're doing good. At the next light, turn right. Why did you decide to bring Max to the conference?"

"It was the weirdest thing. I was sitting in my apartment and I heard a voice." She knew what she was about to say would make her sound bonkers. "It told me go to the conference. May have been the television since it was on. Anyhow, I decided to stop by."

They drove in silence for a few minutes. Nala probably thought she was crazy. Rapid repartee was not Abby's strong point, which made her feel she didn't stand a chance at flirting or even the whole romance game until today.

"I'd like to find the sneaky person who made free with my credit. In some ways, I'd like to know who this person is that is managing to live a much more exciting life than I do while using my name, my credit, and ironically, my general looks. While at the booth, I was joking about it with Karly. She pointed out there was no reason for me not to enjoy the same perks as fake me, except I wouldn't be lifting any credit card digits."

"Working at Harry's booth caused an epiphany of sorts?"

Epiphany made it sound somewhat spiritual, but she wasn't sure if that is exactly what happened. Nala pointed to the left, and Abby started the slow process of switching lanes on the jam-packed city street. Most motorists were more interested in their cell phones or the passengers, which usually included children, or even eating than driving. A man who was stuffing a donut into his mouth allowed enough space between cars for her to slide over.

The theft incident got her thinking. She worked hard, paid her bills on time, lived frugally only to have her ID stolen. "I was angry when I got my identity stolen. Then, when I saw what the thief was charging, it made me madder. Whoever it was had a better life than me. At one point, I started thinking I could be living that life, too.

Not stealing people's credit but going on vacation to an exotic locale. The only thing stopping me was me."

"Why is that?"

Another question that Abby found herself exploring in her booth time. "I guess I never thought I was the type of person who would take off on a tropical vacation."

"Your only qualification is that you want to go. I've heard some cruise ships are making solo accommodations to keep the price down. If you want to go, then you are the type of person who goes on exotic vacations. My grandmother would tell you not to wait your life away. Maybe you're waiting for someone who will whisk you away on the vacation of your dreams, and you can wait, only to find that person never shows up. Too many of my mother's friends have husbands that don't want to travel. Those same women are always complaining that they wished they had traveled when they were young and single. You've got the chance right now."

She *did* have the chance. It was an unexpected realization. Her father had worked so hard to make sure her life was unexciting. Abby kept on keeping her life boring, sure that's what it was supposed to be. Karly, Nala, and Max had opened up new possibilities.

"This is it. I'll get in my car and follow you back to your apartment."

There was a convenient space behind the beetle, which Abby took. The car exchange took less than five minutes, and they were all on their way in a mini-convoy.

Chapter Nineteen

THERE WAS SOMETHING not quite right about the aging building that contained her third-floor office. Nala gave it a backward glance as she pulled out to follow Abby's car. Even Max gave the building a lingering look. Maybe he felt it, too.

"What's up, boy?"

"Don't know." He made a blubbery exhale that shook his lips. "Thought I saw something."

A quick glance in the rear-view mirror showed a lone car parked next to the curb and empty sidewalks. During the day there were a few dog walkers, along with the mail person, but the location didn't attract people. There were no trendy stores, coffee shops, or restaurants. No real reason for any type of foot traffic. Twice a year during the marathon and half-marathon, runners passed through this district. It had less traffic and was easier to cordon off than the major streets.

"A person?" It was the more likely thing, although Max would respond to other dogs, cats, and assorted wildlife.

"Could be. Just a shadow." He managed an awkward turn in the passenger seat to look behind him. "Nothing now."

"I'm sure it was nothing." A prickly feeling at the base of her spine said otherwise, but she didn't have time for this. Currently, she had one client, and she needed to take care of that case. Harry would notice if anything was up when he came back to stock up on any items he sold out of at the Con. She could call him tonight and see. It might make her sound a trifle paranoid, but she had reason to be so. Too bad she'd never got in touch with the super.

"Did you call the lightbulb guy?"

Max's question startled her since it had been exactly what she was pondering. "No, but I will. Guess it won't do any good today, but then again, I can always leave a message on his machine."

"Yep," Max replied as he stared out the window. They passed a car with a yappy dog in the driver's lap. "Bark! Bark! Bark! Bark!"

"Stop it!"

A large canine in a small car was tough enough, but the noise of a large, barking dog was painful, especially with the windows rolled up. Thankfully, Max stopped barking and swung his head in her direction. His brows were beetled together. "First, you tell me to not speak in human around anybody but you. I do that. Now, you're telling me not to use my native tongue."

"It's not that." She hated it when her dog made a legitimate point. "You can talk in your native tongue all day long, but not in the car or at such high decibels. I'm surprised dogs aren't deaf with their sensitive hearing and all."

Max tried a few high-pitched yodeling sounds.

"What are you doing?"

"Testing my hearing. High pitches go first. I'm not deaf if you wanted to know."

"Good. Great." Actually, she never suspected he was, not when he could hear her open a bag of chips three rooms away. "We're headed to Abby's. I want you to go over the scents."

Max moaned. "Not that! I just did that before we came to the Con. The smells are the same. She did have fish a couple of days ago. Not sure what you want if I have nothing to compare it to. The police need to make a smell database."

"I'll tell dad as soon as he gets back." Even though she was joking, her dog lifted his head with pride. "It will revolutionize the crime solving industry."

Max would ask her every day if she had talked to her father. Then again, he might forget, easily distracted by a random dog or cheeseburger. Since it was still daylight, it was easy to keep pace with Abby. Even if she lost her, she still had the address in her phone navigation.

Her investigation relied on being able to question the gossipy neighbor. With luck, the woman would be home. If the woman could describe anyone going into the apartment, she'd hit the jackpot. "I've been fortunate that I never lived in an apartment."

Max glanced away from his survey of the buildings that flashed by the window. He was probably searching for a burger joint. "How so?"

"I probably couldn't have you. Most apartments, if they allow dogs, have a weight limit."

"That's just wrong!"

"I agree. I imagine small dogs could tear up stuff just as well as a big dog. Children, even more so. Adults can trash a place, but they allow them to rent."

"Not fair. Large dog discrimination."

"There's that."

Abby's car turned in to the apartment complex, with Nala keeping a safe distance between them. It wouldn't do to hit the client. Besides basic business protocol, she was really starting to like the woman. They shared a lot of similarities, single professional women with rescue pets, no time for a social life, and no romantic entanglements. There were probably a ton of women that shared similar traits, but Nala hadn't met them.

If she had ever lived in an apartment, she might be better versed in the different things that made up apartment life. Perhaps the intruder came in when Abby slipped downstairs to toss her trash. If so, it would have been a crime of opportunity, which would indicate it had to be someone in the complex, probably nearby.

Nala parked the car, turned off the ignition, and cut her eyes to Max. "Remember, you're looking for a scent. No human conversation and no chasing the cat."

"Geesh. You think I don't know how to do my job."

Instead of answering, she managed a tight smile and climbed out of the car. Too often, she found herself arguing with her dog about the most trivial things. When she caught herself doing it, she stopped, appalled at her actions. At school, she made a vow not to argue with her students. Somehow, she forgot that vow when it came to her canine.

Abby stood by her car and waited as if Nala and Max might not be able to find the apartment they had already visited. They walked up together. Abby was still enthralled by the Black Widow outfit.

"I wouldn't mind working in an outfit like yours. It covers everything and remains classy. Not like some of those other outfits."

No need to describe the ones she meant. They had both seen plenty at the con. "I wasn't too thrilled about any of those and told Harry no way I'd wear those tiny costumes. He didn't insist on it. He guessed correctly he'd be without help if he did."

They both chuckled over the possibility of a pair of fishnet hose or a leatherette bustier having Harry manning the booth alone.

As if part of a cuckoo clock mechanism, the neighbor's door flew open, and a white-haired Barbara popped out with an interested mien. As if delighted, she placed her hands together, just a tad below the glasses perched on her nose. "Goodness, this is Grand Central Station today."

Abby looked around the small landing that only contained three doors. "What do you mean?"

Fate must have taken a hand in this. Nala smiled at the woman, praying she'd elaborate.

"Well," Barbara started and placed a hand on her chest. "I'd hoped to take a nap today. My nerves aren't what they use to be." She pointed to Max "You know you *can't* keep a dog that size in the complex."

The woman was going off course. Nala patted her dog. "He's mine. We're only here for a short visit."

Barbara gave Max a second look, then surprisingly bent to pet him. "I had a shepherd mix when I was a kid. Good dog to have around. They keep a place safe. Might have needed one today with all the comings and goings."

Abby managed to catch Nala's eye and gave a short nod, as if to say this is how the woman talked. Since her goal had been to talk to Barbara, it would be better if she had initiated the conversation. People talked more if they took the conversational lead as opposed to being prodded. "What sort of shenanigans have been happening?"

"Shenanigans sums it up. First," she gestured to the far door, "Loraine has a new man. Not much better than the old one, if you ask me. He moved all his stuff in today. It wasn't much. A big screen television with these huge speakers." She stretched her hands out about a meter, and Abby groaned. "He had a couple of black garbage bags I assume were clothes and a case of whiskey."

He didn't sound like a keeper in Nala's opinion. After her ill-fated relationship with Jeff, she came to the conclusion that any man worth having would ask you to move in with him or better yet, propose. The thing of moving in with a woman smacked of freeloading. Abby's neighbor would find herself cooking and cleaning up after the man for the doubtful pleasure of his company.

Abby stared at the third door either expecting it to burst into flames or maybe hoping to set it aflame with her gaze. Looked like all conversational prompts were up to Nala, as they should be. "Wow! That sounds exciting. Anything else noteworthy happen?"

Barbara's eyes rolled upward and crossed her arms. "Someone's car alarm went off. Can't say if someone was getting robbed or if it was just those annoying skateboarding kids who bump into everything."

Well, that was no lead. "Did Abby get any deliveries today?"

Both Abby and Barbara stared at her if she'd suddenly turned an interesting shade of blue. Finally, the neighbor gestured to the door with the simple welcome mat. "I don't see anything." She addressed Abby, "Were you expecting anything?"

Not knowing what her lines were, Abby managed a weak smile and shrugged. "Not really."

"It's hard to get a delivery when you don't order something first."

The woman's tone was a bit patronizing, but Abby had already informed Nala that being nosy was Barbara's good trait. This was so not going as she wanted. Abby already had her keys out and stepped closer to her door. It signaled the end of the conversation, but Barbara didn't see it that way.

"Hey, I heard you got new lightbulbs in your place."

"Huh?" Abby turned away from the door to face her neighbor. "What do you mean?"

This sounded promising. Even Max perked up his ears to listen.

"The light bulbs. You asked for some new energy saving lightbulbs, and that chick from the front office came by to install them. She told me it was a special service. My question was does special mean *free*? I've been replacing light bulbs all on my own dime. This place never struck me as some place that would do anything free."

Nala managed to catch Abby's attention. From her slightly startled expression, it meant she shared a similar thought. It would be best to nail the possibility down. Nala asked, settling an inquisitive gaze on Barbara. "Is she coming back to install the bulbs?"

"Oh no, she walked right on in. The management has passkeys, you know. Mainly, it's to shut off water or gas when needed. Mostly, I think they use it to evict people. Legally, I think they're supposed to do all this paperwork, but I've seen them more than once drag people's junk out on the landing, then put one of those real estate locks on the door. The kind who get evicted usually aren't the type to hire a lawyer."

The information made her determined to check out the inside of the apartment. Nala smiled at the woman. "It's been nice talking to you, but Abby hasn't been feeling well and—"

Abby wavered a little, then clutched the door handle. Barbara held up a hand to her face and hurried back into her apartment. Nala, Max, and Abby ducked into her apartment and closed the door before speaking.

"That's as fast as I've seen that woman ever move."

Nala held up one finger, "Did you catch that you had an uninvited visitor?"

A strident meow pierced the air as Bruno strolled into the living room with his tail held high. He complained, butting against Abby, but ignoring both Nala and Max.

Instead of focusing on her cat, Abby dashed to the bedroom while Max put his nose to the floor. "Oh boy! It's the same scent."

"Shush!" Nala didn't get to say anymore before Abby returned.

"I locked Bruno in the bedroom. He doesn't mind since his cat box and food are in there. I also noticed my file cabinet had been opened. It wasn't fully closed."

The fact she never even considered the management company bugged Nala. It wasn't necessarily the company, but one or two individuals. "You know the woman Barb was talking about?"

"I've dealt with her once or twice. She's not very professional. Made me wait while she conversed with a friend about an upcoming party."

"Sounds like the type to book a tropical getaway or order a bikini with someone else's card? Better yet, does she look like you?"

Abby's face went through a series of contortions from lips pursed to nose wrinkling to finally brow lifting. It appeared like she was doing those facial exercises that were supposed to stave off the need for a facelift. "I would have said no, but I was trying to imagine her not in the skin-tight clothes she wears and the two tons of makeup. She's about the right height, hair and skin color. I imagine if Barb saw her briefly, she might have thought it was me, especially if she wasn't wearing her glasses, which she sometimes does. I don't even know the office woman's name."

"We'll need it." With a name, hopefully her real one, all types of information could be found online. For a deeper search, she'd need Elvin's connections.

"Then we can report her!" The upbeat swing of Abby's voice told her feelings on the matter. "I can't wait to nail her." She pounded her fist into her other hand.

"We'll get her," Nala promised, but made sure to cross the fingers on her left hand as she did so. "We can't go to the police and say she did it. Not enough evidence. They might see it as people badmouthing each other. To do that we will set a trap—one so irresistible that your particular rat won't be able to help *her*self."

Chapter Twenty

AFTER A BRIEF discussion, Abby and Nala came up with the plan to drop by the front office and report cockroaches in the apartment as an excuse. They needed the woman's name to be able to run a background check.

A discordant meow had Abby opening the bedroom door. "I think it's safe for you two to get acquainted."

"Okay." Nala nodded in Max's direction. "You watch the apartment while Abby and I visit the office."

The canine's ears tipped forward while Bruno gave a meow, perhaps commenting on his exclusion. "Do you think I should have included your cat?"

Abby hung her purse on her shoulder and made a face. "Not sure why. He's allowed the thief to enter at will without even the slightest resistance."

"Not sure what you expect a cat to do."

She paused, wrinkling her nose, then shrugged her shoulders. "Oh, I don't know. Maybe he'd leap on her with his claws extended. Kinda like in those kids' movies."

No need to explain those were trained animals used specifically for television and movies. Her eyes dropped to the overweight cat. Any gymnastic leaps would be beyond the feline. "Oh well, let's go. You report, and I'll be your witness. She should have a nameplate on her desk."

After locking the door behind her, Abby moved around Nala and walked with a confident stride as she proceeded down the stairs. A few jogging steps allowed her to catch up with her client.

"Wow! You're a fast walker."

"Not really." Abby slowed her gait a little. "I guess I'm a little excited about playing a part in this sting to get the freeloader who had the nerve to steal my information. Makes me wonder to how many people she's done likewise."

"As many as possible. It may be a con she has done several times. With the tracking that comes with online orders, she can tell when an order is arriving. All she has to do is to stop by and pick it up. She might miss a couple, and a few people may wonder why they got something or mistakenly think it's a gift. When things get messy, she moves."

The sound of laughter behind them stopped Nala in mid-thought. It was hard to know who was in on the scam. Her companion turned and raised her eyes in inquiry. The best she could do was angle her head to the talkers behind her. Abby's mouth rounded, then a look of comprehension filled her eyes as she spoke.

"Is Harry going to have you work the rest of the conference?"

"That was the plan. I don't know now. Obviously, I'm here. You and Karly were doing a better job than I was."

"That we were. Karly had me check out the other booths to see what their prices were. Harry basically has the best prices. There were a few with lower prices, but not much merchandise. We figured people end up at some booth and buy stuff, failing to come back to the booths they passed. Karly came up with the sale sign to get people to stop. She even offered to meet prices if they found the same thing in the hall at a cheaper price."

The couple behind them veered off as they hit the parking lot.

Nala kept to the subject, aware she had no clue who were her thief's accomplices or if she even had any. Data showed men tended to conduct crimes with other men, which was why they got caught. Women tended to act on their own, possibly not trusting men who often bragged after a few beers.

Abby gestured to the wood-shingled building. "There's the office. Half the time the door is locked. We might get lucky."

"Let's hope so." No need to add she didn't have a lot of time to spend on the case since her spring break was ending soon. She kept hoping to quit her pre-school job permanently, but that hadn't happened so far. Technically, she was her own sub. She'd tried to quit last semester, but her principal talked her into acting as a sub until a replacement was found. So far, none applied for the position. Nala had her suspicions that dealing with rambunctious preschoolers did not appeal. Could be her class's reputation had gotten out to the general public. Too bad she used her one big case payout to pay a year's rent. It helped month to month but didn't pay the rest of the bills.

Abby stepped onto the winding sidewalk that led to the office. Weeds squeezed out of the cracks in the cement. Cigarette butts, discarded candy bar wrappers, and a crushed soda can decorated the walk. Her father would see the trash and bring up his broken windows theory that once someone vandalized a home or a building, the whole area would follow suit unless the damage was cleaned up immediately. That was why a broken window in a vacant house was the kiss of death. At least there were no windows broken in the complex.

The office door swung open, which was a plus. The two of them walked in, unnoticed, as music blared. The lone occupant was a uniformed waitress with her back to them, sitting in front of a computer. On the computer screen was a popular shopping site. The woman's attention was on her phone, though.

The desk was crowded with Styrofoam cups and magazines. A lit cigarette rested in the ashtray. No nameplate in sight or a handy business card holder rested on the surface. *Great.* She'd have to go with the surprise attack. Her father taught her most people told the truth when surprised. It didn't give them the time to search for an answer.

"Lacey! It's me, your old locker partner, Nadine Collins!" She chose a fake name just in case Abby had left something in the apartment with Nala's name on it.

The woman jumped a little and stared at Nala who made sure to block Abby. "I, uh, am not Lacey."

She reached for the cigarette, which Nala knew was a stalling technique and forced her to up her game. Her flat palm hit the desk knocking a few items off of it. "Why are you lying to me?" Her voice was loud and confrontational. "I know you stole my boyfriend. You're welcome to him. I met someone much better. Lacey, what's your problem?"

For a tough character, the woman's shoulders went up. "I don't know what you're talking about. I'm no Lacey. My name is Greta Daniels. Never went to high school with you. As for your boyfriend, he's lucky to get away from such a crazy chick." She took a long draw from her cigarette, then stabbed it out. "What do you want?"

If she were Nadine Collins, that would have put her in her place. Nala took a step back and tried for a wobbly smile. "Sorry. I mistook you for someone else."

"What are you doing here, anyway?"

On cue, Abby stepped up and cleared her throat. "I came about my apartment."

That got Greta's attention. Her chin went up and she asked, "What about it?"

"Cockroaches."

"You must be leaving food out."

"No. I'm not. The place needs to be sprayed."

Nala was ready to applaud Abby as she worked her story. Greta appeared uninterested, yawned and rubbed the back of her neck. "We can't pay for pest control for every sloppy tenant."

Well, this wasn't going the way she planned. She got a new idea. "Forget about it, Abby. You got that big promotion, which means you won't be living here much longer anyhow. Let's go spend some more of that money on all that pretty bling. You need to treat yourself even more and celebrate big time."

Her client picked up the cue and added, "That's right. Think of this as my thirty-day notice."

"Suit yourself." Greta didn't even make a note of the surprising information, which meant Abby didn't have to carry through on the threat.

Act one of their play was done. Nala pushed the door open. Abby followed. They walked leisurely back to the apartment, allowing the cool spring breeze to blow away the stale smoke from the office. Once inside the apartment, it was safe to speak.

"All right, we got the name. I'll call Elvin. It could be an alias, but many of those are listed on the crime database."

Abby knelt to pat Max, then picked up Bruno who meowed his feelings about being greeted second. "They list the criminals' aliases?"

"Yes. Ironically, people tend to stay close to their own names when making up fake ones. Sometimes, it could be a maiden name. Many times, they will use the same first name over and over again. I guess they do it so it's a name they respond to. I hope Greta is the same."

"The name didn't suit her. Can Elvin find out if there are more people at the complex with identity theft issues?"

Her subcontractor shared information, but he didn't reveal his sources or even methods. In the beginning, she thought she'd be able to get him to share his connections, but that never happened. Besides, he was good at what he did and wasn't that expensive, at least for her. "He's already found that the city of Noblesville has had a spate of identity thefts, but I certainly don't lay that all on Greta. She doesn't strike me as smart enough to have a far-reaching scam. At most, she could be a foot soldier."

Abby brought her fist up to her mouth and rested it against her lips for a few moments before she dropped it. "I agree about her not being the brains behind the operation. Still, I'd like to move. Anywhere, but here. Do you know someplace with reasonable rent?"

Max bumped up against her leg. Nala bent to caress the dog's ears. Most of the time, he rubbed up against her because he wanted attention, a treat, or to relay information. What could he be trying to tell her, if anything? The memory of seeing a *For Rent* sign in her neighborhood as she left came to her mind. One of her elderly neighbors and his children balked at the expense of updating the home for a sale that might not happen. Singles usually wanted the amenities of an apartment complex while families wanted neighborhoods with their own church, fire station, and commons.

"There's a place in my neighborhood. Small dated home, probably still has all the avocado green appliances. It can't be too much, considering I live in a fairly modest community."

"Sounds great! If you and Max live there, it must be okay."

Quiet, unassuming, would be how she'd described it. The last excitement was when Max attempted to herd the neighbor's grandchildren against their will. Their terrified screams had alerted Nala. Her dog loved the running and yelling game, but the kids, not so much.

"It's safe. Trust me, there's a dozen Barbaras watching the comings and goings of the residents. Most of the elderly dears are armchair sleuths and have the police department on speed dial. Tell you what, I'll call Elvin, then we'll swing by the house. I'm sure we can get someone to open it up for you to take a look."

Abby rocked up on her toes and clapped her hands together. "I can't believe it. Having my identity stolen should have been a horrible thing, but suddenly I met you, guys were hitting on me like crazy at the Con, and now I may have a better place to move to. Best of all, I got in the final word with Elvin."

Probably not. As verbose as Elvin was, no one got in the final word. Life interrupted the conversation, which he'd pick up as soon as they met again. Even now, Elvin was constructing his reply. Might as well call him. She pushed his speed dial number, put it on speaker while she conversed with Abby. "I admire your ability to look on the bright side."

The phone burbled until, "Yo! Batman here," assaulted her ear.

"You're not Batman, and at no time would the Dark Knight ever say *yo*."

"Spoiled sport."

It was tempting to call him on the remark, but decided not to, especially considering she needed his assistance. "Need your help."

"Expected as much."

His smug tone made Nala rolled her eyes while Abby mimicked gagging. If Elvin ever wanted her client back, he had his work cut out for him. It might be interesting to watch. "All right, boy wonder, we've tracked down Abby's identity thief."

"Hacker junior and crew?"

"No, it appears to be the apartment office manager, Greta Daniels. We don't think it's her real name. She's in her twenties. About five-seven, I think. She was seated, but the neighbor mistook her for Abby since they are somewhat similar in appearance."

Her remark caused Abby to make a derisive snort that could have carried over the phone.

Elvin asked, "What was that?"

"Ah, that. Must be Bruno, Abby's cat, hacking up a hairball. You know cats."

The maligned feline shot her a dark look as if he understood her.

"Anyhow, I want you to check and see if any of the Camelot apartment residences have had their identities stolen. The neighbor had seen Greta entering Abby's apartment without permission. She has the master key, which allows her to come and go as she pleases."

His guttural growl came over the speaker. "I could kick myself. It was so obvious. Of course, the apartment management would have access. I used to live in an apartment. There's a reasonable notice clause that the landlord or his lackeys have to give before entering an apartment. The exception would be in the case of a gas leak or a burst pipe."

"I kinda have the feeling these are not the reasonable notice type of people. I suspect they do very little repair at all."

"It doesn't sound like a good place for Abby. She deserves someplace much nicer and safer."

That man sounded like he cared, which surprised her. Judging by Abby's open mouth, she was in shock, too. "That may be. Just do the work on Greta for me. I'm pretty sure she has some associates here, but we can't finger them. We've set a trap for Greta. We mentioned a big bonus Abby got and how she already spent a bunch of money and we're going out to celebrate later. I know she'll be back for a return visit. I need the spy equipment I bought. The teddy bear nanny cam and stuff. I don't want to leave the apartment to retrieve it because I'm sure Miss Help Herself will be in the apartment as soon as Abby's car clears the lot."

There was a short put-out sigh. "Tell you what. I got similar stuff, except for the teddy bear cam. I'll bring it over and even set it up, but it doesn't prove that Greta took Abby's identity. At best, you get her breaking and entering on film. If you want theft you need to leave some bling around."

"I figured as much."

"Usually when thieves work in groups one will flip on the others for a lighter or no sentence."

"I thought of that, too. How about I go to my parents' house and grab some bling? You can wire up the place while Abby is here, then we can all take off together. We can watch the action go down elsewhere."

"Well, uhm…" Elvin paused, then asked, "Do you think Abby would be cool with me being over there?"

The person in question gave an emphatic nod. No need for him to know how eager she seemed to want his company. "It's a job. Do you think Batman ever asked Catwoman's permission to save the city?"

"That would be stupid."

"Exactly. See you in a little bit. I'll let Abby give you the address." She took the phone off speaker and handed it over. Once Max heard the jingle of her car keys, he strolled to the door.

She glanced back at the smiling woman on the phone. Whatever Elvin was saying, he was making headway. It was hard to say if that was a good thing. In all those romance novels she'd read in junior high school, all a man needed was the right woman to turn him around. Not sure if that would hold true for Elvin, but she was sure a few years of therapy wouldn't hurt, either.

Abby disconnected and handed the phone back. "Your mother's going to be okay using her jewelry as bait?"

"She's still on the trip, and she'll never know. It's not real diamonds, just pretty good fakes. My father would never have bought her the real stuff, calling it a handwritten invitation to a jewel thief. Ironically…" She shook her head, then continued. "The only people who can tell it is fake is a jeweler and a jewel thief. It's not that fashion jewelry you get at the mall that costs a couple hundred as opposed to a couple thousand. If something happens, which it won't, it'll give my father an excuse to buy her more jewelry. Didn't even take it on vacation because the travel agent warned about lavish bling displays. It'll be fine."

Even though, most of the time she'd promised something would be fine or easy, it wasn't.

Chapter Twenty-One

NALA'S GOAL WAS to buzz over to her mother's house and pick up the bling. Since it was still daylight, there should not be an embarrassing repeat of the previous visit. Her parents should be on land by tomorrow morning, although they may choose to stay an extra day to visit with friends on the way home. Her phone chirped. Not a number she knew.

More than likely, it would be someone who wanted to sell her stuff she didn't want or couldn't afford. The persistent salesperson would talk a mile a minute, convinced they would get their proverbial foot in the door. She shamelessly turned the phone off when a simple 'I'm not interested' didn't work.

Max gave her a significant look. She thumbed the phone on and was prepared to be offered a real deal on a funeral plot for two.

"Hello?"

"Is this Gwen Bonne's daughter?"

"It is." Not the way a usual sales call began. "Can I help you?"

"I hope you can, but I don't know with your mother being gone and all. Mona is stealing and she's out to steal your mother's customers and start her own firm."

There was a ring of certainty in the tired woman's voice. "Who is this?"

Her cell number wasn't listed as her business number, even though she gave it to her clients once they signed up for service. If someone had her number, it was intentional or the result of her signing up for the various giveaways to win free vacations. She always went for the places she'd like to go, such as Europe or the Caribbean."

"Raylene. You left me a message."

She had. "I'm so glad you called. Are you still in town?"

"Yeah, I'm crashing at my boyfriend's house. That witch Mona not only fired me, she threatened me, telling me I better get out of town. Wait. You're not working with Mona, are you?"

Nala felt like she just walked into the middle of a movie. "No, I'm not working with Mona. I have no clue what she's up to. Would you care to enlighten me?"

Muted voices sounded at the other end. The boyfriend might be weighing in on the smartness of calling. Finally, Raylene came back on the line. "Sorry. That was Jason. He's worried because Mona is seriously whacked."

"You know my mother."

"Of course."

"Have you met my father?"

"Once or twice. He seemed nice."

The term *nice* made her smile at the ridiculousness of calling Capitan Graham Bonne nice. It would be the same as calling a charging bull *cute*. "Neither one of them would be very happy with Mona. Tell me what you know."

"We've had problems with inventory and deliveries. Two wing chairs might be ordered, but only one gets delivered. I'm sent to go get something from the stockroom, and I could never find it. It was weird to have all these mishaps happening at the same time. One day, I walked into the stockroom while Mona was talking to the driver. He called her Mom."

"I never knew the delivery guy was related to Mona."

"No one does. When he said it, she told him to never say that again around Posh Interiors."

Things were starting to add up. Her father had talked her mother into the cruise since she'd been obsessing about her business. Looks like she had the right to worry. "What else do you know and why did Mona fire you?"

"She didn't know I knew about her son and stuff. I wasn't sure if the son was stealing for himself or Mom, but I heard her on the phone ordering black velvet paintings. Black velvet paintings! Even though I may not have any design training, I know enough not to order that junk. People who want that kinda thing can pick it up at a flea market."

Fortunately, Nala was able to drive the familiar route without too much attention to the road. It was just as well since she found herself immersed in the Mona-goes-crazy story. Had her mother ever said anything negative about the woman?

Her mother *had* made an off-handed comment about the woman having a strong initiative. Not one of those workers you had to tell to do everything. Mona could come up with ideas of her own, but many her mother would not approve or like.

"Do you think she knows you heard?"

"No, that's the weird part. The other day she comes in and starts screaming at me. Tells me to get out of her sight and go back to Mexico."

That would have been right about the time Nala canceled the card and after the order from Mexico. The woman was trying to frame Raylene and scare her bad enough she'd leave town.

"Did you say anything back?"

"I told her I was from East Texas, not Mexico, and then I left.

There's not a lot you can do when someone fires you."

Raylene could be a valuable witness. "Hang tight. No worries. My mother will hire you back when she gets home. I should be able to talk to her in the morning, and I'm betting they'll be on an earlier flight. Don't talk to Mona. Stay out of the public eye. It's going to work out. I promise you."

"Thanks. I knew you'd be like your mother."

That made her suck her lips in. She didn't think she was anything like her ambitious mother. "Ah, no problem. Talk to you tomorrow."

"I'm glad I called you. My boyfriend wanted to leave town, but that would mean he'd give up his job at UPS. Good jobs are hard to get, too."

"No worries. This time next week everything will be back to normal. As for you, don't call anyone. Don't answer the door. Does Mona know you have a boyfriend?"

"Oh, no. Your mother frowns on personal talk at work. Besides, he's kind of recent. Didn't want to jinx it. He's been my pillar since this happened."

"Sounds like you have a keeper. Bye." Nala hung up the phone and found herself a tad envious of Raylene and not for the job. She had no desire to be harassed by Mona or even work with her mother, who could be exacting. What she envied was the boyfriend who supported the traumatized Raylene. It was nice there were men out there like that. Unfortunately, she hadn't bumped into any of them, or had she?

The drive to the house ended uneventfully. Nala made sure to park her very distinctive vintage beetle in front of the house so the neighbors would know it was her. Max moved around on his seat in preparation for jumping out of the car.

"I could frolic on the front lawn, so people would know it's you."

She considered the possibility. At least it would be quicker without her dog trying to sniff out any possible dog snacks. "Frolic is all you better do. You know how my mother feels about her lawn."

"Geesh." He hung his head. "Why do you have to go to the worst-case scenarios?"

No need to mention she had her reasons from previous conduct. Nala applied her parking brake, then switched off the ignition. She swung open the door and waited for Max to climb over the console and exit. He scampered across the yard and yelled "Frolic! Frolic!" catching the attention of a neighbor watering her flowers.

Nala waved at the woman, then went into the house. It just showed that people not only saw what they expected to see, they also heard what they expected. It worked for her.

She took the stairs two at a time, unsure if Abby and Elvin would be at each other's throats by the time she returned. The jewelry was in a conventional box sitting on the dresser. Easy pickings for any thief, her father would point out. The said thief would have to get past the neighbors and the security system, then all they would have was a handful of fake jewels that would be worthless to a fence. In a way, her father considered it a practical joke if anyone was foolish enough to steal his wife's baubles.

A nice tennis bracelet, a ring, and a teardrop pendant should work. Anything more would be overkill. Gwen kept the original jeweler's boxes inside the top dresser. She used them for traveling when it was okay to showcase bling, such as weddings and school reunions. Anyone who had just purchased jewelry would have them still in the box. Once she had the jewelry boxed, she headed out.

In the living room, she made a slow pivot to make sure their visits hadn't disturbed Gwen's perfect living room. Nothing Nala could see, but her mother would notice an errant dog hair. Oh well, she did the best she could. On her way to the car, her phone rang. A quick perusal showed it was Harry.

"What's up? Did you have a run on Black Widow costumes, and you need mine back?"

"No. There's been another a break-in."

Her free hand fisted and found purchase on her hip. "You got to be kidding me! My office?"

"It got a pass this time. I had complained about the previous break-ins, and the super decided to reactivate the alarm system. It must be a silent one, because the thief was inside the building when I swung by. The police wouldn't even let me in until they brought the guy out, cuffed."

"Was it your water guy?"

"Dressed differently. He kept his head down, but I think it was. Super was there, too. He saw me and grumbled about how much trouble the trash in the basement was. Told me to take whatever I wanted. Goes for you, too. Anything you want?

"I have to think about it," she answered, distracted, and sighed. Hearing her culprit had been caught felt like one of the weights that had been riding her back tumbled off. "Well, that's one less thing to worry about."

"I might grab the vinyl couch. Don't have many walk-in visitors, but when I do they should have someplace to sit."

The only decent item Harry nabbed. Just as well, any furniture she sneaked in would earn her the ire of her mother. "Oh, I'll take the dog statue. It's so pitiful that it's cute. I still don't understand, though, why the guy was in the building?"

"According to the officer, he was in the basement, which is what set the super off. They think he might be a squatter looking for a place to set up. When they brought him up, he kept murmuring something about emeralds."

"Emeralds what?"

"I have no clue, but it probably doesn't mean anything. The dude was not okay in the head if you ask me."

"Apparently, if he kept breaking into a building that had nothing noteworthy in it."

"Hey!" Harry protested.

Oops, she had forgotten about his merchandise. "I meant, besides your collectibles, but most robbers don't know about that."

"The market for collectibles is moving fast. Believe it or not, there's a lot of theft or attempted theft at the Con, which is another reason there's so much security around the place. It's also the real reason for our insurance premiums being so high."

The mention of the convention reminded her that she was supposed to be helping Harry, but really didn't have the time to do so. "By the way, do you need me to help tomorrow?

He chuckled. "I can hear reluctance in your voice. No worries. Karly is amazing. I sold more stock than I ever have before. She has a gift picking out the exact right item for a person. She sizes up the shopper and knows how much they'll spend."

The pure adulation in Harry's voice was obvious. "You sound impressed."

"I am. She's such a great person. Easy to talk to. Funny. Pretty. The whole package."

The man sounded smitten. Here, Karly thought he was stuck on her. Even Elvin thought so. A couple hours with Karly and Nala was old news. Her friend *had* gone to the Con to scope out the guys. She couldn't begrudge her a flirtation or possibly a thing with Harry. It was starting to feel like the world was filled with couples while she was the lone single.

"I agree. She's a sweetheart. Is she working with you Saturday?"

"No." The disappointment was evident in his voice. "She has to work on Saturday to match up all the cats and dogs to forever homes. She's coming back Sunday, though. I bumped into an old friend, Sawyer Donovan, who will stand in for you. He's not eye candy like you, but he knows his stuff. He's a standup kind of guy. You should meet him."

"Maybe I will. I can drop by Saturday and give you the costume back." She expected him to refuse and tell her it was hers since it had been worn.

"Wipe it down so there's no body odor. Then, I can resell it. Plenty of people try on costumes, which is all you did really."

Putting it on, running after Harry, sitting around in a police station, and following Abby home was a little more than a five-minute fitting. "Ah, yeah. I'll do that." She wrinkled her nose at the idea. Sure, plenty of stores and online businesses resold lightly used clothing and shoes. She'd even bought some, but none of them fit like a second skin.

"See ya then." He hung up.

Nala stared at the phone, then hung up on her end. Max joined her as they walked to the car. He scrambled into his seat and waited for her to start the car before speaking. "I only frolicked a little."

"Glad to hear it. Don't need anything else to deal with today."

Max turned his head to stare at her. "Why so glum?"

She closed her eyes briefly, knowing her dog was quoting Elvin and his numerous movie quotes. What could she expect when he was around the man so much? Who knows? In a dog world, maybe Elvin was cool as opposed to being borderline annoying. "I'm not glum."

"Angry?"

"Do I sound angry?" As soon as she said the words she realized she did.

"Yeah!"

"What are you, the canine psychologist?"

"Not sure what that is. I *am* being yelled at for something I didn't do. I only frolicked."

Nala hated it when people took out their aggression on those who had nothing to do with it. Sometimes, it was a domino effect. Husband and wife argue, the son gets in trouble, and finally, the family pet gets kicked. She didn't want to be that person. "Sorry. I didn't think I was yelling."

"And?" Max prompted.

And what? "I'm really sorry?" She waved at one of her former neighbors as she left her parents' neighborhood.

"No. What's upsetting you?"

"Besides juggling multiple identity theft cases? Our office building break-in artist was finally caught."

"That's good or were you upset because you didn't nail him?"

The thought made her wonder did she mind if the cops caught her guy? She played with the idea and shook her head. "I really don't need the extra work."

"Not that." Max whipped around to notice the woman walking a standard sized poodle. "Bark! Bark!"

Typical. He lost interest in her as soon as another female came along. Could be her, though. She tried with Tyler, and he couldn't get back to this former gal pal soon enough. Her mother liked to point out she was way too picky. This coming from a woman who refused to use the rough paper towels in a public restroom and kept a hand towel in her purse. She blew out a long breath. If something was supposed to happen, then it would. Right now, she had to set the trap. Once she caught Greta, it would be time to brief her parents on the Posh Interior situation. If her mother was a tornado, teamed with her father they'd be the equivalent of a fusion bomb. She almost felt sorry for Mona, but not quite. The woman was clueless about what was ready to descend on her. Her father insisted criminals were always caught because they were never as smart as they thought they were.

TOBY HAD HIS hands cuffed uncomfortably behind him. He wasn't sure what happened. The obvious situation was he was in a squad car, nabbed for breaking and entering. Basic burglary would be five years—but he hadn't taken anything. He had nothing on his person. If it had been a home, the time would be longer. If he had a gun, which he didn't, it would have tacked on some more time. All he did was slip into the building.

At the time he was nabbed, the cop didn't identify himself. At first, Toby thought it was Gabe, since it was hard to see in the shadowy basement. He may have said something about the emeralds being his—although he hadn't found them yet. That would be just like Gabe to show up when he figured out where the gems were, then walk away with them. Yeah, he still wasn't convinced the joker was dead. It sounded too convenient.

The officers in the front of the car spoke. "You called it in as a B and E?"

"Yeah, I did. The dude was mumbling something about emeralds or maybe it was emerald *city*."

The first officer snorted. "Hard to say, since the suspect didn't identify himself. They'll do that from his prints to see if he's in the system."

Toby gulped. Not what he wanted to hear, although he should have suspected as much. He hoped they might regard him as a slightly crazed homeless guy. Once they got his prints, not only would he be hit with breaking and entering, but with parole violation. The only good thing about this situation was he didn't have a gun.

This was so unfair. That snake in the grass was lying on some tropical beach, drinking a rum punch while a beautiful woman flirted with him, whereas his good partner, Toby, was headed back to the pen.

Chapter Twenty-Two

ROAD CONSTRUCTION HAD Nala weaving around new roundabouts being built. Numerous subdivisions were popping up everywhere on former farmland, which resulted in one lane traffic. Max must have thought the flaggers were signaling him to bark since he did at every one of them. The first woman smiled, but all the rest just glared, and she would have sworn the last flagger growled at him. It looked like they were going to work until the sun dropped behind the horizon, and it was quickly on its way.

Once on Highway 32, it was clear sailing, if she overlooked the stoplights and the Friday evening traffic congestion. Those on their way home gripped their steering wheel with grim resolve as they waited in traffic. The lucky ones who had gone home earlier to change for a night out were smiling, even singing. The warm weather had some windows down and sunroofs open, allowing different varieties of music to emerge and compete in the space between the cars. A twangy country song wafting from a nearby pickup truck complete with buck decals on the back window caused Max to howl along.

She gave her dog a shove. "Stop that! Bad enough I have to listen to music I didn't choose. I don't need you harmonizing."

"Harmonizing? That's what I was doing?"

"Don't go getting a big head. You also do that with the tornado siren, and as I recall, no one appreciates it."

"Your bad energy is splashing all over me. Yuck."

This was new, but truthfully, she didn't know Max's entire history so there may have been a new age healer in there at some point. Still, you'd think anyone who believed all creatures had souls would accept a talking dog. Then again, he could have picked up the conversation tidbit outside the con center. No way was she apologizing to her dog again.

Her lips pressed together, imagining the scene between Abby and Elvin that she'd have to referee. Her shoulders slumped as she considered her spring break was almost over. Most of her school teacher friends had headed to Florida. A few took cruises. However, she worked. Her vacation would include only one job where she'd have an opportunity to rest a couple of days a week. Maybe she needed a partner. There were two rooms in her office, she could get a divider to make a small foyer of sorts. Another partner could bring in more business. What she needed was a partner who already had clientele. Now, where would she find that?

Despite the extra time spent making her way through the construction, she arrived sooner than she liked with no clue what she might say to the warring two upstairs. "Be ready, Max. Fur might be flying."

"Why would they shave the cat?"

"It's an expression, and I didn't mean the cat." She steered the vehicle into an empty space, cut the engine, and opened the door. Her dog had issues with idioms and metaphors.

"Nothing else has fur in the apartment."

"It's an expression for fighting. I'm afraid Abby and Elvin may be fighting."

"Bet ya."

"Okay, Mr. Know-It-All. What are we betting?" She opened the car door and shouldered her purse.

Max stayed inside the car to reply. "Cheeseburger. They won't be fighting. Pheromones don't lie."

"You said the same thing about me and Tyler."

The shepherd worked his way over the gearshift and paused on the driver's seat. "That one is not on me." Max jumped down.

Maybe. She couldn't say. All in all, as much as she loved her father, she did not want to date one who was so similar. That may have been the initial attraction—which was icky in a Freudian way. People are attracted to what they know, but it wasn't necessarily what is best for them.

They walked up the stairs with Nala straining her ears for sounds of fighting. A resident was playing some loud metal music that drowned out any other sounds. Three guys stood by a withered bush, smoking. One stomped out his cig near the bush, which had a layer of butts near it. She'd take living in an old retired people neighborhood over apartments any day.

When she got to Abby's apartment she was surprised to see the door was slightly ajar. Had Greta come in and killed them both? Had they left in a hurry and forgot to close it—never mind lock it?

An amused voice floated through the slim opening. "That one looks like fun. You should definitely go."

"I've considered it, but I'm not one to travel alone."

"Me, either, which has kept me from going to places I wanted to."

It sounded like they were having a civil conversation. She held a finger up to her lips as she pushed the door open a little wider and stepped in. From her position in the foyer, she could see they were both seated on the couch looking at something. They were sitting closer than anyone antagonistic toward the other would, their heads tilted toward one another. Even their legs were pointed at one another, completing a loose heart, which most would call romantic. Seriously, did she need this?

She backed up and knocked on the door.

Abby called out. "It's open. Come on in."

Her pretense was to give the couple time to jump apart, which they didn't. Instead, they smiled up at her from their place on the couch. Spring was in the air, and it felt like everyone was in pairs. Nala forced a smile and shook her bag. "Got the bling. You got the cameras set up?"

"Come on," Elvin protested. "Consider who you are talking to. Got them up and running. They're motion sensitive so you're being recorded now. That's why Abby and I tried to move as little as possible. It's best if we leave now after you put out your tempting display."

"That's what I thought." No, it really wasn't, but she'd go with that excuse. "If I put the jewelry in the bedroom, which would be the natural place for it, would Bruno bother it?"

Max had worked his way to a pet carrier where an unhappy meow sounded. Abby gestured to the carrier. "We're taking Bruno. I can't depend on a thief not letting my pet out."

"True." She had no clue where they were going that would allow both cats and dogs, along with their humans.

"You can show me that rental we talked about."

That thought had completely left her head. Lemon bars! The inevitable conclusion is they would all meet at her house, which wasn't a wreck, but could be better. "I can. I assume Elvin will monitor from my house?"

"I'll start as soon as I hotspot my car. It has WiFi."

Nala wasn't surprised to hear that, but the man seemed to be overlooking a basic issue. "How will you drive?"

Abby volunteered the answer. "I'm driving."

She couldn't have heard right. Elvin never let anyone drive his car. Even when he took it in for an oil change, he insisted on driving it in and out of the bay. "You're driving his car?"

"Yes." Her eyebrows raised a little. "I can drive a stick."

Did the woman think she inferred otherwise? "I'm sure you can. I was surprised since Elvin doesn't let anyone drive his car."

"Oh, really?" Abby smiled. "Good to know."

Nala escaped into the bedroom and placed the boxes on the dresser. She opened a few so the thief would be sure to get an eyeful. She left the bedroom and announced to the happy couple, "Let's hit it."

Abby stood, dashed back to the bedroom for a peek, then returned with a grin. "Looks expensive. What if she doesn't come to check things out?"

"She will." The memory of the woman's interested mien when she mentioned shopping and Abby buying her something nice was almost the image of a cartoon villain. How the woman got away with what she did amazed her. Even worse, Nala hadn't even considered the management company, but she would in future cases.

They trooped out of the apartment and down the stairs, making an unlikely group with a cat carrier and dog. Nala assured Abby she'd drive slow enough for her to follow. If all else failed, Elvin knew her address. *Wait.* She thought of something and held up her hand.

"Abby, your car has to be gone for this to work."

"Good point. There's a Catholic church and school up the road. Maybe a quarter of a mile. I can drive there. You two can follow. We can get the cars situated and head to your place."

"That works."

After everyone was situated in their cars, Abby took the lead, driving very slowly as if to announce she'd left the area. How close of tabs did Greta keep on the residents? Would she think it was strange that Abby already had some noteworthy bling in such a short time? Hard to say what went through the woman's head, but she was a consumer at heart. Unfortunately, her need for stuff was fueled by other people's credit.

AT THE CHURCH parking lot, Abby locked her car, while Elvin moved to the passenger seat and opened his laptop. Even though it hadn't been her intention to get out of the car, Nala did to make sure everyone was clear on the plan. Elvin already had his laptop booted up. The image of Abby's empty apartment filled the screen. There was a metallic sound, then the sound of a door swinging open.

"She's in." Elvin needlessly announced, causing Abby to lean over the console to see.

"I'm barely out of the parking lot, and she's racing to my apartment?"

Nala had her phone out and pushed 911 instead of her usual police speed dial since it was important to get the local police. "I'd like to report a burglary in progress."

The dispatcher asked for the address, which she gave as she watched Greta pocket the jewels sans the boxes. A man showed up in the frame. "Greta. What are you doing?"

"Helping myself."

"Bad deal. Remember what I said. We only hit a unit once. More than once will make people suspicious. Let's get out of here. You need to leave the bling, too."

"Okay." The woman put her hand in her pocket and sighed as

she rested it on the dresser. "I'm ready."

The sound of sirens rushed by the church parking lot. "That's our cue. We can show the police our video evidence."

Abby started Elvin's car before the man could protest he could drive. She took off in a hurry, barely giving him enough time to shut the door. Nala jogged back to her beetle where Max was waiting and not very patiently.

"Hurry! They're getting away."

"No. We have them on film, and they have no clue. Greta is probably back at her desk lighting a cigarette."

By the time Nala arrived, the officers had detained both Greta and her associate who were protesting their innocence.

The male associate kept his cool. "We work here. Had to check for a gas leak."

One officer looked almost convinced. Elvin popped out of his car carrying the laptop. "The entire robbery is on video. Have the chick empty out her pockets."

"Greta." The man growled, realizing his greedy associate would do them in. "I told her not to take anything."

Nala and Max approached the police slowly. "I called, officer. Nala Bonne." Max barked as if identifying himself.

One of the officers placed the jewelry pulled from Greta's pocket on the car hood. There was the bracelet, pendant, but no ring. "The ring, too."

Greta glared at her. "I knew you were trouble when you came in the office and pretended we went to high school together."

The female officer glanced up at her. "You're Captain Bonne's daughter, the investigator?"

"I am. We have a video of these two confessing they hit up the units. Any recent robberies or identity thefts can be laid at these two's door. There may be others in the group, but I'm not sure. Make sure you get my mother's ring out of Greta's pocket."

"Will do."

The red-faced Greta attempted to spit in Nala's direction. "I know my rights! This is entrapment."

"You're wrong. I am not an officer of the law, and no one forced you to steal. That was your choice." She felt like saying you don't know your terms, but that would be overkill.

The officer placed the ring on the car with the other jewelry, and Nala reached for it, but was stopped.

"That's evidence," the officer told her. "You can have it back after the case is heard."

No need to add that it could be months. Her mother wouldn't be happy to hear that, along with the mess with Posh Interiors and Mona. She also knew, for a fact, that her mother had a wedding coming up where she planned to wear the jewelry. "Alrighty, then."

Elvin showed the video to the officers who asked him to send it to them. The older male officer called in the details, then called Nala over to the car. "I heard you and Max busted another identity theft ring today down in Indy. Your father will be so proud, but you gotta leave some crime solving for the rest of us."

The thought of her father being proud made her stand a little taller. "No worries. There's plenty to go around."

Just about the time she was ready to go home, take a bubble bath, and veg out by watching a movie on her tablet, Abby jostled her arm.

"Let's go check out that rental."

What was with the woman? Was she the Energizer Bunny who never ran down?

Chapter Twenty-Three

THE PHONE CHIMED, and Nala pulled the pillow over her head. No one needed to be calling her this early. She finally got her bubble bath and a movie, but not until Abby and Elvin hung around for another two hours. Obviously, the two of them had reconnected but felt the need to include Nala. No, thank you.

Daylight flooded the room, so it couldn't be that early. Max pranced into the room. "Phone! Phone! I want to go out, too."

There was no help for it. She threw her pillow on the floor. She grabbed her cell, questioning her intelligence by putting it near her bed. "What is it?"

"That's no way to greet your mother, especially when you texted me to call you right away."

She did do that and had forgotten. "Sorry, Mom. You woke me up." She scooted out of bed and walked to the back door to let Max out. "Did you have a nice time?"

"Lovely. We both got some sun and met a sweet couple, Herman and Rose. I know you didn't text me for the details of our cruise."

"Ah yes." The expression about killing the messenger who brought bad news always applied to her mother. "Could I talk to Dad?"

"Not sure why you need to talk to him without telling me why you called, but here he is."

"Hello, sweetheart. What's up?"

"How invested are you in seeing your friends in Florida?" She watched Max circle the yard, trying to get the attention of the small yappy dogs next door. It wasn't a complete morning until he managed to draw them into a barking frenzy.

"Depends." Graham Bonne managed to keep his voice non-committal with the slightest hint of curiosity, using only one word.

"I checked out the corporate card, Raylene, and Posh Interiors."

"The fact you're telling me means your mother isn't going to like it."

"You got it. Mona used the card—not totally sure what her initial plans were, but she has been robbing Mother for a while. A chair here, a rug there, an elephant statue."

A low moan came from the other end of the phone, but it was enough encouragement for Nala to continue. "She has her son in on the scam, only no one knows the delivery guy is her son."

Another moan sounded. She could hear her mother yelling in the background. "What? What's going on? Give me the phone, Graham!"

There were sounds of a struggle, and her mother's voice came on the phone. "Nala, what are you telling your father that has him all green?"

This was the part she hated. Her mother would feel so betrayed by an employee that had been with her forever. There would be heartbreak, possibly tears. Fudge! She had to do all of this without the benefit of a cup of coffee. Best to do it quick, like ripping off a bandage. "Mona is stealing from you. She wants to start her own firm. The charges were due to Mona, but then she tried to frame Raylene by charging those black velvet paintings from Mexico. She thinks Raylene is from Mexico, not East Texas."

"That snake! I knew she was up to something after shutting

down the idea of opening up a second store and having her head it. I should have known."

"Known that she'd steal from you?"

"Yes. She's that driven. What happened to Raylene?" Her voice softened when she mentioned her more trustworthy employee.

"She's in hiding. Mona told her to get out of town, so right now, she's hiding out at her boyfriend's place. The woman is your prime witness. She knows so much more than Mona suspects. I didn't let on I knew anything. I figured you and Dad would know what direction to pursue."

Even if her mother wanted to let her old friend go as long as she returned the merchandise, her father wouldn't allow it.

"I want to skewer that rat and her felonious offspring. We'll be getting an early flight. Drop by the house, get the SUV, and pick us up at the airport. We'll call as soon as we get the flight info. Good investigative work. Your father wants to talk to you again."

That went better than she expected. No tears, no dramatics, just a razor-sharp hatred for a devious employee and son. Mona had no clue what she'd gotten herself into. "Hi, Dad. I guess I'll be seeing you two tonight."

"You can count on it. Thanks for looking into this. No one could have done a better job."

"Thanks. That means a lot to me. See you soon."

As she hung up the phone, Max managed to lead the yappy dogs into a canine chorus. Just another day in the neighborhood and her dog's contribution to it. Nala considered the unfolding day. "I have a free day until I have to pick up my parents. What can we do?"

Not having anything to do was a heady feeling. All her cases had been handled. "How about a walk at the dog park?"

Max grimaced.

"You're supposed to like the dog park."

"It's overwhelming. All the barking. The smells. The dogs. The poop."

"I thought you liked all that stuff."

"In small portions. It would be like you eating chocolate ice cream for two hours."

"Okay, you have a point. I so seldom have a free day we should do something."

Max stared off into the distance as if thinking. "How about the Con? You did tell Harry you'd take back the costume."

"Yeah." She sighed, not enjoying the prospect of finding a parking spot or crowds. "I should return the costume so he can sell it. That means you'll have to wait."

"I prefer to wait outside the entrance where participants admire me and try to figure out which movie I was in."

"We'll do that, then we'll go to a people park and have a picnic."

"Cheeseburgers?"

"Sure." No need to add that no magazine ever featured cheeseburgers as a go-to picnic food. It would be nice to be outside. Technically, she and Max were on call, but she didn't think her parents would be able to get a flight anytime soon. Even with a direct flight, it would still be at least four hours from now. They probably called when their ship docked and weren't even off it yet, let alone at the airport.

Since none of her plans specified anything fancy, she settled on jeans and a T-shirt that mentioned *A Woman's Place is in the Rebellion*. Since her hair wasn't complying, she went for her old softball cap. Her mother would feel obliged to make some remark about not being at her best, which made her add mascara and lip gloss. That was it. Her off day should not be spent primping.

After a breakfast of coffee and cereal, she wiped down the Black Widow outfit and folded it, noticing the quality as she did so. It was no dinky Halloween costume, and she could understand why Harry hoped to sell it. It probably cost plenty. Harry was a decent guy, who had looked out for her in the past, but now it sounded as if he had moved onto Karly, which was sort of okay. If she had been interested in Harry, she had her chance. The funny thing was she couldn't ever decide. The few invitations he offered, Nala had brushed aside since it had never been the right time.

That brought her to Tyler Goodnight. Her eyes rolled upward. She was sure he was the right guy at first—but maybe it was the wrong time. Whatever it was, love was not in the air for her. *Accept it and move on*, as her father would say.

With the outfit folded, Nala added a blanket for the picnic since Max couldn't sit at a table, and her fully charged phone since she never knew when her parents might call. "Let's go. Maybe you could talk while you're standing guard at the convention center entrance."

"Me? Talk?" His mouth dropped open.

"Sure. Why not. They expect things like that. It wouldn't be weird or anything." Noticing her dog's look of confusion, she added, "Just kidding."

"You're pure evil."

"Yeah, that's me."

BY THE TIME she arrived at the convention center, her parents had already texted her to let her know they'd be in by three. This meant she'd have to argue with the door guards that she was not a participant, but merely delivering something to a vendor, run in, thrust the outfit at Harry, then hightail it out of there to make the drive to her parents' house and switch vehicles. Never mind the long drive to the airport.

It made her wonder what airline magic her father had worked. He could have offered to help fly the plane since he did have his pilot's license. That would have gone over well—not. More likely, he referred to the change as a police matter of utmost importance. Those who assisted him might be convinced he was saving a major city from being bombed or taking out a terrorist cell. Her father did intense gravity very well with just a tightening of his jaw.

Luck was with her since she snagged an empty parking space on the street. There were not a lot of things her beetle, which she lovingly nicknamed Natalie, could do but street parking was one of them. "Good news, Max. I won't be long, and I don't have the time to dally."

The shepherd cocked his head quizzically. "Not clear on the talking thing."

"What do you think?"

"Got it."

The leash was a necessary evil in the city. It was a requirement, and there were a few people who feared any large dog might attack them. Karly could have informed them that most people are bitten by small dogs. Dogs bite out of fear mainly, not aggression. The bigger the dog, the less he had to be afraid of. Still, she should tie the leash to a parking meter or something.

People crowded the sidewalks. Some were in costumes, others managed with a T-shirt or a hat to declare themselves a fanboy or fangirl. Still others slowly pivoted to take in all the visitors, possibly unaware that Comic Con was even going on. There was an Amway convention in town, too, along with some biker jamboree. It might be hard to pick out the participants since many of the Comic Con folks had such varied outfits that were applicable to different shows as well as comic books. You not only had Batman, but Bruce Wayne, who just happened to be a handsome, well-dressed man. Not everyone could carry that look off, either.

The guards remembered Max, so there was no real problem there, but they insisted on her calling Harry and having him tell them she was bringing in the costume. Even showed them the costume that she'd have to run through a metal detector anyway.

It might be less trouble if she put Max away from the main entrance. Knowing him, he'd deliberately stand in the way. She hooked his leash around an ornamental plant. "Be good."

Sometimes she felt her dog was a teenager since most of the time he ended up doing the opposite of what she said. Oh well, in and out. How long could that take? She got past security and race-walked to the vendor hall. The restful day was slipping away and turning into a stressful day—or what she would call *a normal day*.

There were some people in front of Harry's booth, which boded well. The sale signs Karly had made still remained. Elvin had joked that Harry wouldn't do as well without any eye candy. Merchandise in hand, the customers moved on, allowing her to see Harry talking to some unknown guy. It was a clean-cut guy with a nice jawline in a short sleeve button-down shirt. He reminded her of a character from the show about Superman's boyhood home where he lived in Iowa or somewhere like that. Harry noticed her and waved.

Both men turned at her approach. Her mother's constant reminder that a woman must always look her best suddenly had validity. Why hadn't she taken time to at least fix her hair as opposed to donning a hat? Oh well, it's not like the man with the kind eyes and nice smile cared about her. Probably married or at least had a girlfriend. Harry spoke first.

"Hey, I was just telling Sawyer about you."

Fig bars! That was the last thing she wanted to hear. It made her wonder what he had said. Anything that started with the *crazy chick above me* or the *ice princess* would all be bad. She forced a smile, then a laugh, which sounded more like a cough. "Hope it was good."

Sawyer answered for him. "Harry tells me you do investigations."

"That's me, Nancy Drew." She went to tug on her hat but ended up pulling it off. She shoved it on her head as fast as possible but was sure the man had been treated to the sight of hat hair. What else could she do to make herself look foolish?

Harry held his hands out. At first, she couldn't figure out what he was doing, but then she remembered the costume. "Oh yeah." Nala shoved it into his arms. "Gotta run."

"Nala, wait." Harry managed to grab her hand to stop her. "I wanted you to formally meet Sawyer. He was my roommate at the University of Wisconsin."

She waved, not sure what was expected from a formal introduction. She knew no kiss on the hand or one on the cheek was involved. She wouldn't mind the latter, but her hat would come off again. Nala couldn't chance it.

Sawyer came out from the booth and held his hand out. "Sawyer Donovan Insurance Investigator."

She grasped his hand, appreciating how strong and firm it was. "Insurance investigations? I've done some of those. Like to do more, though."

"That's what Harry said. He even told me you might be open to renting me some office space." His smile grew wider as he spoke.

Rent some space? Where did that come from? Even though Sawyer still held her hand, she cut her eyes to Harry, who shrugged.

"Just a thought. Sawyer is thinking about relocating to Indy. He needs an immediate space to set up his computer, and I noticed you have that outer office you almost never use."

Yes, she did, but it would have been helpful to have this conversation without Sawyer present.

The man released her hand and glanced back at Harry. "I get the feeling you didn't clue Nala in on this."

"She's been busy running down identity thieves and all."

Some extra income would make her life much easier. It might even allow her to quit her preschool job. It would be heaven to march in on Monday and announce she was gone. Her principal would have to work a little harder to find a sub.

The two men politely dickered with one another, and Nala could see the desired money slipping away. "Wait a minute," she struggled to recall his name. It was short and began with an S. "Sean. I'm not against the idea. It's just the first time I've heard it. We could discuss it and see what your needs are. If nothing else, I'm close to your good buddy, Harry."

The man swung back around to face Nala. "Sounds great." He reached into his pocket and withdrew his business card. "Call me when you get time. By the way, the name is *Sawyer*."

Her eyes dropped to the card. There it was in Arial Black font, *Sawyer Watkins, Investigator*. There was a number underneath and that was it. The card resembled the man to an extent—clean lines, no frills, and straight to the point.

"I'll do that. Sorry to run, but Max is waiting for me outside. I'm afraid to leave him by himself too long."

Sawyer held up his hand in farewell, while Harry chose to tease her instead. "Better hurry, he'll be flirting with all the women."

"Oh, he doesn't limit himself to women. Anyone with food will do." She noticed the perplexed expression on Sawyer's face, but she had no time to explain. Harry would.

A panel must have ended since there was a surge of people in the hallway. Nala stayed close to the wall, going against the crowd to the outside doors.

Once outside, she glanced to where she had left Max. A small crowd of people had formed, and Max's voice carried above the crowd. He was doing a rendition of Elvin's movie lines.

"Of all the gin joints in all the towns—"

"Max!" She pushed through the crowd, unhooked his leash, and tugged on it, earning a few moans from the crowd. Most peeled off, talking about what they had seen, debating on if the dog was robotronic or a gifted ventriloquist act.

"Hey, lady! Is that a real dog?"

She gave the man asking a pained look. "What do you think? Just part of the convention scene."

A few snapped photos as they left. She only hoped there wouldn't be any videos popping up on social media but knew better. She'd have to go with a really good ventriloquist act.

Once they were safely in Natalie and on their way to her parents' house, she asked the obvious question. "Why did you do that?"

"I wasn't clear if I was supposed to talk or not. I did ask. You said, and I quote 'What do you think?'"

"It was obvious—you don't talk."

"I had to."

"This I got to hear." Agitated, she swung into the left lane without a signal, causing a cabbie to lay on his horn. "See? I can't even drive straight I'm so upset."

"You can say that again."

She shot her dog a dark look as she mentally did damage control. Even if someone did post a video of Max talking, people would assume it was dubbed. She'd seen plenty of videos of animals speaking that were faked. Cute, but no one really believed the animal could talk.

"Hear my reason, then you'll understand."

"Go ahead."

Max cleared his throat. "It started out okay. A few people came by and petted me. One man even gave me part of his sandwich."

"We talked about you accepting food from strangers."

"I only sniffed it. It was Pastrami"

She knew better. Max had slight Pastrami breath. "Go on."

"Then this chick comes by. She kneels beside me and hugs me really hard. The woman reeked of smoke of some type. She tells me she's going to let me free and tries to unhook the leash. I said in a low voice that I was an alien observing the human race in the guise of a simple dog."

"I can see how you might have seen that as mitigating circumstances. Then what happened?"

"The chick starts screaming about alien invasion and how I talked. Before I knew it, a crowd surrounded me. A few poked me to try to get me to talk. One even suggested I was some type of robot and could be taken apart. Talking seemed to be my best choice. I considered charging, but I was still tied up."

Somehow, she had the feeling that wasn't the entire story. Max wasn't above a little editing to make himself look good. "I can see your point. We'll just see what happens and handle it from there. You gotta learn that most of the time it's not beneficial to speak. Which reminds me, we might get an office mate. This would be a very good thing for us. It might even mean working just one job."

"Bark! Bark!"

"I knew you'd be excited about it. Right now, we've got to switch cars and pick up the parents."

Chapter Twenty-Four

Graham and Gwen Bonne waited outside the terminal with their luggage beside them, sporting twin determined expressions. The two of them epitomized the idiom *loaded for bear*. She slowed and eased into an open spot in front of the terminal and released the door locks. Her father popped the back door open and loaded the luggage while her mother scrambled into the back seat. Max had commandeered the passenger seat per usual.

Her mother spouted orders even before her husband scrambled into the car. "Drive directly to Posh Interiors. I'm afraid that miscreant might burn the place to the ground. She's always been jealous of me."

Her father attempted to reach for her mother's hand, but she pulled it away. "I know you're going to try to calm me down. I don't want to be calm. After all the years I paid Mona's salary and gave her discounts. What about all the nice gifts I bought her for her birthday and Christmas? I even helped her out when her husband divorced her. Let her pick out the basics for her new home at cost. It's no wonder her husband left her. That backstabber!"

Nala pulled out in traffic as her father continued to attempt to calm her mother down. From the sound of things, he wasn't succeeding. If her mother got any irater, she'd combust.

"Now, Gwen, remember you used to be friends."

"I made the mistake of thinking we were. She was a frenemy.

Just pumping me for useful information." Gwen tapped the back of Nala's seat. "Faster."

Her father cleared his throat. "There's no need to speed."

It wouldn't be a good deal to be pulled over with a police officer in the car. Most people thought you got off with a friendly warning, which did happen sometimes. Other times, the officer became the point of gossip and censure. Her father hated gossip, especially when he was the butt of it.

The drive to Posh Interiors took forever with her parents arguing about the right way to handle the situation. Her father might be the go-to person for talking down hostage takers, but he was having no luck with his wife, probably because she had years of emotional investment in both her store and Mona. If Nala could drive with her fingers crossed she would have. The situation had disaster written all over it. A glance in the rear-view mirror showed her father looking down at his phone and texting. It made her wonder who he was texting, but he was probably putting an insurance policy in place.

It was after four when they pulled into Posh Interiors. The store closed early on Saturdays, but Mona's car was still there. Great. Just what she didn't need, a showdown.

Her mother spotted the car, too. "Look Graham! She's inside stealing me blind. Probably breaking into my safe if she hasn't already done so. Block her car in, then exit."

The procedure was one the police use when apprehending perps. Her eyes went to the mirror to see if her father would countermand the instruction. He didn't. That was the way it was going to be.

The four of them bailed out of the car. Nala pocketed the keys and reached for her purse. Gwen sprinted for the back door with her husband trailing her. Anger made her mother fly across the pavement in her classic pumps. At the door, she turned and yelled,

"You got your gun, Nala?"

Her father emphatically shook his head *no*.

"It's my day off. Why would I have it?" She had it and decided before everything was over, she might need it. She motioned to her father that she'd take the front door. The security code was the same as the back door, or she assumed it was.

The showroom was lit up as if the door was still open. Maybe a code wouldn't be necessary. Nala peered into the store, looking for the troublesome Mona when shouting broke out and what she thought sounded like a gun. She swung into action with Max squeezing into the door with her. He went left, and she chose right, sneaking around the perfect room combinations. She could hear yelling. Her father's voice was the loudest.

"Don't do this! You know good and well you'll never get away with this."

"I have so far. I've spent months messing with your orders. Shortchanging you on merchandise and blaming it on the distributors!"

"I had my suspicions." Her mother's voice sounded choked and low, not like herself. Nala figured being betrayed by your friend would do that. A Sheraton dining room suite blocked her clear view of the trio. Once she stepped out from behind the china cabinet, she saw her mother with Mona's arm around her neck and a gun pointed at her head. The sight made her gasp in horror, drawing Mona's attention.

"Stop right there. I should have guessed your nosy daughter was somehow involved in this. I did wonder about your odd little visit the other night. Should have left then, but there were a few more things I needed for my shop." She ran the nose of the gun up and down Gwen's face. The woman didn't cry or shake. At the most, she silently seethed, possibly angry at herself for not anticipating the gun.

Nala kept her weapon near her leg and out of sight. Her father's eyes met hers. He gave a small nod, a signal. It was up to her to distract.

"I'm not sure what you're talking about." She moved a foot closer, making eye contact with her mother. Her father moved behind the woman, causing her to twist to keep him in sight. The slight movement was the opening her mother needed. She dropped and rolled out of the way.

Max soared in an arc toward Mona, who cursed and aimed her gun at the dog.

Not Max!

Without taking time to consider her actions, Nala shot the gun from her hand. Max landed on her with all four feet just as the sound of a siren pulled into the parking lot.

Her mother managed to regain her feet while Graham and Max held down the screaming woman. Nala grabbed a box of tissues from a display and pushed them against the bloody hand. "I didn't want to shoot you, but no one shoots my dog." She lifted up the tissues and looked at the wound. "At least I didn't hit an artery."

It had never been her intention to shoot anyone, but instinct took over. Mona would have shot Max who had never done anything to her, all over a furniture store. Her mother moved closer to her former employee. It was probably a safe bet to say the woman would not be getting her accrued vacation days.

"I trusted you, Mona."

The police came through the front door, identifying themselves as they entered. Her father yelled back. "Back here! Suspect is apprehended."

The two officers helped Mona up, and one called for an EMT when he spotted the bloody wound. She managed to raise her good arm to point at Nala. "She shot me. You should arrest her."

What would happen if she was ever forced to use her gun, had never occurred to Nala.

Her father moved to put his arm around her as he spoke. "It was a hostage situation. She took the shot I couldn't."

ONE OFFICER NODDED, while the other listened to the chatter from his shoulder radio. Her father continued, "There will be paperwork, but you have witnesses."

Gwen smiled for the first time since Nala picked her up at the airport. "You not only have witnesses, I have it on video. I knew someone was stealing from me. I just didn't know it was you. I had new hidden cameras put in throughout the building on Sunday when the store was closed. As for the cruise, it wasn't the indulgent trip most thought. It was a guise to bring my thief out in the open, or should I say, thieves?"

This had been a sting, and no one bothered to inform her? "Gingersnaps!"

Her mother didn't even bother to turn to look at her. "Language."

"You could have told me."

Her mother gestured to her father. "He told me that the fewer people who knew, the better it would work. We had confidence in you."

She was glad someone did. At least Max was safe. "Did you even go on a cruise?"

"We did. Not sure I would have if we knew how bad the WiFi would be. You can buy Internet packages, but that doesn't mean you have Internet. That's why we needed you to check on stuff. We're lucky we have an investigator in the family.

"Yes, you are." Max strolled over to sit beside her, unaware that there had almost been a bullet with his name on it. She knelt and hugged her dog, who whispered, "Glad you're a good shot."

"Thanks to my dad who had me at the shooting range before I could ride a bicycle."

Her father looked up from his discussion with the arresting officers. "You say something, honey?"

"I love you, Dad." She turned and reached for her mother's hand. "You, too, Mom."

The officer cuffed Mona after an EMT bandaged her hand, but she still stood glaring at everyone. "Get me out of here! I can't stand this perfect family ending."

Her mother shook her finger at the departing woman. "I can forgive your rampant ambition, even your greed, but I can't accept how you terrorized poor Raylene. As soon as I can track her down, I'm rehiring her to take your place."

Mona managed an outraged snort and a venomous look that fell short due to her uniformed escort.

Max barked.

"I especially hate the dog!

Max barked twice.

Her father laughed and held up his hand. "Just the way I taught him. Bark twice for danger."

The End

A Bark in the Night

(Book One)

Chapter One

A GROAN ESCAPED the silent watcher as the girl pulled out a bunch of keys to unlock the front door. The dog that had been sitting now silently stood, his ears alert, his head slowly swinging side to side as he emitted a low growl.

"Damn it." He hadn't counted on a dog. Who takes a dog with them to an office building anyhow? He could have knocked down the girl and grabbed the keys, and finally made it into the building. He'd spent the last six months trying to enter the place.

The few remaining offices weren't open to the public. He'd even donned delivery outfits and tried to get buzzed in. All he managed to discover was no one in the building had water delivered or even a pizza. Usually, he received no reply when he buzzed. It could be that the buzzer didn't work. The building itself was circa 1930s and only the bottom floor was stores, while the rest were apartments or offices.

That would have worked fine if there was an actual store on the first floor instead of empty rooms. He'd considered breaking in, but he'd most likely get caught and end up back in the slammer. Something he'd prefer to avoid since he had more enemies inside than he did out. Now, he'd have to rethink the situation. Once the girl and her dog entered the building, he tucked his hands into his jacket pocket to feel the short length of pipe he'd hidden there. A man had to protect himself, but as a felon, a gun would automatically earn a huge fine and possibly incarceration. Things he wanted to avoid.

Hands still in pockets, he strolled in the direction of Monument Circle. Sweat dotted his face due to the early heat wave. He could have pulled off his sweatshirt, but the hoodie provided conformity that made him almost invisible.

In the center of the city stood a huge war monument reaching toward the heavens as if trying to touch the departed or at least send a message they hadn't been forgotten. He couldn't remember when it had been built—sometime after the Civil War. As a kid, his grandfather had taken him there. With each war, more statues and flat memorials engraved with names appeared. He remembered fingering the names thinking the people only became important by dying. That wasn't going to be him. Nope, he'd had enough of being Toby Nobody. Once he got into the building, he'd find what was his by right and buy that sailboat he fantasized about while doing time. Might even sail around the world.

Foot and vehicle traffic picked up as he made his way to the circle. A horse-driven carriage, complete with picture-snapping tourists, passed him on one side. The harness bells jingled with the horse's movements. He was not sure why a person would even bell a horse. The animal was too large to miss. Then again, maybe the owner thought it made the experience more festive. Toby stopped and watched the slow-moving carriage. He'd never taken a carriage ride, never took a gondola ride down the canal, either. Nope, those things were for tourists or people with a lot of throwaway money. Soon, that would be him, as soon as he got rid of the obstacles.

NALA PLACED ONE hand on her hip and kept a tight grip on the leash clipped to a handsome black German shepherd mix as she surveyed the building. The stone façade building rose a good five stories, nothing compared to the other buildings looming behind it on a more visited street in Indianapolis. The morning sun revealed chipped parts of the façade and the crumbling entrance steps, exposing the underlying concrete block structure.

"The building has character." She glanced up and down the street, noticing the lack of foot traffic during the early day. The ground floor windows revealed empty rooms inside where light spots on the industrial gray carpet revealed where furniture once sat. "I was never shown a ground floor office or even one with wraparound windows." Her shoulders went up in a shrug. "It is just as well. Anyone visiting a private eye doesn't want to be on display. I probably couldn't afford it anyhow. Let's go see *our* office."

The dog gave a bark as if he understood. Nala's straight hair swung into her face as she bent to pat the animal. "That's right, Max. It's a new start for both of us."

Max and Nala climbed the first flight of stairs in silence. By the time they reached the second flight, a young man with a dark hipster beard and arms full of labeled boxes met them.

"Hey, a dog, cool!"

A bark greeted his assessment while Nala offered her hand, then pulled it back as she realized he couldn't shake. "Hello. Do you need any help with your boxes?"

"No, I'm good. I'm sure you're not coming to see me. I'd remember if I had a beautiful woman and her equally handsome dog coming to see me."

A nervous laugh greeted his remark. Blatant flirting rattled Nala since it was difficult to pinpoint if it was sincere. Extroverts could reply with clever comebacks in a second, while people like herself struggled for an appropriate reply long after the person had left. "Yeah, right."

Instead of insisting he meant it, the man grinned. "I'm Harry Chafant. I run a mail-order business on the second floor. Didn't know there were any other businesses in the building. There are some apartments in use, though. Maybe you're here to see one of the residents."

Nala shoved her hands in her jeans pockets since she didn't know what to do with them. "Ah, I'm Nala, Nala Bonne." *Oops*, she had lost a chance to try out her new name. "I'll be opening my business on the third floor. Max," she gestured to her dog, "and I are going up to check out the office."

"Really?" Harry drew out the word, and his smile grew bigger. "Today must be my lucky day. I'm headed to the post office, but when I get back I'd love to show you around."

"Thanks, but I've already seen the building." Regret stabbed her as she watched the man's smile slip. No good would come out of being too friendly to her neighbors. Even if they did hit it off, eventually they'd break up and she'd peer out her door every time a woman got buzzed in, wondering if it was her replacement. Still, she didn't want to sound unfriendly. She held up one hand. "See ya around."

"Yeah," Harry agreed and continued to descend the stairs.

If her best friend, Karly, had witnessed the scene, she'd take Nala to task, telling her she shot down another perfectly good prospect. Maybe she had, but she also avoided a messy emotional entanglement and the possibility of placing another crack in her heart. Some women threw themselves into the dating game with all the intensity of a bullfighter. A failed romance never seemed to get them down. They would just move on to the next guy. The most amazing thing about it was that there was always a next guy. In her experience, most men never passed her father's background investigation test. Oh, the joys of having a father in law enforcement.

On the third-floor landing, Nala withdrew her key to the office and opened the door. The entry office remained dusty and empty. The furniture fairies hadn't appeared overnight, not that she'd expected them to. A few words to her mother would have her scouring the design warehouse for office furniture, but she wouldn't mention it. This was something Nala wanted to accomplish on her own. With helpful, somewhat overprotective parents she seldom felt like she did much on her own. Even with school projects, she had felt they were more a group project.

Her father had built a circuit board that allowed an electrical circuit to run several items at once for the science fair. She, however, had wanted to grow plants and play music to them. When she didn't ace the science fair, her father demanded to know if the fair was fixed. It was obvious the circuit board was the superior project. Her petite teacher went toe to toe with her father and pointed out the circuit board was beyond the ability of a seven-year-old. A third-grader won with an experiment that showed tomato plants grew taller with regular shots of diet cola.

"Let's hit it." Nala dropped the leash and allowed Max to wander at will while she withdrew window cleaner, a rag, and some press-on letters. Her first project would be the exterior door.

"I'm not sure about the clear glass. If a person wants privacy they don't want everyone and their cousin peering in at them as they come to me to consult about a philandering husband or wife."

"Do people even do that anymore? I just thought they divorced, divvied up the stuff, and sometimes offloaded the family pet to a friend, relative, or took him for a ride in the country."

Nala blinked, knowing good and well no one else was in the office. She dropped her gaze to Max, who had his head cocked as if waiting for her answer. *No, it couldn't be.* Dogs didn't talk, at least not in a raspy baritone. She pinched herself just to be certain she wasn't dreaming. It hurt. *Maybe she just thought he said something. The best thing would be to test out her theory.* "Did your last owners divorce?"

Something must have happened to Max since she had picked him up at an animal shelter the day before he would have been put down. Grown dogs were only kept for a few days at the most. Then again, it could be she wanted Max to talk so she'd have someone to converse with. A fellow traveler in this new life she'd plotted out for herself.

"Nope." He grimaced, showing his teeth. "I made the mistake of talking again. Not the first time I've been ousted from a comfortable home. This last time I was driven from the house by my former owner holding a crucifix and calling me *devil dog.*"

"Weird." She shook her head hard still not convinced she wasn't dreaming. I would have thought someone would have put you on the David Letterman show. Whoops, I keep forgetting he retired."
Was she really having a conversation with her dog?

"You'd think that." He barked a couple of times before continuing. "You gotta remember English is my third language and some things don't translate."

"You speak three languages?"

He lifted his nose with pride. "I do. Dog, of course, the silent language of scent, and I'm reasonably conversant in English. One potential owner tried to speak to me in German. Despite my muddied bloodlines, I couldn't understand a word he said. I wanted to tell him I was born in America. I didn't, since I wasn't totally sure."

"Ah, of course." She nodded her head as if she understood. *Was there anything understandable about a talking dog?* "So, when did you start talking? Are there a lot of talking dogs out there?"

His nose dropped as he stretched out and laid his head on his paws. "All dogs talk in the accepted canine dialect, except for basenjis who do this strange yodeling thing. I haven't met one who speaks English, although most do understand it very well. They might pretend not to know phrases such as stay off the couch, not for you, or not now. They do. Even though they understand English, they freak out when I say something. Something about it being us against them, meaning your kind."

"Ah." Nala searched her mind for how she had treated Max in the few days she owned him. Had she offended him somehow by treating him like a dog? "You never answered how you came to talk."

"Oh, that." He managed a few sharp yips that resembled a laugh. "Funny story. My first owner was a close-mouthed male. Not one to share his feelings or general observations about life. While this didn't bother me all that much, it was an entirely different story for his girlfriend, who happened to be a witch. She always fixed extra scrambled eggs and bacon for me when she visited, so I liked her. Anyhow, one day, she says to the man, 'If you don't talk to me, then your dog will.'"

"Just like that?"

"Took me a while to become a good conversationalist. At the time, I was so excited I voiced every thought." He lifted his head enough to display a doggy grin. "Imagine a constant litany of me listing everything I saw. Tree, grass, dog poop from the poodle two houses down, smells like she likes me. After all, she left it in front of my house. Well, you get the idea."

"Irritating."

"Yep, I discovered immediately that while people yack non-stop, they don't appreciate a talkative dog, especially my first owner who didn't even make the effort to talk to his girlfriend. One day, she was gone. Not sure if they agreed to separate. I just noticed the house smelled less like the sandalwood incense she always burned. After that, I got relocated, too."

"Where?"

"A family with kids. They had a little boy I adored. He wasn't that good at walking so he often hung onto me when he was unstable. It was only natural that I tried to encourage him. His parents were worried about his developing psyche and the dangers of believing a dog could talk. They thought I was a bad influence." Max stood, paced to the hallway and returned to his original place before circling and flopping back down on the floor.

"That's too bad about the kid. I'm not sure what I'll do with a talking dog."

A foul smell permeated the air. "Sorry." Max offered her an apologetic expression. "The Chinese food you gave me yesterday doesn't agree with me. I love it, though. Besides, stress has that effect, too."

Her intention had been to get a dog for companionship. Karly, who worked at the shelter, had emailed her pictures of dogs that would be put down. *Talk about guilt.* Even worse, when they met for lunch, she'd talk about the abandoned dogs, giving them names and listing their idiosyncrasies. Nala pointed out more than once that if Karly wanted someone to adopt a dog it was better not to mention things such as its tendency to rip up anything vaguely chewable or its midnight howling. Karly insisted people had to enter relationships with open eyes.

As if that would ever work. There was a reason woman shoved themselves into shapewear, piled on the makeup, and clipped on hair extensions. Men didn't want reality, and she was sure women didn't either. On occasion, when they needed a reality check, they'd hire an investigator. She'd specialize in date research. No woman wanted to go on a date with an online prospect or even the cousin of a co-worker and end up battered, broke or, worse, dead.

"We'll have to limit your intake to the weekends. Can't have you scaring off the clients with your toxic farts."

A hopeful gleam appeared in Max's eyes as his ears pitched forward. "Do you mean you're going to keep me?"

"Why not?"

"The talking usually scares people off, but Karly assured me you'd be okay with it. Since you're into magic, psychic skills, and all that." His long tail wagged, hitting the floor. The empty room magnified the sound.

"Karly knew? The woman who never believes in too much information withheld the fact from me that you could speak?"

"She never told you she didn't like Jeff, either."

Nala looked up from pecking at her cell with her index finger. "You mean you and Karly talked about my ex-boyfriend?"

Max swallowed hard. "You know, I could be an immense help around the detective agency."

"How so?"

"Scent. I can tell if people are lying or not by their scent."

She shook her head, imagining how well a large German shepherd mix sniffing them would go over. "I'm pretty sure my future clients and suspects wouldn't go for you sticking your nose in their crotch."

"Please." He managed a huff. "I have excellent scent ability. The nose in the crotch thing is something dogs do just for fun. It's a game we like to play with humans. If you didn't react so strongly, then it wouldn't be as hilarious."

Requiem for a Rescue Dog Queen (Book Two)

Chapter One

THE SUNLIGHT PAINTED the lake with a golden shimmer. Nala leaned back in her boat seat as her handsome companion expertly guided the craft toward the pier. He'd mentioned reservations at a lakeside restaurant that had received a stellar review in The Indy Star newspaper. The thought of the renowned grilled rainbow trout had her mouth watering, or maybe it was her date. She glanced back to the tall figure at the wheel. With his broad shoulders and thick, wavy, dark hair, he was almost movie-star handsome, which caused her a momentary pang. What was he doing with her, a preschool teacher turned private eye? She'd never stop traffic with her cute nose and average figure.

Forget about it and enjoy the moment. Her hair streamed behind her as the boat picked up speed. Even though it had been a hot Indian Summer day, going this fast on the water chilled her. The windbreaker she brought just in case would solve the issue but would cover up the flirty top she'd donned for the date. Should she be comfortable or becoming?

A loud noise interrupted before she could decide. The lake remained empty and calm, except for the wake behind the boat. Using her flat hand as a sun shield for her eyes, she peered toward the shore to figure out who might be playing the same trio of notes repeatedly. No one on the shoreline, which only deepened the mystery. It sounded so familiar. In an *aha* moment, she realized it was her phone. Unfortunately, the realization forced her to open her eyes in her dark bedroom.

The red numerals on her clock indicated it was one-thirty in the morning. It was too late or too early for anyone to call. The sound stopped when she realized the tune had been the one she assigned to Karly, her best friend. Karly would only call her this late if it was an emergency. A cold canine nose touched her hand as she reached for her phone on the nightstand.

"Go back to sleep, Max. It doesn't involve you."

Even though it was dark and Max was a black German shepherd mix, she would have sworn the dog cocked his head and gave her an *oh, really* look. The damp nose disappeared with the sound of dog nails on the wood floor as Max settled on the floor. She could hear him mutter under his breath, "We'll see."

Yeah, dealing with a talking dog could be problematic at times. Her fingers found the phone which now had a glowing dot on the dashboard for notifications. Before she could call back, the phone rang again, vibrating in her hand. Karly again.

"Why in the world would you be calling me in the middle of the night?"

Her friend's breathless voice gasped out. "We need your help!"

"We?" Her friend had never been a steady *we* since she tended to form relationships with men that were strictly *me* people. She usually figured it out after a few dates when she sometimes ended up splitting the bill or paying for everything since her companion conveniently forgot his wallet. Karly couldn't afford a love life.

"Fiona and me. I'm at her house, and the police just left. They aren't taking this seriously."

"Not taking what seriously? Did you need to call me in the middle of the night?" No need to add she'd ruined a perfectly wonderful dream, which was about as close as she got to romance, lately.

"I had to call you. There was no one else I could depend on. It's important someone in authority knows what's going on."

If she were trying to reach someone in authority, she'd misdialed. The only thing Nala had control over was Max and her own life, and neither one ever did what she wanted. "You called me as an authority?"

"No, not really. I thought you could pass it on to your father, who, as a captain on the police force, could exercise some control in the matter. Maybe give the officer who blew us off a good talking to."

She shoved up into a sitting position and turned on the lamp, even though it made her wince with the sudden explosion of light. Max shot her a disdainful look and padded out of the room, possibly for a darker sleeping area. "You haven't told me anything. Who's Fiona? What happened that you had to call the police?"

Karly gave an audible inhale before starting. "Fiona Bridgewater, she's the woman I told you about who inherited all the money and started a personal no-kill dog shelter on the county line."

A slight memory surfaced of her friend gushing about a lucky woman who had a boatload of money and was constructing her own giant kennel for homeless dogs. Karly met her because the woman had relieved the shelter of twenty dogs at one time. She usually took the handicapped and elderly dogs, the ones that had the least chance of adoption. Nala remembered thinking at the time if she'd inherited a boatload of money she'd pay off her credit cards and take a luxury cruise.

"I remember."

Karly gave a little sniff, an indication she was very upset and had been crying or the autumn pollen was getting to her, possibly both.

"Well, she built her kennel, which is really nice. Very state of the art. It's like those stables for thoroughbreds."

"Karly," she gently reminded, knowing her friend could get wound up about kennels the way some women did movie stars. "What happened?"

"Yeah, that. Someone has taken exception to Fiona's personal dog sanctuary."

"That might be understandable, having twenty dogs barking constantly." Whenever Max decided to go into a full-out barking frenzy, it got old very fast. At least her dog understood her when she demanded he stop.

"Oh no, it's not like that. She's out in the middle of nowhere. Fiona bought forty acres and stuck her kennel in the middle of it next to the old house. You need to drive down a long stretch to reach it. There's no zoning, which is why she purchased the property. A quarter horse farm, about a half mile away is her closest neighbor."

"Okay." Her lips twisted as she tried to figure out what caused her friend to call. "Why did you call the police?"

"The idiots who have been harassing her returned. She thinks it is just teenagers out on a lark, but this time they went too far. I remember your dad saying something about the police couldn't do anything without a chain of evidence. I was trying to establish that chain."

"In the middle of the night?"

"Fiona and I were working on a campaign to raise money for my shelter and the need to neuter their pets to prevent more homeless cats and dogs. Time got away from us since we were both in the zone."

Even though her friend couldn't see it, she smirked, knowing very well what her friend could be like. "What's been happening?"

"She received threatening phone calls about silencing her dogs permanently."

She could see how that would be upsetting to a dog lover. "Did she try to star 69 to find out who it was?"

"Blocked number."

"That could be problematic. Anything else?"

"There was a note placed on her car, describing what they'd do to the dogs. It was graphic." Karly made a shivery groan into the phone.

"What happened to the note?"

"The police took it, but I managed to snap a shot of it for you."

She really rather would have had the actual note. At least that way Elvin could have lifted prints from it and have some of his borderline legal associates run them. No need to mention that more serious crimes, such as murder and extortion, would take precedence over nasty notes about dogs. "Thanks. You called the police about that in the middle of the night?"

"No. It was the fire."

"Fire!" The news started her neurons firing on all cylinders. "Are you okay?" Then she remembered the rescues. "The dogs?"

"Yes. Thank goodness Fiona spared no expense with the kennel. The perimeter alarm went off, which was something she had installed recently, startling us. We ran outside and saw the flames by the kennel. Fiona had fire extinguishers, which put out the blaze. I insisted we call the police. They came. Told us we had nothing to worry about since the kennel was concrete and had a slate roof. It would have to be an intense fire to touch it. Officer Daylen took the report and the note. In my opinion, Daylen didn't seem too concerned about the phone calls since Fiona had no record of them, only her word. Probably wrote it off as crazy dog ladies starting a fire for attention."

"Hmm." She stalled, wondering if Karly might be right. Her father had related some bizarre tales around the dining room table on occasion, everything from spurned lovers being locked outside in their birthday suits to adults dressed up as Indy 500 drivers holding up a Dairy Queen and requesting payment in dilly bars. It might not be as heartless as Karly thought to take their complaint with a grain of salt. After all, both were awake and dressed, which at that time of night could be viewed as suspicious. "I'm sure it's not that. Officers are trained not to show too many emotions."

"Ha! He showed emotion all right. It was no secret we were wasting his time."

"Everyone has good and bad days. Maybe he wasn't at the top of his game. What do you want me to do for you besides complain to my dad?"

"Well," Karly hesitated.

Nala rolled her eyes knowing whatever the request was she wouldn't especially like it. "Spit it out."

"I thought you and your wonderful detective dog could come out and look for clues."

"It's still o' dark-thirty, if you haven't noticed."

"I thought Max could question the dogs, while the incident is still fresh in their minds."

Apparently, her friend had more confidence in her dog's ability than she did. "It doesn't work like that. Max pretty much avoids other dogs. I don't ever remember him having a conversation with one. Now and then he senses something from body language, and he does get info from smell."

"Bring him out and at least let him do that. I've told Fiona so much about him that she wants to meet him. I think it will help get her mind off this awful situation."

Even though she had no desire to do so, Nala knew she'd end up driving to some unknown destination. Karly had such a soft heart. "Where are you?"

"It's near Tipton, off one of those country roads. Once you get to Tipton, call me, and Fiona will walk you through getting here."

"Okay." Nala was already up and searching through her closet for something that struck the right balance between private eye and preschool teacher. Her sudden decision to quit her preschool job left her school with no certified teacher. She'd agreed to sub until they found someone. It wasn't a bad deal, since at present she had no cases. It provided some money but not the amount she'd earned as a regular teacher for doing the exact same things. "Talk to you soon."

"Thanks, Nala. You're a saint."

Easy touch, gullible, anxious to please, all of those might fit, but not *saint*. If she had any saintly attributes, she'd not be resenting her impromptu trip in the wee hours. After she dressed and pulled on her shoes, she whistled for Max.

"Guess what? We get to do a middle of the night investigation, courtesy of Karly." She expected some whining since her pooch never withheld his feelings.

"Yippee! Wow! Wow." He shook his head. "Sorry about that last bit. I just sounded like a yodeling basenji in my enthusiasm. What's the case?"

"Not sure if it's a case or not, but there's a local woman who built her own dog shelter and is getting threats for doing so."

"Fiona," Max added as he pushed up from his place on the couch and stretched.

"How do you know her? Were you listening to my call?"

He wiggled his shoulders then shot her a doggy grin. "While I may have many superb talents, hearing what is being said on the other end of the phone while asleep is not one of them. Fiona Bridgewater is the canine answer to Daddy Warbucks from *Annie*. She sweeps into a shelter and takes all the hard luck dogs home to endless T-bones and beef scented bubble baths."

"I doubt the dogs have it that good. Who'd want a beef scented bubble bath? Yuck."

"Don't knock it until you try it."

"When have you ever had beef scented bubble bath?"

He hung his head. "My companion is too miserly to buy me my own bubble bath."

Max, due to Karly's influence, insisted on referring to her as his companion or business partner. At times, it both amused and irritated her. "Grab something to eat and drink since we're heading out. And what's more, I've never seen any meat scented bubble bath anywhere."

Her pet headed to the kitchen for a quick drink and begrudging bite of kibble. He managed to talk around a mouth full of dog food, dribbling it on the floor. "You can buy bacon soap online."

How would he know that? It was enough that Max had favorite shows he liked to watch, but she did not even want to consider he could be surfing the net using her computer or phone. It was probably her phone since it had voice commands. "End of subject. We're on the clock. If I get this done in a timely fashion, we'll both be able to grab some Z's. If not, I'll drop you off on my way to preschool."

Max joined her at the door. "Preschool. Children. I'd love to go with you. It's so much fun playing the running and screaming game. I make the short humans run in a circle, waving their hands, and screaming for all their worth."

"Which is why you're never allowed at preschool. Besides, little Kellum is allergic to dogs." Nala flicked on the porch light and waited for her dog to exit before locking the door.

They strolled to her vintage Volkswagen Beetle as Max continued to talk. "Allergic to dogs? I don't believe it. It's the same as being allergic to air. Dogs are totally natural and essential to a good life."

"Dogs aren't essential to life." She opened the passenger door for Max and waited for him to settle. He had to get in the last remark before she closed the door.

"I said dogs are essential for a *good* life. Plenty of folks are out there living sad lives without a canine companion."

She shut the door without answering and circled to the other side of the car. Nala slid into her seat and closed the door. It was eerily quiet in her neighborhood, not a peep from a dog or a meow from a cat. Only the silent older sedans parked in driveways indicated anyone lived there at all. A few neighbors had resorted to electric golf carts to cruise the neighborhood. All the same, she shouldn't have been conversing with her dog outside.

"Max, you know you're not supposed to speak outside."

"Yeah, I know, but it's dark and late. The worst people might think is you're getting good at throwing your voice. You could have your own Vegas act. I could be your dummy, although I hate the word. On the other hand, some of your little, old lady neighbors might be excited to think you have an actual love life when they hear my beautiful baritone."

Nala rolled her eyes. "Not only do I have a talking dog, I also happen to have one who thinks he's a comedian."

Author Notes

A Bark in The Night (the first book) was written after many requests from the local readers for a story set in Indianapolis. I certainly knew the town and surrounding areas. Many of the businesses and streets mentioned in the story do exist. The characters and the very lovable Max are entirely my creation.

Come and visit Indianapolis some time. You might be surprised at its several first-class restaurants and venues. I even have an adorable bed and breakfast to recommend too, The Nestle Inn.

Love to see you. In the meantime, stay in touch via my newsletter. Sign up at www.morgankwyatt.com.

Subscribers find out about exclusive freebies, contests, and personal appearances.

If you feel like writing a review, please do.

Reading takes you to your happy place.

MK Scott
www.morgankwyatt.com

Made in the USA
Coppell, TX
05 October 2021